THE MEASURE OF DISTANCE

THE MEASURE OF DISTANCE

مسافة البعد

An Immigrant Novel

Pauline Kaldas

The University of Arkansas Press
Fayetteville
2023

978-1-68226-235-1 (paper)
978-1-61075-800-0 (electronic)

27 26 25 24 23 5 4 3 2 1

Manufactured in the United States of America

Designed by Daniel Bertalotto

∞ The paper used in this publication meets the minimum requirements of the American National Standard for Permanence of Paper for Printed Library Materials Z39.48–1984.

Library of Congress Cataloging-in-Publication Data

Names: Kaldas, Pauline, 1961– author.
Title: The measure of distance: an immigrant novel / Pauline Kaldas.
Description: Fayetteville: The University of Arkansas Press, 2023. |
Summary: "The Measure of Distance is a saga that follows four generations of an Egyptian family. Beginning in the late 1800s when the British took control of Egypt and culminating in 2011 with the Egyptian Revolution, the story alternates between the lives of those who migrated to America and those who remained. The novel surveys the larger landscape of immigration through the eyes of the family members, revealing how migration impacts the ties of kinship"—Provided by publisher.
Identifiers: LCCN 2022061324 | ISBN 9781682262351 (paperback; alk. paper) | ISBN 9781610758000 (ebook)
Subjects: LCSH: Arab Americans—Fiction. | Emigration and immigration—Fiction. | Egyptians—Fiction. | Immigrants—United States—Fiction. | LCGFT: Novels.
Classification: LCC PS3611.A4326 M43 2023 | DDC 813/.6—dc23/eng/20230104
LC record available at https://lccn.loc.gov/2022061324

For my family,
dispersed among the continents
and ever evolving

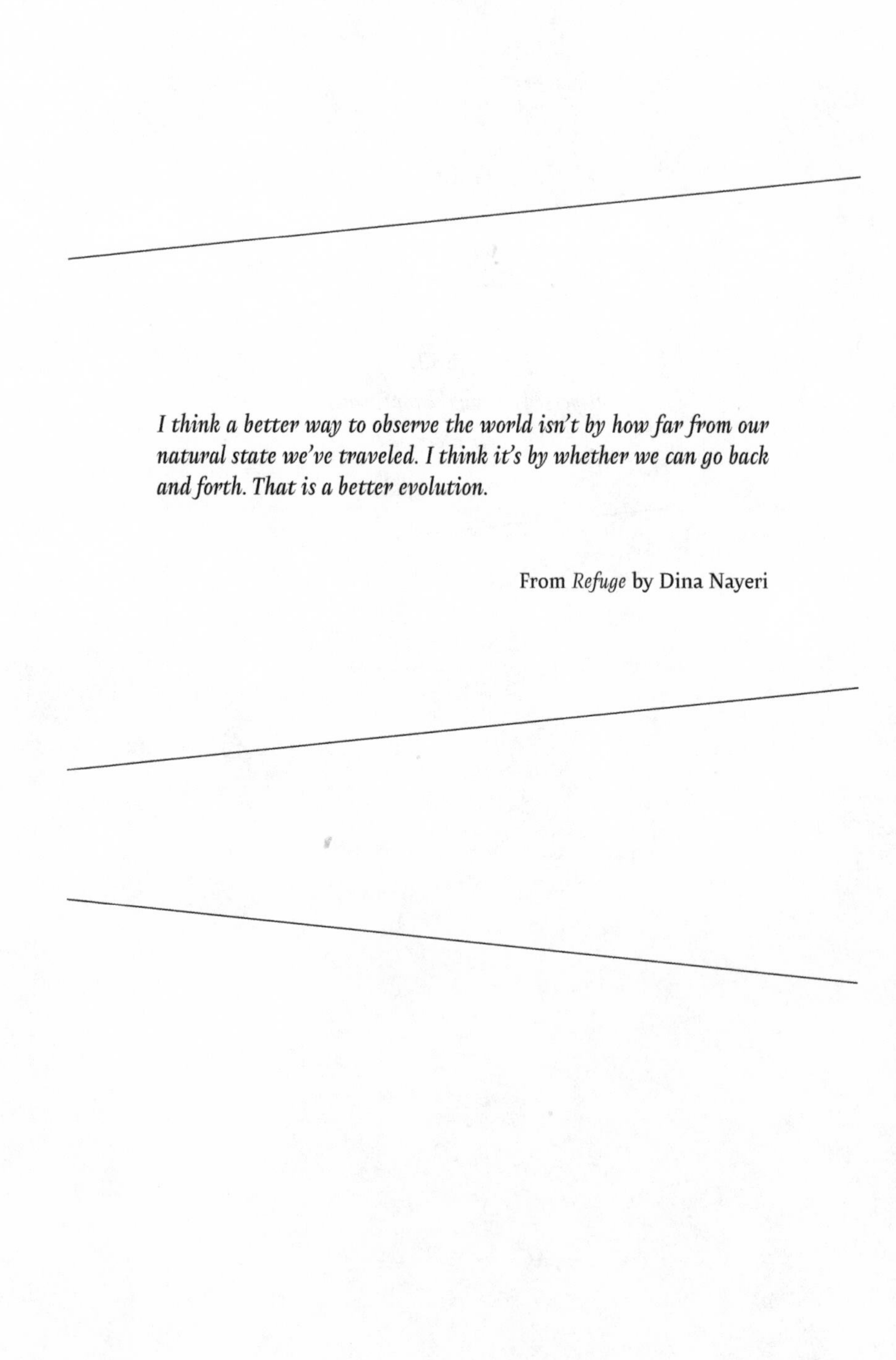

I think a better way to observe the world isn't by how far from our natural state we've traveled. I think it's by whether we can go back and forth. That is a better evolution.

From *Refuge* by Dina Nayeri

Contents

Acknowledgments

With deep appreciation to those who helped me on the journey of writing this novel: Khaled Mattawa, Lisa Suhair Majaj, Marcia Douglas, Maggie Hosni Awadalla, and Ayman El-Kharrat.

I offer my gratitude to the amazing people at the University of Arkansas Press, especially Mike Bieker, David Scott Cunningham, Daniel Bertalotto, and Janet Foxman, who believed in this novel and brought it to life.

I am honored to have been in residency at MacDowell, the Virginia Center for Creative Arts, the Writers' Colony at Dairy Hollow, and Green Olive Arts in Morocco, which gave me the gift of time, space, and the companionship of other artists, so I could find my way to creating this novel.

My heartfelt thanks to my husband, T. J. Anderson III, and my daughters, Yasmine and Celine, whose love and support carries me through each day of writing.

Author's Note

When the characters are speaking or thinking in Arabic in this novel, I have attempted to maintain the syntax of the language, and I have not used any capitalization. This choice was made because the Arabic language has no capital letters. When the characters speak English, I used capitalization. This differentiation between the two languages is intended to highlight the bilingual nature of the novel.

Family Tree

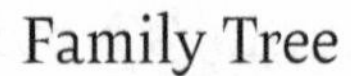

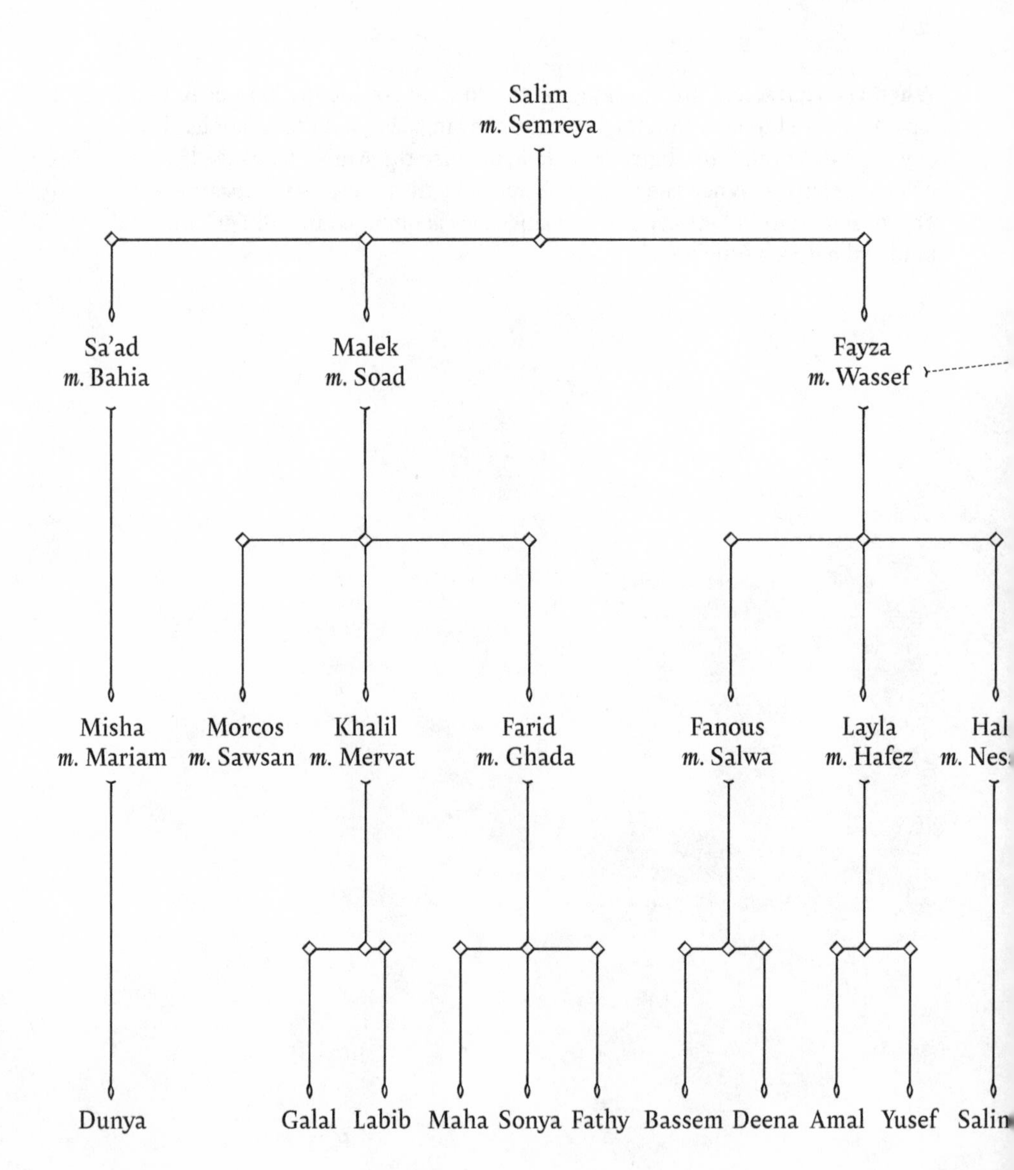

Salim
m. Semreya
Sa'ad
m. Bahia
Malek
m. Soad
Fayza
m. Wassef
Misha
m. Mariam
Morcos
m. Sawsan
Khalil
m. Mervat
Farid
m. Ghada
Fanous
m. Salwa
Layla
m. Hafez
Hal
m. Nes
Dunya
Galal
Labib
Maha
Sonya
Fathy
Bassem
Deena
Amal
Yusef
Sali

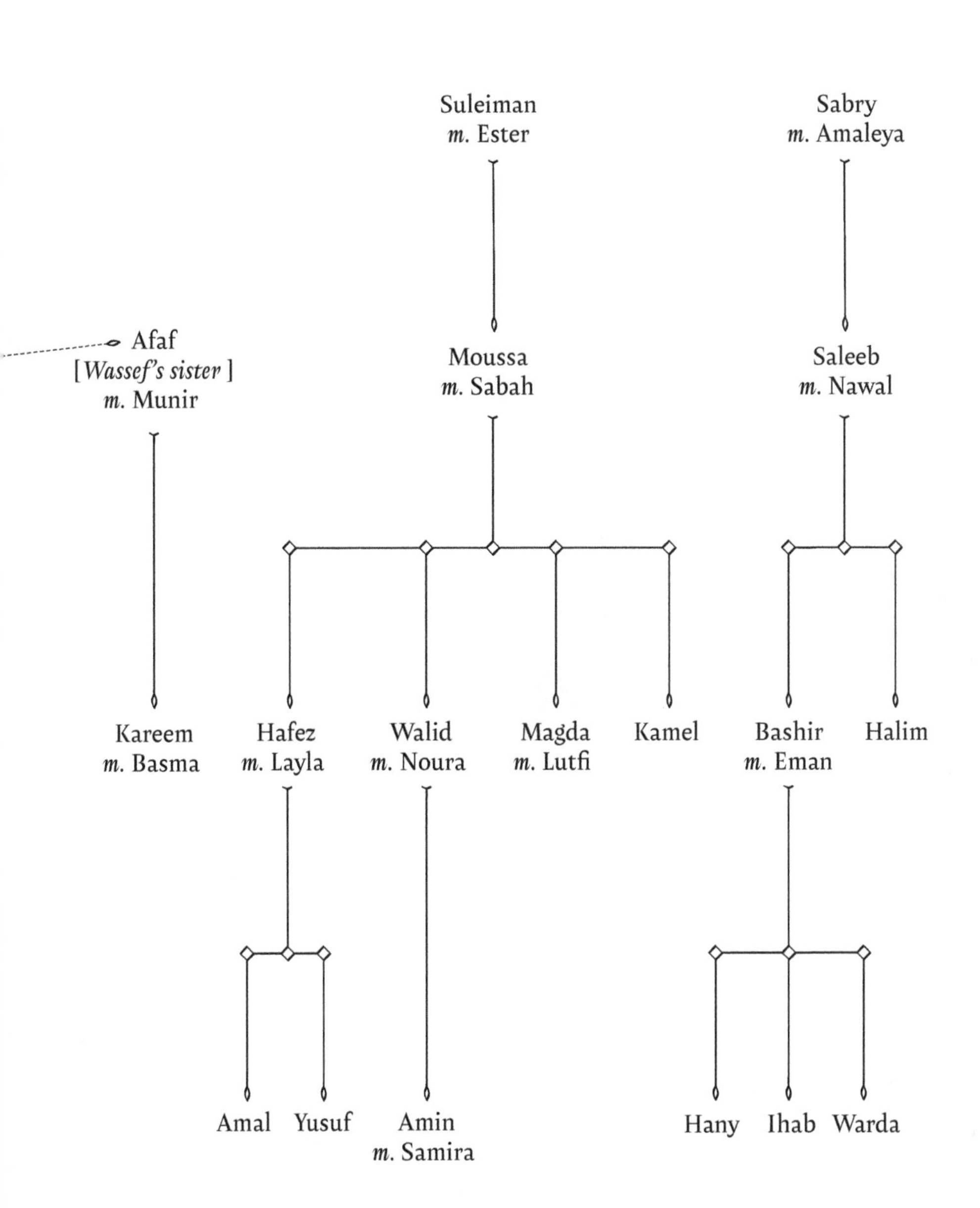
Suleiman
m. Ester
Sabry
m. Amaleya
Afaf
[Wassef's sister]
m. Munir
Moussa
m. Sabah
Saleeb
m. Nawal
Kareem
m. Basma
Hafez
m. Layla
Walid
m. Noura
Magda
m. Lutfi
Kamel
Bashir
m. Eman
Halim
Amal
Yusuf
Amin
m. Samira
Hany
Ihab
Warda

THE MEASURE OF DISTANCE

Kom Ombo – 1880s

The three brothers—Salim, Suleiman, and Sabry—grew up alongside each other in the village of Kom Ombo, where their parents, grandparents, and all the generations before them were born. The village of Kom Ombo sat fifty kilometers north of Aswan and persisted on agriculture. Its main crop was sugarcane, and the stalks rose from the earth to reach upward with their slender green leaves as if the sky longed for their sweetness. The fields stretched across the land and sustained each family. The sugarcane was sold to be peeled and chewed or turned into juice, fulfilling desire in people's lives.

Facing the Nile as master of the landscape stood the temple of Kom Ombo, its columns planted firmly in the clay soil of the earth. Built in honor of two gods—Sobek, the crocodile god, and Horus, the falcon god—it stood in perfect symmetry equally divided in worship of the two deities. The crocodiles associated with Sobek found sanctuary here and came to be both worshipped and feared. Horus, known as the creator of the sky, was carved on the temple walls, his right eye representing the sun and his left eye representing the moon.

During the day, the temple seemed to sleep alongside the flowing of the river, allowing the inhabitants of the village to pursue their farming, their planting, their cooking, and their quarrelling. At night, the temple rose higher from the ground, reaching toward the sky to communicate with its past. Its columns lit up as the sun set, and it kept watch over past and present as the inhabitants of the village rested from their days.

Salim and Suleiman grew up as close brothers, only a year and a half between them. They travelled the same path each day from home to school to the daily chores. Salim was the serious one and Suleiman was the joker. As they grew, Salim's seriousness settled into him, but Suleiman's joking disappeared with the hardships of life. The youngest brother, Sabry, arrived ten years after the birth of Suleiman. He was a peaceful child, always content with what he was given.

When Salim finished school at the age of twelve, he started working at his uncle's bakery, beginning as a delivery boy. After a few years, he grew tired of balancing the tray of loaves on his head to make the deliveries to each house, occasionally getting admonished for being late as the family waited for the hot bread, so they could have their morning meal. He told his uncle he wanted a different job, and his uncle apprenticed him to the head baker. At first, Salim enjoyed being engulfed in the smell of flour and using the strength of his arms to knead the dough. He liked the idea that he was creating something, but of course the bread was quickly consumed and each day he had to start over. After two years, he grew tired of waking before the sun to start the baking, and he asked his uncle if he could help with the accounts. His uncle's eyesight was diminishing, and he looked at the boy who was not afraid to ask for what he wanted and agreed. Salim spent two years learning the accounting of the business. By then he was twenty, and, without anyone's knowledge, he had been steadily saving his money, one coin after the next. He came to understand that money, unlike the bread that was consumed daily, could accumulate and last.

In 1880, the majority of Egyptians still lived as poor peasants in the countryside, but the migration to the city of Cairo had begun, increasing with the British occupation. Salim had been born in 1882, the year the British took control of Egypt, although the Ottomans continued to hold power. Despite the uncertainty of who was in charge, most of the country's citizens paid little attention and remained focused on their daily lives. By 1900, Egypt's population was ten million, with two and a half million residing in Cairo.

When Salim announced his intention to move to Cairo, his uncle wailed at the thought of losing him. Catching his breath, he looked at his nephew, addressing him as if he were his son. "ya ibni, i have just daughters and you are like my son. the store will be yours one day."

Salim's uncle sat in his brother's section of the house, the home that had expanded to accommodate each marriage, making room for the family to remain together as it grew. They were all the same family, marrying from among each other to keep what little property and wealth they had and to ensure the inheritance of their descendants.

The uncle directed his gaze at his nephew. "life in the village is good and there is enough for us to live."

Salim looked at his uncle, noted his eyes that could no longer focus easily, the sunken cheeks, and the mud-earth complexion of his face. He knew that his uncle had never left the village, that his life had always been bound by the enclosure of this plot of land.

"my uncle, i want more. in cairo, i can build a bigger bakery, make more than bread. you are the one who taught me."

Salim's parents sat quietly in the room. His mother had placed the tray of konafa she made that morning on the table, the warmth of the shredded phyllo dough and the cream seeping from its center held together by the honey poured over it. In front of each person, she had placed the customary cup of tea, knowing exactly how many spoons of sugar each of them required without having to ask. Despite the tempting aroma of the konafa, none of them had yet taken a bite to sweeten their tongue. Salim's uncle looked at the resigned faces of his brother and his sister-in-law and knew there was no use in uttering words.

Salim took the train from Kom Ombo to Cairo. He arrived in 1902 and found a city moving and growing at a pace that exceeded the slow rhythms of his native village. He secured a job in a downtown bakery and spent his spare time walking around the city, making plans to open his own shop while he observed the layout of the neighborhoods: Old Cairo, where the poor did their best to survive; Zamalek, which was reserved for the foreigners and diplomats; Garden City, where the middle class had carved a space for themselves. He considered one of the poorer neighborhoods, Old Cairo or Sayeda Zeinab. The poor ate bread with every meal, filled their stomachs with what they could afford. But he looked at them only with pity. They accepted their place in society, existed through each day as if it were a chore to complete. They procreated, and the children repeated the pattern of their parents' lives.

He wandered further away from the center of the city and south of Cairo, where he discovered the area of Maadi. The Egyptian Delta Land and Investment Company had recently founded Maadi, planning its streets and building its first houses. Now, they were going to reconfigure the railroad so it would make stops there on its way to Helwan. Road 9, which was closest to the railroad station, had already designated itself as the main shopping district. It was only a two-block stretch with a few stores, mostly owned by Greeks. There was a grocer, a pharmacy, a stationery store, and a hairdresser. Salim saw the potential for growth. He settled on a storefront in the middle of Road 9 and opened his own bakery.

His was the first bakery in Maadi, and it became known quickly, as he offered delivery, hiring a young boy to carry the bread to the various homes. The population of Maadi was small; perhaps only thirty homes had been built, and most were occupied by foreigners. This is where some of the Germans, Italians, French, and British chose to build their villas. But not everyone accepted the presence of the colonizers with ease. The protests and uprisings were ongoing, culminating in the 1919 revolution. Egyptians wanted to rule themselves, not be subjects under the thumb of the British.

The uprisings led to the installation of King Fuad, creating the illusion of independence. Egypt flourished, and Christians took a leading role in the growth of the country, establishing newspapers, universities, banks, theaters, and new businesses.

Salim's bakery did well, and he acquired steady customers. The population of Maadi grew, and by the 1930s there were almost three hundred homes. When the business began to plateau, Salim looked around and understood that the well-off wanted more than the simple loaves of bread, something to distinguish them from those who could afford nothing else. He hired another baker who could make the soft Italian loaves, and especially the French baguettes, which he displayed in the front window to entice the women who spoke French as they walked down the street, having layered their Arabness with the cultured contours of their previous colonizers.

When Salim's father became ill, Salim returned to the village. People called him Pasha and bowed their heads when he passed. Now he was viewed as a city person, no longer one of the villagers. He held his head high and accepted the image bestowed on him. He discovered that his uncle's health had deteriorated and that his brother, Suleiman, had taken over the bakery. It was in dire straits, making no money and losing customers steadily. His new authority enabled him to change the direction of his family's life, and he convinced his uncle to sell the bakery before it was in complete ruins. He told both his brothers that they should follow him to Cairo. Suleiman agreed, seeing Salim's success and knowing that once the bakery was sold, he would have nothing in the village. But Sabry hesitated. He was content with his life, helping to cultivate the family's plot of land, so he refused to join them despite his eldest brother's persuasiveness.

Salim was already in his mid-twenties, unmarried, and the village knew it, placing its young women in his path. He presented his proposal to the daughter of one of his father's cousins. Semreya was a woman with a mild demeanor and strong arms—someone who had the strength to work. He went about to select a wife for Suleiman, but his brother rejected the women he suggested, preferring someone who was marked by her beauty rather than her strength. Salim grew tired of his brother's naivete and finally presented a proposal to Ester, a young woman who had beauty and looked like she had some sense. The proposals were accepted based on Salim's status, and he paid the dowry for both his wife and his brother's wife. They went to Cairo, leaving behind the adobe houses built along the edge of the Nile and the villagers who all knew each other and who had lived on this land for more centuries than their names could count. Behind them, they left the imprint of their footsteps for others who might follow.

Bashir and Salima – 2010

"that's the best decision they made."

The taxi driver steps on the gas quickly to gain the few meters of space that open in front of him when the traffic moves. As he presses his foot on the brake to stop directly behind another taxi, his bumper threatening to capture the other car's taillight, he joins the chorus of agitated horns. It's a call of screeching hyenas in the torment of stalled traffic on Cairo's Airport Road.

"this country doesn't deserve to have someone living in it. mafeesh amel. there is no hope of change."

The intersection up ahead clears, and the rows of cars push forth, eager to make progress toward their destination. Although it's still early, the streets have already become congested with the movement of eighteen million people. The shroud of nighttime darkness has lifted, and it's possible to see the outlines of buildings and lights blinking on. The city seems to be taking a breath, stretching itself to make room for the onslaught of lives about to move within its boundaries.

The taxi driver turns his head back to the young woman who has told him that her parents immigrated back in 1984. The woman notices the driver's thinning hair and the etched lines around his mouth. She guesses he might be only in his forties, but he looks like he's edging toward sixty. The man turns his gaze back in front of him, takes an opportunity to switch to another lane that appears to be moving more quickly.

The driver speaks as if continuing a story. "my brother, halim, waited too long. he left in 2005. in '67, people left egypt carrying just their bags. today, you have to be a millionaire to do that. he couldn't get to amreeka, so he went to canada. it's cold there. he says the air is ice that slaps your face. and jobs are hard to find. they wanted him to have canadian experience, but no one would give him a job. he was an accountant here, but every day, he had to mix up numbers to make his boss happy. you know the problem with this country? there is no morality. everyone takes and puts in his pocket. now my brother washes dishes in a restaurant. he says it's honest work."

The traffic stalls again as it approaches the Airport Bridge. The driver gives a side glance into the rearview mirror. The woman's face is turned to the window, looking in concentration as if she were keeping track of each sign. Her long black hair is loose, and the sharp angle of her nose clearly identifies her as Egyptian. He realizes that she is unaware of his glance, so he looks more closely. Her wide eyes are a lighter color and her chin small, dimpled under her full lips. Probably Coptic, he assumes. There is no doubt she was born from this place, but she is thin and at ease in her body, one leg crossed over the other as she leans toward the window, and she is wearing pants that drape the curve of her thighs. When he picked her up at the airport, she had lifted her own bag into the trunk of the cab with ease. Only foreign women were accustomed to carrying their own load.

"where you born in amreeka?" he asks.

She shakes her head toward the window. "i was eight years old when we left."

"when was the last time you were here?"

She turns her face and looks around as if just becoming aware of the fact that she is inside a taxi. "twenty years ago," she answers, her voice carrying the weight of each word. He can tell that she needs to retrieve the Arabic sounds, her tongue unaccustomed to moving across the distinct letters.

"you must've been very young, just a child."

She looks up at him through the rearview mirror. "i was fifteen," she says, her tone flat. Before he can respond, she turns her face to the window again.

* ⁂ *

At the sharp age of fifteen, nothing fit, not the blue dress with white ruffles around the sleeves, not the shiny, black, buckled shoes her mother made her wear. Not her cousin, with whom she had spent long childhood days playing hide-and-seek and who now chanted "you're not egyptian." She took the words and swallowed them whole, unable to digest their sharp edges. She had looked ahead to this three-week visit with anticipation, imagining a return to what she had left behind at the age of eight—the smooth feeling of her body running through the schoolyard, the afternoons playing jump rope with her older cousins, the downtown excursions with her uncle Farid who took her to Groppi, where she sat at a table eating cassata ice cream among adults who talked about art and politics. Her uncle's embrace used to lift her feet off the ground, but when she returned, he had not pulled her close. She felt only the air of distance between them.

Her mother told her what to wear each time they were invited for dinner at a relative's house, and she felt herself placed as an adornment to show her parents' success. "look how much you've grown" with hugs and kisses to greet her, but then the adults turned to each other, and she sat in itchy clothes outside the hum of their conversation.

Only when her cousins were there was there a place for her, but all of them had grown, and the games they had played were now packed away. "what is it like in amreeka?" they asked, but when she answered with the reality of her family's life, relaying work and school and church and loneliness, she saw their faces withdraw as if she were lying, so she learned to embellish with enlarged descriptions of the hamburgers they ate and the oceans where they swam. And when her cousins asked her to say something in English, she spoke words that remained damp on her tongue.

* * *

They leave the bridge behind and enter El-Nasr Road. The traffic moves steadily now.

"what's your name?" the taxi driver asks, his eyes looking ahead.

There is a hesitation as she opens her mouth to respond, then pauses before saying, "salima . . . my name is salima. they named me after my grandfather, salim."

"a good name," he says. "my grandfather had a brother named salim. it means whole, complete," he adds. "i'm bashir, the one who brings good news. i don't know if that's true, but if someone wants a taxi and i arrive, then i guess that counts as good news," he says with laughter fluttering around his mouth.

* * *

Salima looks out at the city bourgeoning around her. Yes, her name was Salima, and she had been called by it for the first eight years of her life and still was by her family. But when she entered school in America, the name lost its fluidity and purpose. When teachers found it on their class rosters, they looked up before even attempting its pronunciation, wondering who might be carrying this unwieldy assortment of sounds. When they attempted to hook the letters together to create some semblance of a name, most said "Salyma," eliciting a round of giggles from the class, while others only allowed the first three letters to leave their tongue, saying “Sal” with a questioning tone as if the rest of the name would come as a response. Her classmates twirled the name to laughter by calling her “Salami” or ridiculed her by saying she had a boy’s name. She kept quiet and learned to hide herself in the corner of the schoolyard when the assaults of language hit hardest.

When it was time for high school, she had come to understand that in America, there was some freedom to choose, and she claimed the name “Linda.” At each teacher’s hesitation before calling her name the first time, she was quick to say, “It’s Linda, I go by Linda.” She saw relief relax their features as their pen crossed out one name and replaced it with the other.

* * *

The skyline of the city emerges from the morning fog, and taller buildings make their appearance as the pollution rises above the clouds. Every nine months, the city increases by one million people. Their presence presses against the limits of inhabitable land, pushing open the desert like a womb.

“what do you think of egypt now, eh ra’yek?” asks Bashir, wondering how the city appears to someone who can see its transformation from the passage of time.

Salima looks from the window at the emerging landscape.

“we were living in mohandessein when i was young,” she offers. “i just knew my house and school. the city has grown.”

“but it’s not big like amreeka,” Bashir says. “when you left, there were only thirty-five million in the country and five million in cairo. now we have become eighty million in the country and eighteen million in cairo.”

The cars congeal at a point, not moving. There are no traffic lights, and it’s unclear why they have stopped.

“yes, amreeka is big,” she says. Then adds, “we get lost from each other in it.” She notes the squint of his eyebrows in the rearview mirror. How can she explain the vast expanse of land that seems to swallow people once they arrive? “california is six hours by plane from new york,” she says.

Bashir’s eyes widen, and he nods, showing that he can see the image she has created.

* * *

Her mother’s sister, Layla, and her husband, Hafez, had arranged an apartment for them when they immigrated to Boston. It was the first floor of a house on a side street in Cambridge—two bedrooms, a living room, a kitchen, and a bathroom. Just enough space—a table in the kitchen where they could eat, no dining room, nothing here to suggest they might have friends or family over for dinner. They planned to buy a house after one year, maybe even sooner, her mother said, the images of homes from watching *Peyton Place* in Egypt dancing behind her eyes.

They stayed in that apartment for five years, making do with the dream they had brought with them. Her father found work with the help of Hafez, but Salima could tell it was not what he had hoped for. The crinkles in his forehead multiplied, and his eyes drooped at the corners as if too tired to remain fully open. After a few months, her mother found a job at a Hallmark store. Occasionally, she came home with discarded greeting cards—ones with black balloons wishing someone a Happy 50th Birthday or ones that sounded out a few squeaks when opened instead of the song that played before the batteries expired.

* * *

"you haven't seen the citystars mall," Bashir says, pointing with urgency at the six-story structure that occupied a square block of the city's land.

"that's a mall?" she replies, her eyes stretching the girth of the building.

"yes, they say it has over six hundred stores. it was built in 2004. i've never been there. my wife went once, but she got lost and it took her an hour to find her way out. but this is normal for you—just like amreeka."

"i haven't seen anything like this," she responds. "where are we?"

"this is heliopolis, where the wealthy live and shop."

The traffic congeals around the mall, and they find themselves in the misaligned lanes of cars trying to maneuver around those entering the shopping area. On one side of them, there is a white Mercedes. Salima looks over at the car. The driver is an older man. In the back seat, three young women sit in conversation with each other, oblivious to the tight weave of cars around them. Their black hair is long and straightened, sliding across their shoulders at an identical length, and each of their faces displays the perfect lines of their makeup.

"those are the kind of people who go to the mall," Bashir says, gesturing his chin in the direction of the car. "in amreeka, everyone must be like that," he adds.

Salima continues looking inside the Mercedes as if the response she wants is there. "not exactly," she answers.

* * *

The house they bought was not like the expansive homes of *Peyton Place* or the mansions of Hollywood they saw on their American TV. It was a small Cape Cod on a street with similar homes, all in a row like perfect Lego pieces. There was still no dining room, but a counter in the kitchen created a separate space for the eating area. It was another five years of paying off car loans and credit card debt and her father earning more money before they could shop at the malls instead of the discount stores. Salima looked back at the mall and wondered if she would have been able to shop here if they had stayed. And if that would have mattered. Would her mother have been happier if she had been able to buy expensive clothes, would the aching of her legs from standing behind the cash register all day have been relieved if she could have bought a prettier dress? And would her father have resisted the stoop that settled on his shoulders had he been able to buy a designer suit?

* * *

"but amreeka is abundant," Bashir asserts.

"every country has its poor," Salima responds, feeling the weight of America's myth in his words.

"but surely the poor in amreeka are not like here."

How could she describe the homeless of America to him, the people curled up against walls, the city streets filled with those in makeshift homes. If she explained, she knew she would shatter something.

"being poor is always hard," was all she could offer.

* * *

Each year, Bashir took a day off from driving his taxi. He woke early before the cars tackled the crumbling streets of the city, and he drove in the relative quiet of morning, ignoring the stop signs and red lights. He made his way from the outskirts of Helwan, with its narrow streets and low buildings, where he lived with his wife and three children in a first-floor apartment. The two-bedroom space sank with the weight of five people. His two sons, Hany and Ihab, slept in one room, and he and his wife had the other. Their six-year-old daughter, Warda, slept on a narrow cot in the corner of their room. Other than the two bedrooms and small bathroom, there was the kitchen where his wife spent most of the day. The kitchen ran like a hallway half the length of the apartment, a stove and refrigerator on one side and a counter on the other. At the end, against the corner, there was a table that offered just enough room for three people to sit. There was no other space except the narrow front hallway where they had placed one chair. This is where Bashir sat when he came home late in the evening and where his wife handed him a plate of food.

Driving on that early morning when the streets offered room for movement made Bashir feel some hope. He could let his body take a deeper breath, fill the space around him. And he imagined a room, a square room with windows that allowed light to enter, with a couch and two chairs. He saw his three children seated together on that couch, enough space for each one, and he and his wife each occupying a chair. It was enough—he lengthened his breaths, able to overcome the tightness he usually felt in his chest. Each day, he came home and sat in the chair in the hallway, the air settling heavy on him. His breaths would come short and hard. When his wife expressed concern over his health, he blamed the long day in traffic, inhaling the smog of old engines. And he would ask her to open the small window above his chair, even though it only looked out on the building's stairwell.

When he arrived at the edge of downtown, he followed the turns of the streets until he saw the American Embassy, a concrete structure of thick walls surrounded by a wall and confined behind multiple enclosures. Already, there was a gathering of people outside, mostly men at this early hour. Each year, more of them looked familiar. He knew it was an annual ritual for others as well. At the beginning of October, they gathered here and lingered outside until the gates opened and they were allowed to enter after being scanned and patted down, the Americans assured they were not a threat. They made their way to filling out the forms with their name, address, place of birth, education, and family members. It seemed impossible that this simple process could lead to the dream of streets paved with gold. But each year, Bashir repeated the ritual. When he released the form into the slot, he felt the box swallowing some part of him, as if the application required the sacrifice of a pound of flesh.

Rumor had it that over a million Egyptians applied every year for the green card lottery and that only a few thousand were selected. Each time, he hoped his name would be chosen, but the pattern of his life remained the same. His wife kept constant vigil over the mail. She couldn't read beyond a few basic words, so she studied the images that decorated the letters, and when he came home, she greeted him in the narrow hallway, holding the thin pile of envelopes, having pulled out the ones that looked official. Now he kept his glance focused downward when he answered that there was nothing. He didn't want to watch the way her wide eyes stared at him with the expectation of wonder and then blinked into the gray film of what he believed was disappointment.

* ⁂ *

"do you have a big house in amreeka," Bashir asks.

Salima catches his eyes in the rearview mirror, and they hold each other there for a few seconds. She pulls her gaze away and responds, "i live in a small apartment."

"your parents did not buy a house?" he asks, raising his eyebrows and turning his head slightly before readjusting his vision on the road.

She realizes she has given the wrong answer. "my parents own their house, but my job is in another state. it's far away."

"no husband?" Bashir quickly retorts.

Citystars Mall is now behind them, and up ahead is the Ramses Hilton, its brown, lanky body rising with ease.

"no," she allows a slight pause, "no husband."

In the mirror, she watches his eyebrows squint into a puzzled look.

* * *

By the time Salima was ready for college, her parents' financial situation had improved. Still, the expectation was that she would remain at home. The notion that she would live in a dorm was an unspoken taboo. She chose Northeastern University, attracted to their job co-op program. She was able to work full-time every other semester, putting her business major into practice and getting the experience she needed to eventually become a CPA specializing in taxes.

After they had been in America for two years, her parents received a letter from the IRS telling them their taxes were overdue. No one had told them how the system worked, and when her father brought home the tax forms, Salima watched him sitting at the kitchen table with the papers spread out, squinting his eyes, running his fingers through his hair, and scratching at the back of his head. After an hour, he became still, his eyes fixed on the wall in front of him. Salima looked up from her sixth-grade history book and glimpsed the wetness in the corner of his eyes.

"papi, can i look at the papers?" she asked quietly.

Her father looked up, realizing that she had been sitting there. He gestured outward with both hands as if offering her everything he owned and then rose from the table.

She scrambled through the papers, reading the tight print of instructions, and filled in the numbers on the forms, sometimes going back and erasing. It was a simple form. They did not yet own a house or have any assets. She double-checked the numbers, and even with the fine for not having filed on time, it seemed they would receive $200 back.

When her father returned, she explained to him what she had done. He looked at her like he was trying to bring her image into focus and said, "without you, there is no life."

* * *

They approach the Ramses Train Station, and the traffic becomes denser. Bashir turns from the main road and catches a narrower street.

"this is a quicker way to get to tahrir," he says, keeping his eyes focused on the road. "it shouldn't be too crowded yet," he adds. "in another hour, it will be packed and we could be stuck in tahrir forever."

* * *

America is a big country, he thinks. He had heard about the different states, and that even the weather was not the same in each place. Perhaps it was necessary for people to move so they could find work. And she appears Coptic, he thinks to himself, as he glances down at the cross he keeps taped under the dashboard so it's less visible to the passengers.

When he first started driving the taxi, he had placed it dangling from the rearview mirror. But he noticed how some of the passengers would begin with a friendly remark and then quiet down when their glance caught the swing of the cross. When they stepped out, they handed him only the minimum fare. On the rare occasion when he picked up a Copt, the conversation always turned to religion, to the futility of trying to succeed in this country when you were a minority. These conversations drained him, and the larger tip from the customer didn't lift his spirits. He would have to stop at a café, sit for a few minutes, and drink a cup of tea with mint, holding the glass cup with the tips of his fingers. Finally, he decided to tuck the cross where it couldn't be seen and keep his religion to himself.

* * *

"you're coptic," he says, without any preface.

Salima looks toward him. "yes, how . . . how did you know?"

"there's something in us. we know each other," he says, making a turn so they can now see the length of the Nile.

* * *

Salima's mouth curves into a smile. The Coptic church in Boston had grown quickly, with more immigrants arriving and searching for a place to worship and relieve their fear and loneliness. From a handful of families, it grew to hundreds. It was the one place where there were others like her who had been brought to America as children, and they felt at ease with one another, with no need to explain, no questions to answer. Each Sunday, her family went to church, having fasted without food or water that morning so the communion they received could be the first thing that entered their bodies. But what Salima looked forward to was the gathering after church—the kisses on both cheeks, the sharing of stories, and the Arabic flowing from everyone's mouth. It became an enclave, a place of safety away from the hostility of where she had to exist each day.

* ⁂ *

"life is hard here for us," Bashir ventures. Her silence encourages him. "we can't reach a good position, and each door closes in our face. there was a day when this was our country, but today we are just a few, and each day is harder than the last. that's why so many leave the country. but i hear that there are many churches now in amreeka. my brother says there is even one in canada. it's two hours from him, but he tries to go so he doesn't feel he's alone."

* ⁂ *

Salima never told her parents. After college, she had lived at home for over ten years while she worked. No suitable marriage offer had arrived. The ones her parents were willing to accept, she rejected. When she was in early thirties, she requested a transfer to a position in another state. She told her parents that her job required her to go to Atlanta, that it was likely to be for a short period. And for those nine months, she made multiple excuses, coming up with elaborate lies about how she was required to travel, so she couldn't come home for Easter or Thanksgiving. Her parents believed in the values of their faith. A woman remains virtuous until marriage, a child obeys their parents, a daughter takes care of her parents. They had raised her in the Coptic Church, and she had followed the rules of prayer and fasting, never letting them know that after a while it felt more like ritual than faith to her.

* ⁂ *

"do you have brothers or sisters?" asks Bashir as they approach Tahrir Square.

"no, i'm an only child," she answers.

Bashir doesn't say anything, and she feels her response requires explanation. Egyptians rarely have only one child. "my mother had health problems, and she couldn't give birth again."

Bashir nods in understanding and says, "it's too bad."

The Nile moves closer as they begin to circle the outskirts of Tahrir.

* ⁂ *

Last Friday, Bashir had taken his daughter, Warda, with him to the store to pick up some groceries for his wife. Each Friday, his wife's sister and her family came to eat with them. It was a habit they had stumbled into after his wife's parents had died and her sister had moved to Cairo. He didn't mind the ritual. It forced him out of the taxi one day a week, one day when he didn't feel encapsulated in the confinement of metal and glass, breathing the smog of exhaust. The first time he had volunteered to go to the grocer, his wife objected, but he insisted. He stretched his legs as he took each step and swung his arms like a wind-up toy, feeling invigorated by the physical movement of his body. He always went alone, but last Friday, Warda pulled his hand as he was about to step out the door and insisted, "baba, i want to go with you." His rebuttal that it was a long walk and she could stay and help her mother was met only with a tighter grip on his hand. His wife nodded as she entered the kitchen; he knew she preferred quiet when she cooked, not the constant interruption of children.

The noise of the city was rising after Friday prayers. They walked through old Helwan as the streets became crowded with other shoppers.

"i like the day of friday," his daughter said.

He looked down at her, almost surprised to hear her voice. "why is that?" he asked.

"because you're at home. why do you leave us the rest of the days?"

Bashir rarely gave attention to his daughter, worrying more about his two older sons and the unpredictable future that lay ahead for them. Most days, his only contact with Warda was the goodnight kiss she gave him. It surprised him that she even noticed his absence. He stopped as they were about to cross a street and stalled to look at her. Her black hair fell below her shoulders, and he realized he couldn't remember it growing longer. It was held in place with a red headband. She still wore the turquoise earrings that were placed in her ears as a baby. He looked at her face and noted her large hazel eyes—they were his mother's eyes—and he saw now that her features had grown, and she was not so much a child.

* ⁂ *

"i have a daughter," Bashir says, "she is six years old."

"may god keep her for you," Salima gives the correct response.

"may god keep you," Bashir returns the response.

* ⁂ *

Salima had relinquished what she had been given. She had lived inside the denial of her body, avoiding the mirrors that reflected the changing contours of her shape, insisting she felt no movement inside her, and convincing herself this was a momentary passage of time without consequence. But denial became impossible with the pain that caught her breath for twelve hours. She was alone with the passing shifts of nurses. They counted her heartbeats, measured her blood pressure, and reminded her to breathe. But she saw pity in their eyes when they asked if family would be arriving, if the father would be attending the birth. She slept on and off between the pain. At two in the morning, she woke with the cry of a sharp contraction. A nurse came in and sat next to her, placing her cool palm on her forehead. "It's quiet tonight," she said, "I'll sit here for a while." The nurse asked no questions, and Salima was grateful for the silent company.

* * *

"are you staying with family?" he asks, thinking this might elicit a response.

"naam?" she responds, looking up from her trance-like state.

He repeats his question and senses her body sighing.

* * *

She wasn't sure where she was staying or if it had been a good idea to come. The ring of the telephone had travelled from Egypt to the United States, reaching her mother, who then called to tell her that her great-aunt Afaf was not well. She could never decipher her relationship with this aunt. Her mother tried to explain it to her, tracing it back to her grandmother Fayza, and through Fayza's husband, Wassef. Her aunt Afaf was younger than her grandmother, who had died when Salima was only two months old, leaving no imprint on her memory. When Salima was born, her mother was only twenty-two. Her pregnancy had come too soon after her marriage, and she was left perplexed by her status as a new wife and the caretaker of this infant. It was Aunt Afaf who had seen her mother's clumsy fingers as she tried to pin the diapers, snap the clothes, and bundle the child, so she took over caring for Salima.

When Salima heard the news of her aunt's illness, the recollections of her childhood surfaced: her aunt brushing her hair, her aunt offering her a bowl of warm lentil soup, her aunt teaching her how to make the cross-stitches in her embroidery. These memories lived like impressionist paintings in her mind. After her mother told her the news, she remembered her aunt's full body embracing her as she entered her home, when she returned at fifteen, and the way she kissed her on each cheek back and forth multiple times. She felt safe in that embrace, for a moment forgetting her awkward belonging in this world.

After she hung up with her mother, Salima retreated into the corner of the couch where she had been sitting for the past week, encapsulated in a white blanket. Her body pushed against its catatonic posture, and she rose to find herself searching on her computer for tickets to Egypt. The website automatically led her from one page to the next until her clicks resulted in the purchase of a plane ticket.

When she told her mother that she was going to Egypt to see her aunt, her mother insisted that she couldn't stay in a hotel, that it would be an insult to the family, and she gave her the addresses of two of her uncles.

* * *

"i'm not sure. i might stay with my uncle farid, or perhaps with my uncle fanous," she responds. "uncle farid has a bigger apartment, but my mother said it would be better to stay with uncle fanous. the two of them have children, but i'm not sure if they're married or still at home."

"children," Bashir says almost in a whisper as if to himself. "they are a blessing," he adds louder, "but also a burden we carry."

His tone surprises her. She knows that children are viewed as a valuable commodity here, their birth an accomplishment that reflects on the success of their parents. The burden of raising children is tucked beneath the pride parents exhibit when they talk about their offspring.

"how many children do you have?" It's the first question she has asked him.

The car next to them shifts sharply and pulls into the small opening ahead of them, forcing Bashir to push hard against the brakes, which is followed by the screeching of the car behind them also attempting a quick stop and the resulting cacophony of horns and shouts emerging from rolled-down windows.

"no one knows how to drive in this country," Bashir mumbles under his breath, and then louder he says "sorry" with a turn of his head toward Salima.

They continue, and the traffic floats into a steady but slow movement as they enter Tahrir Square. Bashir takes a deep breath and rolls up his window. "three children," he says, "two boys, eleven and thirteen, and my daughter. thanks to god."

Salima shifts her body slightly, moving her legs from right to left. "may god provide for them." She gives the proper answer.

Bashir's glance shifts to the mirror for a split second before he refocuses his attention on the road ahead.

* * *

She allowed herself two options.

When she was sixteen, the niece of one her mother's friends came to the States for a visit. They invited them over for dinner, and the niece, who was nineteen, sat quietly and ate little. Her aunt made excuses for her, claiming that she was having difficulty adjusting to American food even though they were eating kofta and stuffed peppers that night. After dinner, her mother urged her to show the niece her room. Salima thought there was little to show, but she obeyed.

As soon as they entered the room, the niece closed the door and said, "i came here to have an abortion."

Salima stared at the young woman with her makeup and straightened hair who seemed so much older than her despite only the three-year difference.

"i did it two days ago. there is still pain. that's why i can't eat much," she said, as if she were only explaining her rudeness in not eating.

"but why?" asked Salima.

The niece laughed, a throaty laugh that sounded more like a sneer. "because there can't be a child without a husband. you've been in amreeka too long."

"do your parents know?" Salima pulled out her desk chair and sat down, finding that she needed something to lean her body against.

The niece remained standing in the middle of the room as if she were about to perform a dance. "of course," she answered. "they are the ones who sent me here, and when i get back, i'll do the surgery."

Salima looked at her quizzically.

"you really don't know anything?" she declared as she sat down on Salima's bed. Then added, "so i can be a virgin again."

The idea that you can undo what you've done and reconstruct the past stayed with Salima. When she made her decision, it was with the intention of achieving the same result.

* * *

"when did you get married?" she asks Bashir, the question suddenly arising from her.

"it has been fifteen years," he answers. "it's hard to get married in this country. everything is expensive. no one can afford an apartment or furniture. there are people who wait years."

* * *

He couldn't get married until he was thirty, and by then he could already detect a few gray hairs around his temple. He had attended the School of Economics at Cairo University and had done well. When he graduated, he had entered the workforce with eagerness, submitting his resume to the top companies, but each response came back a rejection. If he pushed for a reason, he was told they weren't hiring right now, or he didn't have any work experience, or they needed someone fluent in English. He stopped asking, lowered his standards, and applied to smaller companies.

At first, when his parents asked if he had heard anything, they did so with a smile and a reassurance that something would come, that God would provide. But as the months stretched into each other, they stopped asking, as if they couldn't bear the words he would hand them in response.

The evenings became silent, his father on the balcony drinking his cup of tea, the sprig of mint floating in the hot liquid, his mother in the living room focusing on the stitches of her needlepoint, his younger brother at the kitchen table doing his homework. Sometimes, the silence of the apartment closed in on him, taking on weight and pressing down on his shoulders. He would push back the chair he was sitting on, the noise scraping against the floor, causing everyone to momentarily pause in their action and look in his direction. Startled by the shift of energy in the apartment, he would announce that he was going for a walk. "tayeb," his mother would respond, and then as he was stepping out the door, she would ask him to pick something up—a few loaves of bread for breakfast, a kilo of mangos if they were in season, a bag of rice because they were almost out. She asked as if she had just recalled this urgent need for the particular item, but each time he sensed fear in her request, that he might continue walking, might disappear into the city streets, and the item she requested was like a trail to ensure he would find his way home again.

After almost a year with no job prospects, Bashir stopped imagining his future. He didn't live beyond each day. Each morning, he scoured the paper for any possibilities and spent the hours following all leads. The days when there was nothing, he lied to his parents, claiming he had an interview or had heard about another opening. He moved in perpetual motion, his daily routine circling his life as if he were repeating an endless pattern.

One day with summer approaching, the family sat around the dinner table for their midday meal. His mother had made stuffed zucchini, one of his favorite dishes. He noted that his parents' mood seemed lighter, a smile from one of them or a joking comment went around the table. His brother relayed his school day's events. He was now in his second-to-last year of high school, and next year he would have to prepare for the exams that would determine his college admission and his discipline of study. But the weight of that time had not yet entered their lives, and Bashir wished he could hold this moment of his family permanently.

At the end of the meal, his father turned to his wife and said, "ya nawal, make us some tea." As his mother went into the kitchen to prepare it, Bashir made a motion to get up, but his father gestured back to the seat and said, "wait, sit with me on the balcony, have a cup of tea."

Something in the pit of Bashir's stomach moved, and he remained standing for a moment as if leaving were an actual option, but of course he accompanied his father to the balcony and sat down with obedience, "aywa, ya baba."

His mother came out of the kitchen, carrying a tray with two glass cups of tea and a bowl of sugar. She laid it on the table and scooped four spoons of sugar into her husband's cup, stirring the crystals till they dissolved into the liquid. Then she raised her gaze to Bashir, "how many spoons?" she asked. He always took two, but she still asked as if hoping for a different response.

"two," he said.

"just two?" she inquired as if she were insulted by his unwillingness to accept her generosity.

"just two, ya mama," he responded, calling her by name as if to comfort her. He had never had much of a sweet tooth, unlike most Egyptians, some of whom took as many as five or six spoons of sugar in their tea. The sweetness tasted bitter in his mouth. Even the two spoons of sugar stung his tongue, and he would've preferred to take only one, but he was afraid of the repercussions.

His mother stirred his tea and then retreated into the kitchen on the pretext of cleaning up. Bashir sensed a plan behind his parents' choreographed movements. He was part of a production and expected to play a role, although he had not been given a script. He lifted the glass cup to his lips, but the liquid was too hot and his taking a sip was only a pretense. He placed it back on the table and inhaled deeply. Then he waited for his father's words.

They could both hear the water of the kitchen faucet and the ring of the aluminum pots as his mother washed the dishes. A sharp breeze reached them on the balcony. Bashir felt it whip past his shoulders, and its unexpected coolness helped him to exhale. His father buttoned his sweater and stared at his tea for a minute as if it held the script with his lines.

Keeping his hands wrapped around the glass cup, he directed his words downward. "ya ibni, you've been looking for a job for almost a year now."

It was neither a question nor a statement, so Bashir kept his gaze straight, looking slightly above his father's head.

Letting the pause settle, his father continued. "you have a good degree, but it seems this country is faltering and has little to offer even an educated man."

He took a sip of his tea and released his words. "we left kom ombo because there was nothing there, no path that one could walk on to reach somewhere. your grandfather sabry said no when his brothers left and went to cairo. he tried to cultivate the land, but, in the end, it yielded nothing, and he could only sell it. he told me to walk after your great-uncles salim and suleiman, that maybe the city would give me something, and inshallah, my children would at least prosper there."

His father's gaze reached back to a place that filled his imagination, and for a moment, even Bashir stepped into it, remembering his early childhood in the village.

The pause settled between them, a memory holding them hostage, until his father looked down and seemed to remember his tea, lifting it to his lips and taking a long sip. He straightened his posture and leaned back to open his gaze and take in the room with Bashir sitting across from him, the sip of tea seeming to have rejuvenated his energy. "inshallah, something in accord with your qualifications will come. but it's not good for you to sit empty, doing nothing." Bashir turned to look at him, knowing the next words mattered. "your uncle has a friend who owns a supermarket in zamalek, and he can give you a job. you can work at the deli. they will train you. lots of foreigners shop there and they have money to give tips. it's a good job." His father uttered the final words, then closed himself, the effort to speak having taken all of his breath.

Bashir remembered himself in college, walking to class, laughing with his classmates, flirting with the girl who always wore her hair in a ponytail. Their hopes had been high then. They believed they would get good jobs, be able to get an apartment, marry, and live a decent life. He had been close friends with three others. One of them had a good job, but his family was well-connected and had made the arrangements for him. Another was working at a small travel agency, answering phones and designing ads. The other one was like him, floundering, unable to find anything. Two weeks ago, he had run into him on Qasr el Aini Street, near the hospital. They greeted each other, and Bashir asked what he was doing there, knowing he lived out in Shoubra.

His friend shuffled his feet against the dusty sidewalk and then looked straight at Bashir. "it has been a year for us, bashir," he said with a hard conviction. "and there is nothing." He paused, allowing an ambulance to screech its way through the traffic toward the hospital entrance. "i was at the saudi embassy, applying for a job."

"but what kind of a job?" asked Bashir. "doesn't saudi arabia only want manual laborers?"

"yes," responded his friend. "but they pay well, and any job is better than sitting around waiting for someone to have pity and give us something."

Bashir looked at his friend, young and handsome, one of the top students in the class. "best of luck to you," he said, and hugged his friend with a kiss on both cheeks.

The thought of Saudi Arabia floated in his mind, but he couldn't think of leaving his brother, his parents, the world he knew. He wondered if he suffered from a loss of imagination. And he had heard how the Egyptians were treated in Saudi Arabia—as second-class citizens, brought there only to do the hard labor none of the Saudis wanted to do.

The deli counter of the supermarket rose in Bashir's imagination. A long glass case filled with rolls of cheese and luncheon meat. And behind him the whirring of the slicer. A flock of customers making their demands—"a kilo of mortadella thickly sliced"; "a quarter kilo of swiss, medium"; "a half of salami, thin." His existence would blend into the counter, a server to the expanding hunger of people, a smile, a nod, an assurance he would provide what was requested. In exchange, a tip slipped into his palm, the paper note flattening against his life line.

Bashir looked up at his father and noted his thinning hair, the crease of his forehead, and the way he carried his body with heaviness. By the time they had moved to Cairo, his father already appeared old. He moved as if carrying a burden. He seemed to bend under the weight of his name, Saleeb, meaning "cross." Perhaps the burden was Sabry's decision not to follow his brothers to Cairo, and it was Saleeb who had to take the path intended for his father.

Bashir knew that path was meant to lead to his success, that the burden continued to rest on his shoulders. Now, if he refused this offer, he would be seen as ungrateful, rejecting a favor from a family member. If he accepted, he would have to acknowledge defeat, accept his degree had led nowhere. But he had nothing to suggest as an alternative. Not one single job offer that would reward him with some sense of accomplishment.

He nodded toward his father. Bashir noted his father's chest deflating with a slight exhale of breath, a slackening of his mouth as if he were disappointed by his response, but it passed quickly.

"alhamdulillah," his father said. "you have a job and, god willing, something better will come in the future." His father rose from his seat, announcing he was going for a walk, as if eager to escape from the heavy air of the apartment.

* * *

"how long have you been driving a taxi?" Salima asks as they enter Tahrir Square and the heart of the city. The day is now in full motion and the noise of the city begins to escalate—more cars edging into the traffic, more people making their way to the bus stops—an energy permeates through the streets and expands like the fingers of the delta.

Salima rolls down the window as far as it will go and closes her eyes for a minute, allowing the day's sounds to enter her. She can distinguish the car horns, the heavy dragging of the buses already getting flooded with passengers, and the Arabic words hovering through the air. It has been a long time since the language entered her, its sounds demanding more of the throat than the lightness of English.

"a long time," he answers. "it's over twenty years that i've been driving a taxi."

* * *

He had spent five years slicing behind the deli counter. The customers gathered in front of the glass, demanding their orders, and he served them, rewarded with the small tips they slipped into his hands. At first, he smiled, tried to engage in conversation with the customers. But often, they didn't seem to hear him, preoccupied by the choices they were making as their gaze wandered across the case filled with an abundance of possibilities. When his boss was watching him one evening, he told him to keep his remarks to "what would you like today?" and "thank you." "this is a grocery store, not a taxi," he had added.

Bashir learned to restrain his friendly chatter, and instead, his hearing sharpened as he listened to the conversations around him. There were the two women who always came in together, complaining about their wandering husbands. He would prepare their order a little slower, allowing them more time to vent their frustrations. He learned to recognize the woman who arrived, led by her mother-in-law instilling instructions on what and how much to buy. Every time the woman tried to buy mortadella, the mother-in-law vetoed her choice, and he noted the downcast gaze of the woman in response. After he wrapped her order, he would slice a piece of mortadella and hand it to her—"just a sample we're offering today," he would say as she reached out her hand to accept it and thanked him only with the momentary glow in her eyes.

He learned to be efficient when the few men came in to make a purchase. They had been given instructions, he knew, by their wives or mothers and were slightly embarrassed at having to run this domestic errand. But it was the woman who ordered only a quarter of a kilo who tugged at his heart. He took note of how her gaze ran across the case piled with meats and cheeses, filling her hunger with the imagination of abundance she could only take in with her eyes. And he saw how her shoulders fell when he asked what she needed, ordering less than either her heart or stomach yearned for. After he measured the quarter kilo she had ordered, he added a few extra slices, as much as he could without anyone taking notice. He saw the Egypt he lived in with its tiered lives, the layers of eighty million people sequestered in their prescribed places, unable to move beyond the position into which they had been born.

After five years behind the counter, he found his breath heavy and his heartbeat unsteady each morning he had to go to work. He wanted a way out, but every avenue seemed closed.

It was his mother who came home one day, out of breath and flushed, who offered a possibility. "ya lahwee," she breathed out as she entered the apartment and plopped herself into a chair. She fanned her hand to cool her face as her breath calmed. "ibn el kalb," she swore at the unknown culprit, calling him the son of a dog. "it's a five-pound ride and he asks me for ten pounds and when i refuse, he locks the doors. what has this country become when this is what we do to each other?"

Bringing his mother a glass of water and helping calm her down, Bashir decided at that moment that he would become a taxi driver. At least there he could charge what was fair and maybe make a small dent into the injustice of this world. Now, after all these years, the streets of Cairo had imprinted on his palms that held the steering wheel, moving the vehicle through the maze of the city.

* * *

"there is the nile hilton," Bashir points to his left, where the hotel curves to align with the corniche.

"is that the mogamma?" Salima asks, gesturing toward the enormous gray building jutting out of the ground like a mammoth boulder.

Bashir lets out a small laugh. "yes, that is the heart of all our bureaucracy. it's where they make sure nothing ever gets done."

"and that's the american university?" she asks, leaning toward the left side of the taxi to see the building at the far end of the square.

"yes," he answers, "but the university moved to a large area in new cairo. now these are just offices."

Salima takes in the building that was originally a palace and wonders if that is where she would have gone to college if they had remained in Egypt. If she would have married a doctor, if she would have lived in Heliopolis, if she would now be a wife and a mother.

Bashir turns on the radio and a distinct melodic voice fills the air.

"do you know umm kulthum?" asks Bashir.

"of course," she says, "when my mother missed egypt, she would play one of her tapes."

* * *

Salima had hoped it would be a boy. A boy she could keep distant, but a girl, she feared, would be too intimate. After those hours of screeching pain and the pushing that made her body feel like an erupting volcano, the doctor announced it was a girl, and Salima surprised herself by feeling relief. One nurse was about to take the bundled baby out of the room, but the one who had sat with her during the night asked if she wanted to hold her. She responded to Salima's almost imperceptible nod by bringing the infant to her. The child's eyes were open, and the nurse commented on how unusual that was. Salima stared at the tiny figure in her arms. She had a full head of black silky hair, and her eyes were wide and dark, the irises almost black in their intensity. The child stared at her as if demanding an answer. "I'm sorry," Salima said, although she was not sure if she had spoken the words aloud.

The child's wail came unexpectedly out of the quiet, and Salima shuddered, unsure what to do. "She must be hungry," the nurse said, taking her from Salima's arms.

The father was a man she had dated a few times, someone who was lost, looking for something to ground him. He dreamed of being a chef but only worked as a cook in a diner. He told her he wanted to open his own restaurant, food from around the world. When she asked for specifics about the menu, he gestured his arms open and said, "Everything." After a few dates, their contact with each other naturally ended. When she found out, she knew there was no need to tell him.

⁂

Bashir rolls down the passenger side window as they make their way to the Nile Corniche, heading toward Maadi. Something in the soft air entering the taxi and the tight weave of the traffic makes him braver. "and why did you come back to egypt?" he asks.

Salima inhales the question, holding in the desire to reveal her answer, to say what she has left behind. "my aunt is sick," she says. And after her breathing evens out, "i was very close to her when i was young."

⁂

What she remembers is her aunt Afaf feeding her. From as far back as she could retrieve memory, it was her aunt holding a spoon for her. She mixed the molekhia and rice, offering it to her and allowing her to take each bite slowly. When she returned home from school, her aunt was always there to greet her, offering her a sweet lemon or a mango or an apricot, depending on the season. In the winter, there were pomegranates that her aunt peeled and dissected, pulling out each seed to make her a bowl of red jewels that she mixed with sugar. Salima sat at the table, spilling the day's contents to her aunt, who listened to stories of her school, the teachers, the lessons, the games they played, and the boy who caught her in a game of hide-and-seek behind a tree and tried to reach his hand under her shirt. Her aunt nodded at all her stories, accepting each one. But within a week, that boy had been moved to another class, and when he passed her, he dropped his gaze to the ground. Her aunt lived in the same building as her family, and her presence was a constant in Salima's life until one day her aunt unexpectedly married and moved away.

⁂

Bashir waits to see if she will say anything else, but he senses her leaning back into the worn plastic of the seat.

"distance is hard," he offers.

She looks up and catches his glance in the rearview mirror.

Misha and Mariam – 1954

Misha arrived in America in the fall of 1954. The trip took two weeks on a ship that rocked his family across the ocean's waves until it dropped them unceremoniously at the shore's edge. Before Misha bought the tickets, his uncle Malek, who everyone knew hoarded his money like a thief, whispered Misha aside one day and handed him an envelope. He placed it in his palm and put his hand over it while he spoke: "buy second-class tickets. don't think about getting tickets in steerage or you'll never get there. they'll put you and your wife through purgatory before they let you touch the land of that country. no need for first-class tickets. second-class is enough to get you off that boat and into the country."

Misha was still tempted to buy steerage tickets and keep the rest of the money. But he looked at his wife holding their two-year-old daughter's hand, and it seemed more like the child was supporting the mother than the other way around. His wife was small; even pregnancy had done nothing to expand her. Her belly grew and the rest of her remained the same. After she gave birth, she retreated to her tiny frame. She was only twenty when Misha married her. He had just graduated and was establishing his career as an engineer.

* * *

In my last year of college, Mariam walked into my life, and it seemed I could do nothing but follow her around like a lost puppy. My classmates laughed at my obsession. I ran into walls, I forgot to turn in my class projects, and with my eyes searching everywhere for a sight of her, I regularly spilled my tea, my mother becoming frustrated at the spots she had to scrub out daily.

Finally, I trailed her into one of her classes and sat next to her. I was not enrolled in the course, but the lecture hall was large enough to camouflage me. When she turned and smiled at me, the sweat ran from my head all the way down. Her glance said she knew why I was there, and that she had been waiting. I had not spoken a word to her, but I knew she had seen me, could not have missed the way I was there at every turn she took. As the instructor began his lecture on Charles Dickens, intoning the struggle between man and society, I could only focus on the shaking of my hands. Finally, I managed to pen a note, asking if she would be kind enough to share a cup of tea with me at a café across the street. It was 1950, and mine was a bold move, asking a woman to meet alone with me. She read the note, folded it, and put it in her purse. Nothing else.

When we sat across from each other in the café, my tongue seemed to go numb. She let me stay in my awkward silence. Finally, she spoke, "and what can i do to heal you, my sick friend?" I laughed, and our ease with one another began as if we had been childhood friends. When she indicated that she had to attend another lecture, I placed my hand across the table, reaching toward her but not touching her. "can i request a visit to your family?" Despite her clear confidence, her brown eyes blinked, and she turned to look directly at me as if expecting me to answer my own question. I took in the beauty of her complexion, the strength of her posture. "your response is the most important. i will not ask if you don't want me." I felt the breath she took. It was parents who approved or rejected, and she knew I had stepped over cultural bounds by asking her directly. The question and possible answers hovered above us. She pulled a pen out of her purse, and on a small napkin, she wrote something and passed it to me. The word *aywa* was carefully penned by her hand. When I looked up, she was already stepping out of the café.

* ⁂ *

Misha was born in 1928, the year the Muslim Brotherhood was founded. He learned about business from his father, Sa'ad, who had learned from his own father, Salim, who had come to Cairo from Kom Ombo and established a successful bakery. Sa'ad's father urged him to attend college, saying the prestige would pay off. Sa'ad was not the smartest when it came to books, although he managed to get accepted into the Faculty of Commerce at Cairo University. After two years of making his way from Maadi to the university to attend his classes, he dropped out, partly because of his low grades and mostly because he felt the time spent sitting in a classroom and reading books was wasted. His father was furious. "i get the money to send you to college and you do this. what will people say. my son is stupid like a donkey." Sa'ad was the first in the family to enter college, and it gave his father the right to hold his head high. Now, his father would have to cower among his brothers, unable to hold his stature in the family. But Sa'ad persuaded his father to allow him just one month to come up with a plan. They achieved a truce, and the father left the son in peace for a short while.

Once Misha's grandfather had established his bakery and was assured of his financial success, he considered the possibility of investing some of his money. Salim enjoyed watching the accumulation of his wealth and was reluctant to release any of it, but owning something alongside the bakery appealed to him. A friend mentioned that there was cheap land for sale near the pyramids, and Salim decided to acquire a few acres. Over the years, he had considered selling it, but it was worth little. The area surrounding the pyramids remained bare, an uninhabited arena of sand that created the monotonous landscape everyone drove through to arrive at the ancient structures.

"i want to build something on the pyramid land." Sa'ad had asked his father to sit and talk. They had retreated to the salon, a room usually reserved for guests, with its formal furniture and heightened European décor.

Salim leaned forward as if to hear his son's words better. "and what exactly would you build?"

"a hotel. a small hotel at the beginning." His son kept his voice steady, an even tone. He knew his father did not trust passion. He was a solid man who weighed the consequences before he took action. "there are many tourists who come here so they can see the pyramids. we can build a hotel that looks from every direction on the pyramids. instead of the land sitting empty, we can use it and make money from it."

"and how will you build this hotel?"

The son had prepared a detailed plan to support his proposal. He had called on every friend he had made since primary school to ask for their help. Now, in front of his father, he laid out the architectural drawing for the hotel and the figures outlining the cost of construction and the potential income. He went through, step by step, beginning by explaining that while this would begin as a two-story hotel, the foundation would be built to sustain an eight-story building if expansion were a possibility in the future. Salim did not look at the drawings or the accounting columns as his son spoke. He looked at Sa'ad's face and watched his eyes move from drawing to drawing. He followed his gestures as they pointed to the numbers anticipating profits, and he noted the even tone of his voice even as the blood rose to his cheeks. He remembered the plans and charts he had created when he was opening the bakery and the excitement that flooded his body as he worked through every detail. When his son finished, catching a breath to resuscitate himself from the energy expended on his speech, he looked up. Salim nodded. "mashee," was all he said, indicating that his son could move forward.

The small hotel took a year to build. Each day, Sa'ad made the hour-long drive out to the pyramids through empty roads of sand with hot air flying into the car windows, whipping against his darkening skin. At the building site, he heard the whispered laughter of the workers: "who will stay here? maybe the pharaohs will come out and sit on the balcony?" He knew they thought it was a losing endeavor. But Sa'ad looked over at the pyramids rising toward the sky and closed his ears to the gossiping workers. He gave instructions, focused on the details he had envisioned in his drawings. His friend Hosni was the architect overseeing the project, and he stood by his side although Sa'ad knew that he too had his doubts.

When the hotel was complete, he asked his father if he wanted to see it, but his father shook his head. "when the hotel fills with people, i will come to the desert to see it," he said. Sa'ad went to every travel agency in the city, offering a percentage to anyone who sent tourists to stay there. Six months passed and nothing; the hotel sat with closed shutters. It was on his drive out to check on a problem with the electricity that he stumbled on his solution, when he had to stop and wait while King Fuad passed through the city. The traffic had halted to let the king and his entourage drive through the streets undisturbed.

Once the traffic cleared, Sa'ad drove quickly, until he arrived at Hosni's apartment in Garden City. "do you know anyone in the government?" he asked, even before his friend could invite him in.

Hosni raised his thick eyebrows in response. And Sa'ad explained that if the hotel could only receive an endorsement from someone in a high position, it would succeed.

Hosni laughed. "why don't you just send an invitation to the king?" he said.

Sa'ad felt the weight of his friend's ridicule on his shoulders. Hosni must have seen the disappointment in his face, so he said he would see what he could do. A few days later, Hosni had connected him to one of the top ministers, who accepted the invitation to spend a few days at the hotel. It worked. The picture in *Al-Ahram* newspaper of the minister and his family eating on the terrace of the hotel overlooking the pyramids circulated, and the reservations started to come in.

Within two years, the hotel was a success. The profits accumulated, and Sa'ad's accomplishments gave pride to his parents, who could hold their heads up high. Everyone forgot that Sa'ad had not earned his college degree. He married Bahia, a young woman from a good family, and they lived as young couples did in the late 1920s, building a life. The city of Cairo was growing, approaching two million inhabitants. And the country was flourishing with theater, cinema, and music. Naguib el-Rihani created his theatrical comedies, Talaat Harb Pasha highlighted Egyptian cinema with the creation of Studio Misr, Mahmoud Saeed's paintings pushed against Egyptian conservatism, and Mohamed Abdel Wahab, Farid al-Atrash, and Umm Kulthum created a musical renaissance.

Maadi was attracting the upwardly mobile. The Maadi Sporting Club offered tennis and swimming, and more shops opened on Road 9, including the Bata shoe store, the Greek hairdresser, a pharmacy, and a bookstore. With the profit from the hotel, Sa'ad bought land in Maadi, around the corner from Road 9, and built an apartment building, renting mostly to foreigners and diplomats. In this way, he was not subjected to the rules of rent control. Once one tenant left and another came, he could increase the rent by however much the market could bear. The tenants stayed for short periods, none of them willing to settle their lives in this colony, with its dark inhabitants who spoke in guttural sounds.

Each day, the city of Cairo vibrated with people's lives, but beneath the daily routines, a discontent was broiling. The independence of 1922 had proven to be a farce, and protests sprouted around the country. In the 1930s and 1940s, demonstrations against the British continued and were often met with force from the government. These acts of resistance escalated when, on January 25, 1952, British soldiers opened fire on Egyptian police in Ismailia, killing fifty police officers and wounding many others. The next day, Cairo erupted with riots in the downtown streets that resulted in the burning and looting of stores, cinemas, theaters, nightclubs, restaurants, hotels, and the opera house. The earth shook as rioters targeted British-owned businesses and moved through the streets with determination.

ON JULY 23, 1952, EGYPTIANS WAKE TO THE NEWS OF THE REVOLUTION, THE DEPOSED KING, AND THE NEW GOVERNMENT. IT IS AN OVERNIGHT UPRISING, OVERTHROWING THE YOKE OF COLONIALISM. THERE IS NO RESISTANCE MOVEMENT AND NO GUERRILLA TACTICS LIKE THE ONES THAT LED TO THE END OF COLONIALISM IN MOROCCO AND ALGERIA. A GROUP OF ARMY OFFICERS TAKE OVER AND SEND KING FAROUK INTO EXILE. THE PEOPLE GO TO SLEEP WITH COLONIALISM ONE NIGHT AND WAKE THE NEXT MORNING WITH INDEPENDENCE. SOME CELEBRATE THE END OF BRITISH CONTROL; SOME MOURN THE END OF THE EMPIRE; AND SOME WONDER IF THE FREEDOM THAT COMES WITHOUT STRUGGLE HAS LESS VALUE.

Mariam and Misha were married in January of 1952. By July, Mariam was in her sixth month of pregnancy and her health seemed precarious. She had little appetite throughout the pregnancy, and the doctors worried about her ability to carry the baby to term. Misha's thoughts focused on Mariam's health and the baby she was carrying. But in the back of his mind, he knew Egypt had made a turn from which it would never recover. He feared the arrogance of these young soldiers who had so easily succeeded in gaining control of the country. The officers' accusation of the monarchy's corruption and bribery made him uneasy, and he felt that this new government might simply follow in the footsteps of the old. The talk of the army operating in the national interest made him wonder how that interest would be determined.

He wanted to leave, but he told no one. It was rare for anyone to emigrate. Egypt didn't let go of its citizens easily, and America had set up sharp restrictions. The only person he knew who had left was one of his mother's cousins, and he had gone to Australia. Once he was gone, it was as if he had been erased. Misha made some inquiries, but Mariam's condition forced him to wait and watch.

In September, Mariam gave birth, a few weeks too early, but the baby was healthy, a little girl with a halo of dark-brown curls and Mariam's large brown eyes. The birth was difficult, and Misha stayed in the room even though that was unheard of in those days. But he couldn't leave her. He sat next to her, held her hand. They let her carry through the labor for twenty-four hours, and in the end, her exhaustion required releasing the child from her body with forceps. Their daughter came out loud and crying, then her eyes opened and, as if she understood where she was, she immediately quieted. Mariam remained weak after the birth, her breath shallow and her face pale. Her eyes blinked, striving to remain open. They had never discussed names, fearful of the evil eye, worried that something might go wrong. Now, holding the bundle of his child, Misha turned to Mariam and said, "she needs a name." Mariam brushed the baby's cheek with her hand. "dunya," she said, naming her as the world.

Mariam recovered slowly, and after a year, she seemed well. That's when Misha began the paperwork for immigration. It took time as he came and went to the embassy, gathering the necessary documents, paying the bribes. He contacted an old classmate who had recently gone to the States on a scholarship. But he told no one, not Mariam or his parents.

In 1954, Misha's father lost his hotel. As Misha expected, the country closed like a fist. Nasser held it in his firm grip, establishing a socialist regime and passing the Land Reform Act. The government began confiscating property from its owners, claiming it was a way to equalize the wealth of the country. Misha believed these attempts at socialism were all doomed to failure, that the stolen wealth would end up in the pockets of government officials, and the people would have less than before. Many who lost their land and businesses were Christians who had worked hard to achieve their success. Misha felt like they were tugging at the rug beneath people's feet and that one misstep would allow them to pull it all the way out from under everyone.

The government claimed the hotel as public property. Sa'ad took the blow of the loss hard. That hotel had been his pride, the accomplishment that enabled him to hold his head high, to be called Pasha, to do right by his parents. With its loss, his age settled into his body, and he spent his days sitting on a chair in the living room, watching the fluttering of the curtains. At night, he woke in terror, repeating "there is nothing. there is nothing, mafeesh." His wife did what she could, but she knew that he had lost more than land and property.

Misha was an only child. His mother had two miscarriages. Each time, when she entered her third month, it seemed her body could no longer hold the child and it was released. With the third pregnancy, she remained in bed from the beginning, taking no risks, barely moving for nine months until Misha was born. Now, he was the one responsible for caring for his parents as they aged. But he felt the doom of the country approaching. His parents were not yet old, and he believed his father would recover. He still had the building in Maadi, and both his parents had siblings to look in on them. Misha imagined that he would return every year to see them.

When he told Mariam, she looked deeply at him without saying anything. "is that what you want?" she asked.

He nodded.

"i'm with you from the beginning of life until the end of life," she responded.

He kissed her hand and folded her into his arms.

He approached his mother and told her of his plans. Sorrow swept across her eyes, but she only said, "this is your life and your family. life is a trial."

When the plans were firm, Misha told his father. "i have nothing to give you. khalas," his father said, waving his hand to indicate it was over. With the loss of the hotel, Sa'ad felt as if the legacy of their family had been snapped.

Toward the end of 1954, Misha and Mariam left on the *Khedivial* steamship, one of the last ones to arrive at Ellis Island before it closed. Misha followed his uncle Malek's advice and bought second-class tickets, allowing them to have a room of their own with some comfort. It was a good decision, as Mariam became seasick after the first few days when they hit turbulent waters. Dunya lay down as Mariam slept, and Misha would see her bright eyes looking at Mariam's face as if there were something there she needed to decipher.

By the time they arrived, Mariam was pale and had lost so much weight that her clothes draped loosely around her. She put on makeup and did her hair before the inspectors came on the boat, trying to give the appearance of health. She was tired, so Misha dressed Dunya in her best outfit and put bows in her hair. When the inspector came to look at Mariam, she was holding her daughter, and as he approached Mariam's face to look more closely, Dunya laughed and pulled at his sleeve. The distraction worked, and the officer was captured by the the child's precociousness, neglecting to notice the yellow tinge of Mariam's skin, and so they were allowed to disembark.

* ⁂ *

Misha had contacted his friend who was studying at Boston University, and he found an apartment for them in an area called Central Square. Given the name of the location, Misha had expected something like Midan Tahrir. But there was little to observe—just apartment buildings, a main road with shops and restaurants, and strange people walking around.

Their building hugged the corner of two streets as if it wanted to be able to see in all directions. Misha stepped into the apartment with Mariam and Dunya behind him. The space contained two small bedrooms, a living room, and a simple kitchen. Mariam said, "it's good." But Misha knew that this was not the glamour of America that she had expected. He turned to her as they stood in the bare living room and said it was temporary, that they would buy a grand house soon like the ones they saw in American movies, that it was just a few weeks they would be here. But she only repeated that it was good.

Misha noticed that Mariam's face remained pale, so he contacted his friend, who helped them to find a doctor. She was diagnosed with jaundice and given the medicine she needed. As Mariam's health improved, Misha's sense of hope rose. The English words still stumbled on his tongue, but he found a job making drawings at an engineering firm. He had hoped for something better, but this was a good start, and he assured Mariam that something better would come.

Misha felt their first two years in America fly by. He came to understand that they did not live in a good neighborhood and urged Mariam to look for another apartment with him, but she told him she just wanted to get settled before moving again. On the weekends, he took her out to explore beyond their neighborhood, going to downtown Boston. One day, they discovered Filene's Basement and quickly their apartment filled with kitchen gadgets, clothes, and toys for Dunya.

Once every two weeks, Misha sat down to write a letter to his family. He did not want to tell them how small the apartment was, how their furniture was mostly bought on sale already damaged, how in the evening they stayed in because of the drugs and prostitutes that occupied the streets of their neighborhood. Instead, he wrote about the toaster and the electric mixer they had bought, the apples in the grocery stores, the pistachios and hazelnuts they could easily purchase. He assured his family that they were doing well, exaggerating the comforts of their life, the luxury of their material accumulations. It would be another fourteen years before he would learn that it was his letters that enticed his younger cousin Layla and her husband, Hafez, to also immigrate.

The first letter that came from home was written in his father's hand, recounting his optimism about getting the hotel back. Misha read about his lawsuit and the time he spent meeting with different lawyers who promised him success. Most of the letters came from Misha's mother, who only wrote of the family news—who got married, who graduated, who gave birth. At the end of each letter, she added, "your father wants me to tell you that he has hope that the lawsuit will succeed and then you can return home."

It didn't occur to Misha to send money back. Even with the loss of the hotel, he knew his parents were still well-off. His salary did not lead to any abundance in their lives. He paid the rent and utilities, gave Mariam money for food and clothes for her and Dunya, and made payments on the car they had bought. There was little left to put aside.

* ⁂ *

Misha's father had spent the morning meeting with a new lawyer. He had grown tired of the slow process the previous one was making. This lawyer assured him it would take no more than a month to get his hotel back. He didn't let his face falter when the lawyer mentioned his fee. It would all be worth it. Misha would return and help to run the hotel. And then Misha and Mariam would have a son, and what he had built would continue. Something for the generations after him to stand on.

"we'll have to sell the maadi apartment building," he told his wife when he returned home that afternoon. He sat at the dining table, waiting for her to bring his dinner.

Bahia turned back to the kitchen after he spoke, although there was no more food to bring out. She allowed herself a single moment of inhaling her breath as she leaned on the counter and looked out of the small window into the center of the building. She glanced around for something to take and settled on a glass of water.

At the dining room table, she sat down and pulled her chair in. "belhana wa elshefa," she said, wishing him a good meal as they started to eat.

"may god bless your hands," he responded.

"is it necessary?" she asked, keeping her gaze on the plate, "is there no other way?"

"what we have saved is spent. there is nothing left except the building. but i'm sure of this lawyer. he will win the case," he said, nodding to affirm his words. Then he added, "and as soon as misha returns, everything will be as it was."

His wife held on to the thin promise of Misha's return. Misha had started sending small pictures of Dunya in his letters. The child was growing. Her dark-brown hair fell to her shoulders, and she noted the bows Mariam put in it. She wanted to hold her, to hear her say "teta."

"whatever you see is best," Bahia told her husband.

* ⁂ *

The phone rings in the middle of the night. Misha has not heard the voices of his family for two years, and, jolted out of sleep, his ears have trouble recognizing the person on the other end.

"alloo, alloo. misha? i'm malek."

Misha can't register the voice until he hears Malek call him Michele, his given name. Then his brain retrieves the memory of his uncle's voice.

"aywa, aywa," he affirms, "how are you uncle?"

"alhamdulillah," his uncle responds, thanking God for his well-being. The response feels sharpened, but Misha assumes it's just the distant connection of the phone. His uncle doesn't ask how he is, and the silence on the line prompts Misha to say his uncle's name to make sure they have not been disconnected.

"misha," his uncle says, "your father . . . your father is gone. he is at peace now."

Misha's hand clutches the phone like a lifeline, and he holds the receiver as if it can transport him not only across the ocean but back two years, back enough to retract his decision to leave. His mind returns to a moment far in the past: *He sits across from his father playing a late-night game of backgammon. His mother's breathing floats from the bedroom to the living room, where he and his father counter each other's moves, measuring the possible alternatives. The moon shines through the curtains, and they only need a small lamp as they study the movement of the circles across the board.*

Misha hears his uncle speaking and realizes he is answering the question he should have asked. "he spent everything he had saved on lawyers who promised him that he could win the hotel back. when what he had saved was gone, he sold the maadi building. finally, he found an honest lawyer who told him that he would never be able to own the hotel again, so he closed the case. when he returned home and your mother asked what happened, he said 'there is nothing, mafeesh haga,' and then he collapsed on the floor. we will bury him tomorrow."

Misha responds with "tayeb" as if he were a pupil in a class obeying a teacher's command.

"your mother wants to talk to you." His uncle's voice lowers, and he is gone before Misha can gather his courage. He hears the tears on the phone before the words come.

"ya ibni, ya ibni," she says as if she could summon her son, "where are you? your father is gone. what will we do? ya rab, ya rab!" Her words rise as she calls upon God. "he wanted to leave you something. he would say that if he could just have the hotel again, that you would return and the hotel would be yours. that is why he tried with everything to get it back."

She takes a breath and Misha can only say, "i'm sorry, ya mama."

"ya ibni, may god be with you in the country that you are in." And the line is gone.

Misha holds the phone after the connection is severed. When he places the receiver back, he sees that Mariam is awake and Dunya is sitting on the bed next to her. They both look at him, but he has nothing to offer. He leans his body against the headboard. The three of them stay in bed with the silence until the sun slowly rises and they can enter the day.

* ⁂ *

As Misha was getting dressed, Mariam asked him almost in a whisper, "do you want to go back?"

"there is nothing there," he answered. Later, Misha wondered if she were the one who wanted to return, if that was the only way she could say it.

* ⁂ *

After the funeral, Sa'ad's brother, Malek, drove Bahia home. He asked if she wanted him to come in, and she shook her head.

"i'll be back with the rest of the family in a couple of hours. just rest. we will bring everything," he said.

Bahia dreaded this part—the ritual of people coming to your home after a death, filling your house with their voices and food. She didn't let Malek walk her upstairs. She climbed the three flights, the heaviness of her breath making her stop and rest at the end of each one.

She unlocked the door, entered, and closed it behind her. The silence of the apartment wrapped itself around her like a shroud. She walked over, sat on the couch, and let the silence descend. She could feel her husband's body in the apartment—resting on the couch next to her, lying in bed for his afternoon nap, sitting on the balcony for the evening breeze. She settled into the cushions as if to feel his body against hers. The sun entered through the open curtains, and in the chair across from her, she saw her son's absence. She imagined how he should have been with her, should have put his arm around her during the funeral, should have guided her to the cemetery, should be sitting here with her: *My son walks next to me as we enter the church. He is dressed in a black suit, and I, too, am in the clothes of mourning. As we step through the door, the eyes of those who are there turn with sideway glances, and I hear someone whisper, "Thank God, her son is standing with her." We slip into the front pew, and as the priest intones the service, my tears flow and my son places his arm around me, leaning me close to him. At the cemetery, he stands on one side of me, and his wife on the other. They grip my hands, steadying my balance until it's over. He sits next to me now, sharing this mourning.*

The knock on the door came, and everyone who attended the funeral descended on the house.

* ⁂ *

The day when Misha knew his father was to be buried, he left the apartment early and walked the streets of Central Square. The stores were still shuttered closed, and he saw a few homeless people leaning into dark corners. An air of smoke and stale alcohol entered his breath. He tried to resist the images that seeped into his mind. Looking at his watch, he noted that it was six, which meant it was noon in Egypt. His mother and his relatives would be preparing to leave the house for the church service. His mother shrouded in black, her face the color of earthy soil without her makeup. His uncle Malek would have come to get her, and he might have sent his wife, Soad, to spend the night with her at the apartment. His mother would lean on his uncle's arm as she made her way to the car, her face stoic. And the priest's chanting and the incense filling the pews. The wailing of those mourning. How many would attend his father's funeral? Would his mother's tears flow silently or loudly? He walked to Harvard Square, where the day was beginning with students and professors and businessmen eager to arrive at their destinations. He wandered through the spiraling streets of this academic city, finding a small diner on Brattle Street where he ordered a cup of black coffee. After the funeral, everyone would come to their home to drink the small cups of Turkish coffee without sugar. An offering to acknowledge the grief of the mourners.

That afternoon, when Misha knew it would be nine in the evening there, he called, but it was his uncle who answered, his voice tight and crisp over the phone lines.

"she's sleeping," he said. "it was a difficult day," he added, as if Misha would not know.

Misha said he would call tomorrow and heard the click of the phone before he hung up.

What if he returned? What life would he step back into? The family wealth was gone. No matter how hard he worked, no matter how much he accumulated, he had no son to inherit. His wife and daughter would receive only the modest sum allowed by Islamic law, and the rest would go to his uncles. Here, he could leave everything he earned to his wife and daughter. But as an only son, he had a duty to fulfill. He should return to care for his mother. But what would his presence offer her? At least here, he could send money to make her life more comfortable. He tried to imagine himself back in the land where he had grown up, but the image evaporated even as he attempted to conjure it.

His uncle took care of his father's business, and Misha learned that his mother had moved in with her sister and brother-in-law. No one asked him to return, but in every phone call, he heard their reprimand. He knew that his absence had become a cavern from which none of them could climb out.

* ⁂ *

A year after his father died, Mariam began to feel unwell. Her breath came in short spurts, and she had trouble standing up for more than ten minutes. Misha took her to the doctor, who asked quick questions and examined her as if her body were made of plastic. He requested blood tests and told them they would be contacted with the results. A few days later, a nurse called to say that Mariam had an autoimmune condition. When Misha asked for clarification, she only said that it would make it hard for Mariam to fight off illness, so she should not get sick.

Misha did everything he could to keep Mariam well. She was reluctant to go out on her own, but she had come to know a few people in the building who had children and would sometimes visit them, so Dunya could have someone to play with. To get her out of the house, Misha enticed her with trips to the ocean on the weekends, where he knew she loved to sit and watch the waves. "it reminds me of alexandria" she told him, "of the summers i spent there as a child with my family."

Her favorite beach was the one they had accidently discovered when they went to Rhode Island to look at the Vanderbilt mansion. Misha looked up at the gigantic chandeliers and wondered at the vision that justified a family living in a seventy-room house. He saw Mariam leaning against a wall and Dunya pulling on her dress. It was clear the mansion did not impress Mariam, and Dunya had become restless with the tedious movement from one room to the other. They left before the tour ended.

On their way back, halfway through Rhode Island, Mariam saw a sign that pointed to a beach and asked Misha to drive in its direction. It was an early evening at the beginning of May, and only a few people were scattered on the sand. They took off their shoes and walked, holding Dunya between them. She giggled when the water touched her toes, and they lifted her up simultaneously, swinging her above the ocean. They kept walking, over an hour, until the sun faded and it was time to leave.

* ⁂ *

The next winter, when already the temperatures were dropping and it was clear snow was coming soon, Misha came home one day to find Mariam dressed and waiting for him at the door.

"please," she said, "can we go to a pharmacy? i'm so itchy everywhere."

Misha drove quickly, and they stepped up to the pharmacy as soon as they entered the store. The pharmacist asked Mariam to show him where she was scratching, and she pulled up her sleeves to reveal her arms, red with protruding dots.

"Have you had chicken pox?" he asked.

They stared at him, trying to make sense of how chickens could be related to Mariam's itching.

"It's an illness that young children get," he said when he saw their perplexed looks.

"Please, can you help us?" Misha asked.

The man seemed to understand the pleading look in Misha's eyes, and he came out from behind the counter to lead them down an aisle to the correct medication, handing it to Misha and explaining how often to put the cream on Mariam's skin. As they walked to the cash register, the pharmacist added, "It's not a good disease for adults. If she spikes a fever, go to the hospital."

When they returned home, Misha went to pick up Dunya from the neighbor's apartment, and that is when he saw that the little girl she played with also had the red dots. He woke up the next day to Dunya wailing at her itchy skin. Misha stayed home from work, did his best to cook and feed both of them. He put gloves on Dunya, so she wouldn't scratch. She was furious against the dots popping up on her skin, and, already, she had created scabs on her face. After a few days, Dunya's itching calmed down, but Mariam remained the same, her skin filled with punctured wounds. Misha felt her tossing and turning on the sixth night, and by morning, it was clear she had a fever.

He left Dunya with the neighbor and took Mariam to the hospital. They sat in the emergency waiting room, listening to the groans of other patients, observing those who came in holding their arms or hopping on one leg. After two hours, Mariam was called. Misha waited while they examined her. Finally, the doctor came out and said she had to be admitted.

"I don't understand," he said. "Is it just a fever? Can you give her medicine?" Misha's brain took in the words: "dangerous" . . . "adults" . . . "watch her" . . . "IV" . . . "complications." He couldn't string them together to create meaning, so he asked if he could see her. The doctor nodded. Misha sat with Mariam, telling her that she would be fine, that she just needed some special medicine. He stayed until the nurse told him visiting hours were over and he had to leave.

When he returned to the apartment, he called the neighbor, who said Dunya was already asleep. He asked if they could keep her for the night since there was no sense in waking her.

* ⁂ *

When the phone rings at 6:15, Misha is already awake and dressed, a lukewarm cup of coffee in his hands. He picks up the receiver and says "hello," careful to pronounce the soft *h* instead of the hard *a* that is used in Arabic for the same greeting. He hears the voice on the other line—a man, perhaps the same doctor from yesterday, but he can't be sure.

"I'm sorry . . . we tried . . . stopped breathing in the middle of the night . . . no immunity."

Misha nods silently as the man repeats, "Mr. Sa'ad, Mr. Sa'ad, are you there?"

* ⁂ *

After Mariam died, Misha couldn't move. It was as if Mariam's absence had glued him permanently in the apartment.

Farid's Departure

I had just turned twenty when I drove Farid to the airport. Like every Egyptian citizen, I grew up seeing King Farouk's red cars moving through the streets of Cairo. He owned Rolls-Royces and Bentleys as well as the Mercedes Benz 540K given to him by Hitler. His preference for red cars ensured that everyone knew when he was driving. His father had given him his first car at the age of eleven, and he drove it around the palace gardens. In 1936, at the age of sixteen, he became our king. He was known for his lavish lifestyle, his desire for drinking, gambling, and women. Whatever he wanted, he collected: watches, stamps, coins, Fabergé eggs, medieval suits of armor, and aspirin bottles. He filled his palace with baroque furniture in the style of Versailles, and the wealthy followed suit, creating ornate French-style salons in their homes.

We thought this monarchy would last forever and that one day King Farouk's son, Fuad, would take over. But within hours of the 1952 revolution, the king had been driven out of the country and was on the way to Italy with his family. When he died in 1965 in Rome, no one in Egypt paid attention. But when Farouk was king and he drove through the city, everything stopped for him.

When I was young, I fancied myself as sophisticated as the king. I took to wearing a French beret and dressed in cuffed pants and white shirts. For me, it was a bit of game, this putting on of a style. To complete the picture, I saved my money and bought a Cadillac. No one else in the family had a car that big, so when my cousin Farid asked me for a ride to the airport, I agreed.

Farid's departure was joyous enough that his family gave their farewell without accompanying him to the airport. He had received a two-year scholarship to study for his master's in engineering. It was an accomplishment, and they were proud of him, assured that afterward he would return. It was a momentary exile, and in their minds, my cousin Misha remained an anomaly. No one saw his departure as a precedent for what would follow, not yet.

By the time he left, Farid's parents, Malek and Soad, were gone, and the night before, it was his siblings and cousins who gathered to bid him farewell. We came together for a meal of lamb, grape leaves, and rice that my mother, Fayza, made, and the jokes abounded about the American women, red convertibles, and whiskey he would find. We made our requests for gifts when he returned—chocolate, perfume, cigars.

By midnight, everyone had returned to their homes to catch a few hours of sleep. Farid and I sat on the couch, our eyes drifting from sleep to startled wakefulness. At two in the morning, we gathered ourselves and Farid's two suitcases into the car and entered the darkness of the city. Neither of us spoke for a while, as we fought against the desire to drift back into dreams. When we approached Airport Road, I glanced over at Farid and noted the slight tremble of his mouth and the blinking of his eyes.

"it's a good opportunity," I offered.

"yes, yes, you're right, ya fanous," answered Farid as if just waking up.

"you'll learn new things and return with a degree from amreeka. that has meaning."

"inshallah."

"and for sure you will have fun. they say there are beautiful things in california."

Farid looked straight ahead as if he had not heard my words.

"i heard the weather is good in california," I added.

Farid rubbed his hands together as if to warm them.

I tried again, "buy a camera and send us pictures."

This seemed to bring Farid out of his silence. "yes, yes," he said, "thank you, fanous. i'll send pictures." Something about the idea of transporting images of himself and what he would see across the ocean seemed to quiet his nerves, as if he had found a lifeline to keep himself from drowning.

The remainder of the ride floated quietly until we arrived at the airport, and I walked inside with him. At that hour, only those travelling overseas were there, and the tension hit against the tiredness of passengers and security guards. Farid seemed to be sleepwalking through the passport check, the luggage check, the search for the gate, and I stayed with him, assuring him he was moving in the right direction. When we reached the gate, I sat next to him and waited. Across from us was a young couple, the woman holding an infant, perhaps not more than a few weeks old. The man looked agitated, shifting from crossing one leg over the other, and the woman kept closing her eyes, but they would open, startled by some sound. I thought, *it's too much trouble, this moving from place to place.* I wanted to know where I was sleeping each night, not wake to wonder where I was and why. Perhaps it was at that moment that I determined the course of my own life, the decision to bind myself to the land of my birth. This unmooring of oneself, this letting go of one rope as you reached for another was not for me.

Farid's flight was called. We hurried our movements, gathering his belongings. Our hug and kisses were speedy, rushing Farid to the plane that would transport him.

Farid – 1966

Farid could have followed in the footsteps of Misha, his eldest uncle's son. He knew there were jobs in America and that engineers were needed. But it was rare that anyone heard from Misha. Farid knew that once a year, on January 7, Misha called his mother to wish her a happy Christmas feast. His phone calls were quick, enough to ask about her health, to assure her that he and Dunya were well. A two-minute call that was meant to compensate his mother for the absence of her son and granddaughter. She had to sustain herself on that phone call for a year, use the few words he had spoken to carry her until the next call arrived.

Farid decided to come back because of family, knowing that this is what he wanted to build. When he returned, his two older brothers, Morcos and Khalil, along with their wives, Sawsan and Mervat, folded him into their homes. He came back with a master's degree in electrical engineering. Quickly, he discovered that in Egypt, that American degree had meaning, and he used it to carve his place in the country. It opened doors, and he walked through them until he reached the highest position. He became a minister, and his words carried weight. In America, he knew that he would always be a foreigner. He had noticed the way people turned their eyes away from his brown skin, stopped listening when they detected his accent, scoffed at his suggestions. Each night he sat in a room to eat alone.

* ⁂ *

At the age of sixteen, Farid was a child pretending to be a man, but when his mother, Soad, died, he shed tears like a baby. Everyone knew she was sick, but they hid it from him. He was the youngest after his two brothers. He heard murmurings that his mother had lost a child before he was born, another boy who died at only a few months. Afterwards, everyone said two boys is enough, a blessing for any family and to ask for more was to anger God. But Farid arrived unexpected. His father, Malek, turned away from him, thinking his wife had tricked him. So, Farid became his mother's son.

As the baby of the family, he was coddled by his mother and his brothers. It wasn't until his mother died that he realized the distance of his father, that he barely knew him except as a shadowy figure who entered the room with a scowl. Farid didn't remember his father speaking to him except once. He was about eight years old and it was Easter. Everyone was at their house to celebrate, and the rooms were filled with noise and laughter. His mother was smiling that day, and Farid was playing with his cousins. They were attempting a game of hide-and-seek, crouching behind chairs and sneaking through the legs of so many adults. Farid snuck a cookie from the platter on the dining room buffet. It was a piece of ghorayeba, the kind made for holidays, each one shaped like a flower, one circle in the middle surrounded by six circles. Farid had watched his mother make them, her hands rolling each small ball and then attaching it to the others until the flower was complete. They were made of butter and sugar, the cookie melting in your mouth, retreating to the soft dough that had created it. Farid took a bite, then saw one of his cousins and started running.

In the living room he paused, scanning for a hiding place when the remaining part of the cookie slipped from his hand to the floor. His father's image appeared. He was standing, already using a cane by that time, his body at an angle as he leaned into it. He pointed his finger at the crumbs that had scattered on the floor. "pick that up," Malek shouted, each word a single syllable hitting against the walls. Farid stood paralyzed, the voices in the room holding their breath in silence. "the butter and flour that made this ghorayeba cost money. money doesn't get thrown on the ground." And Farid knew that in his father's eyes, the crumbs of that cookie had more value than him.

Farid's father believed in money. He followed in the footsteps of his father, Salim, who had left Kom Ombo to make his success in Cairo. Malek used to say that a man who had one piaster was worth only a piaster. After his two elder sons finished high school, he dissuaded them from college. "four years of looking at books and not earning a pound, what's the point of that?" he said. So, one after the other, each son was set up in a job. When Farid's turn came, he assumed that he would follow the same pattern, but Morcos took him aside and said, "you're smart, you should go to college. i'll pay the fees." Farid studied hard that last year and did well enough in the exams that he could attend the Engineering College at Cairo University. His father paid no attention. He died two weeks before Farid graduated.

* ⁂ *

Farid enrolled at the University of Southern California for his master's degree. The campus occupied a large city block, and an iron gate kept everything intact. Inside, the buildings stood apart, as if afraid of each other's proximity. Open space dominated the campus, and the sun layered itself over everything, no clouds to distract it. Outside the gate, there were no stores or restaurants, barely anyone walking. The area was marked by empty streets, a vast expanse with nothing to fill it. It felt like a deserted land mine.

The morning after he arrived, he called his cousin Misha.

"misha, misha . . . this is farid. i'm in amreeka," he announced over the phone.

Misha's voice faded as if he were taking steps backward. He asked about everyone's health in Egypt and responded to Farid's questions about Dunya and himself.

"i want to see you," said Farid.

"where are you?" asked Misha.

"in california," he answered.

"you're six hours away," said Misha.

"that's far," said Farid, disappointment entering his voice. "but you have a car, you can drive," he added, hopefully.

"farid. it's six hours by plane."

Farid had assumed that he would be able to see Misha, that there would be a familiar face in this new country. The conversation ended with vague words about finding a way to see each other, but both knew that, at most, they might share one or two more phone calls. America stretched like a piece of dough, rolled so thin that it threatened to tear.

Farid spent the few days before classes wandering around Los Angeles. He had expected to see the glamour of America, but along with the tall buildings and large cars, he also saw the drunken, the homeless, the ones who fished what they could find out of garbage cans, and the unstable who wandered aimlessly. He breathed in the smog that descended on the population and looked around him. He sensed no happiness in people's faces. The city felt almost tragic. People existed here, but they were not connected to this place, their identities had not fused to the landscape.

Inside the campus, students marched with their books from one class to another, their steps intent on their destination. Farid tried to follow the layout of the campus, but so many of the paths curved and he found himself returning to his starting point. When he stopped someone for directions, he often had to repeat himself as they adjusted to the accent of his voice. They pointed him in the right direction, but there was no lingering conversation.

There was one other Egyptian in the engineering program. The young man had approached Farid after one of their classes. He introduced himself as Ahmed, and Farid found himself cautious, knowing he was Muslim. But his loneliness had already deepened, and he was glad to at least speak to someone in Arabic. Still, every time Ahmed suggested they get together, Farid hesitated and excused himself with the amount of work he had to do.

It was rare for a Copt to receive one of these international scholarships, and Farid had struggled for his chance to study in America. He had ingratiated himself with those in higher positions, played the subservient position. He had ambition, and he knew the only way to rise was through eliciting favors from those in power. Even then, Farid suspected that the committee camouflaged his acceptance. To show that they had not placed a Copt before a Muslim, he was chosen as an alternate for the scholarship, and then the person who received it was offered a better opportunity, so the scholarship went to Farid.

One day, having come down with a particularly bad cold, Farid was unable to attend his classes. Late in the afternoon, there was the first knock on his door. Ahmed stood there, looking alarmed, almost as if he feared finding Farid dead.

After ascertaining the situation, Ahmed left and came back an hour later with an assortment of cold medicines and orange juice. The next afternoon, he returned armed with a large pot and notes from the classes Farid had missed.

"don't blame me if it's not good," he said, lifting the lid of the pot to reveal the rising steam. "i called my mother yesterday and she gave me the recipe. it's her chicken soup, and she said it would for sure cure you."

After that, Farid pulled open the curtain of his mistrust. Ahmed became a good friend. He had already been in the States for a year, and he helped Farid find his way around. Farid appreciated his company and relied on him for direction. Ahmed was always willing to help, and Farid wondered if perhaps he had misperceived other Muslims. He had grown up hearing his family speak about how Muslims always gained the advantage, about how Copts were never allowed to come in first. He heard that when Morcos and his wife's nephew was first in his class, the teacher provided answers for the final exam to the Muslim child in second place to ensure that a Copt would not have the top ranking. He heard about his father's cousin's son who applied over and over for a scholarship to Europe, and that each time it was given to a Muslim. He did not doubt the veracity of all he heard, but here Ahmed was the one who rescued him out of his complete loneliness. Once they graduated, Ahmed decided to remain in the States, but Farid carried their friendship back to Egypt with him. It changed the way he interacted with his Muslim colleagues, and, although he never considered it, it may have contributed to his success.

Through Ahmed, Farid came to know a few people, mostly other foreign students. They gravitated to one another, carrying their loneliness in their bags along with their books. Some were from India, a few from Malaysia, one from Ghana, and two from Kuwait. Their religious differences dissipated in front of their foreignness. They ate together and occasionally gathered at someone's apartment where the host cooked food from their country. Each meal tasted like home even when its origin was from another place. It was a reprieve from the blandness they encountered daily in the cafeteria. When they gathered at Ahmed's apartment, the music of Umm Kulthum and Abdel Halim Hafez came through the tape player, shrouding Farid in a fog of nostalgia. But despite their few gatherings, they remained cloaked in their isolation.

Each day, Southern California rose with the sun. The bright light spread itself like an omen of good tidings, but soon Farid realized that it laid itself like a blanket covering the underside of the city. Already, he had been warned to stay away from Skid Row, an area east of downtown designated for those who had little to nothing. It was set within such defined boundaries that it seemed as if the area had been created by city planners. And when he made his way to Beverly Hills at the suggestion of his cousin Layla, who told him he must see this famous area and tell her about it, he unearthed the illusion of America. Only a few miles from the rest of the city, the wealthy and famous inhabited large, pristine homes. Those who lived here owned more than the houses they purchased. The polished shoes of men and the click of women's heels imprinted on the cement.

The sun was constant, each day the same as if there was no passage of time, and Farid felt himself revolving inside this bubble. Days, weeks, and months went by, and he couldn't mark any single day on the calendar as being more important than another. When the summer after his first year arrived, he learned he could take extra classes and complete his degree in a year and a half. He made the arrangements, knowing that he might lose himself if he remained here too long.

* ⁂ *

The day Farid came back from America, the family told him that his cousin Layla and her husband, Hafez, had decided to emigrate, that their paperwork had been approved, that they had already done the interview, that they were waiting only for final confirmation. Hafez had told everyone that he would only be going for a couple of years, just enough to get his master's. That he would do what Farid had done and return. Farid had received a scholarship to go to the United States, and all the arrangements had been made for him.

But Hafez was not in the same position, and Farid knew that the story he was telling the family was already torn.

* ⁂ *

Farid knocked on Hafez and Layla's door the next afternoon unannounced. He was still suffering from jet lag, and his eyes had trouble focusing, seeing what was in front of him instead of what he had witnessed over the past year and a half. Hafez greeted him happily with a tight embrace, but Farid could feel the pebbles rippling beneath his skin. As Farid came into the living room, Layla folded him into her arms.

"sit, sit. let me bring you some tea," she offered, rushing back to the kitchen. She returned, carrying a tray with the tea and a plate of petit fours. She placed it on the table in front of the sofa where Farid was sitting. She poured the tea, handing one cup to Farid and another to her husband, who had settled in one of the chairs next to the sofa. She neglected to pour herself a cup and instead perched on the chair across from Farid and said, "tell us, tell us . . . about amreeka." Her tone was urgent, as if there was only so much time to reveal the story.

Farid jumped into her question and began explaining the hardship, the expense of life there, the loneliness that wraps around you, but Hafez interrupted.

"why are you saying this? you know we're going. you want to scare layla?" The blood rising to his face betrayed the even tone of his voice.

"hafez, i don't want to lie to you. amreeka is not all gold and money. the life is hard and the people strange. they don't know the meaning of family." Farid moved to the edge of the couch, as if by being closer his words could reach more easily.

"what do you want to say?" Hafez asked, his body leaning away.

"don't go, ya hafez. it will be a mistake."

"you were given an opportunity," Hafez said. "your family has wealth and you have connections—you found a way. i must make my own."

Farid directed his glance at Hafez. "and indeed you've done that. you're already successful. stay here, may our children grow up together."

Hafez winced.

Layla leaned in and asked Farid if he wanted more tea, and although he shook his head, she poured him another cup.

The room retreated. A weight settled, and the cups of tea sat untouched, whispering in the silence.

Hafez let his heartbeat calm to a steady rhythm and tried to keep his tone level. "you weren't here, ya farid. you didn't see the war and you didn't see what the war did."

Farid tucked in his lips and looked down at his shoes. He had bought them at Macy's department store a few weeks after he arrived in America. They were Florsheim shoes, and the salesperson had told him they were the most popular and best-made shoe in America. The leather was a deep brown with a design decorating the front, and the laces tied neatly in the center. The shoes had kept their shape well, showing wear only in the slope of the heel.

"i know that the war had an impact on all of us," Farid said, raising his head but not directing his gaze at Hafez.

"you weren't here, ya farid. you didn't sit with us in the dark every night waiting for a bomb to be dropped, and you weren't here when we heard how many men lost their lives in this war."

Farid held his body still as if any movement could shatter the very earth they stood on.

* ⁂ *

On the morning of June 5, 1967, Farid and Ahmed were planning to go to Santa Monica together. But the ring of the telephone woke Farid at five with Ahmed's voice on the other end.

"did you hear the news? there is a war. and egypt will be victorious!"

A few hours later, they were sitting on the sand, facing the Pacific and debating the outcome of the war. Ahmed was certain of a win for Egypt and its role as the savior of the Palestinian homeland. Farid was reluctant to voice a strong opinion. He had often heard his family argue that Egypt should stay out of Palestine, that it would only mire itself in the problems of others when it needed to solve its own. But now, hearing the news while away from his own country, he wondered at the loss Palestinians felt, the distance that separated them from their homes and their land. He wondered if this war would change anything.

They rallied back and forth a bit, with Farid mostly listening. Around them, the beach filled with women in bikinis, families with children, and tourists taking pictures. They kept their voices low, noticing that at times someone's glance in their direction lingered too long. At one point, a man came by selling cotton candy, and they bought two. The sweet taste coated their tongues until the texture became too sticky. They left shortly afterward. The sun had wearied them, and they returned satiated by the day.

* ⁂ *

Farid, Hafez, and Layla sat as the silence folded itself into the cushions.

"i want a better life," Hafez said, "for me, for layla, for our children. this is not the country we know. cairo now has five million people. there is not enough for everyone. you didn't see the men when they returned from the war. the army took them and returned them bent in half, their eyes locked into the horror they'd seen. this country is over."

Farid opened his mouth, closed it to take back his breath. "i'm sorry about your brother." He paused for a moment as the words lingered in the air. "but you're making a mistake," he said, looking directly at Hafez.

Hafez shook his head.

"stay here and build your life, with the family." Seeing the curtain over Hafez's eyes, he added, "don't take layla away from her family. you will leave us with empty chairs."

Hafez opened his mouth to respond, but it was Layla who answered. "if we don't like it, we'll come back. but at least hafez can get his master's degree."

Farid looked at his cousin, only in her second year of marriage, still so young, and something in him did not want to tell her what he knew would happen, the way life in America can sweep you away until you can't stop.

The quiet of the afternoon began to tremble, and from outside, they could hear the city rising from its rest with the honking of a car, the scraping wheels of a cart, and the voice of a child. It was time to begin the second half of the day. Hafez looked to the window, the white lace curtains Layla had sewn so carefully, a small protection against the cool air of winter.

"i thank you for this visit, ya farid. inshallah, we will see each other in good health."

Layla turned to Hafez, but he had already risen and was extending his arm. Farid attempted to say something, but the power of his voice had deflated. He had no choice, so he rose and shook Hafez's hand in farewell.

* ⁂ *

When I came back from America, I was ready to get married, to settle down and build my family. There was a tailor in Dokki where I went to have my suits made. Back then, there was almost nothing ready-made. The downtown streets were lined with fabric stores, and each neighborhood had its tailor. I had admired the suit of a friend, and he directed me to his tailor in Dokki, saying he was the best. I made my way there, even though it took close to an hour, going along the Nile Corniche and across the Cairo University Bridge. Dokki had been just a small area until the foreign embassies moved there and along with them came the villas for the foreign ambassadors. I suspected that this tailor had been there before the area became so desirable.

When I entered the store the first time, it was the tailor's sister who greeted me. She stood behind the small counter of the kiosk. Behind her, there were shelves piled with folded fabric—mostly grays, browns, and blacks, since this tailor specialized in men's clothing. Each folded pile was pinned with a piece of paper and a customer's name. Even the counter was cluttered with a tower of finished pants and an assortment of pins, chalk, scissors, all the accoutrements of the trade. What struck me was the small jar in the corner of the counter that held a single yellow daisy. It was clearly out of place, the water in the jar a threat to the multitude of fabrics.

The tailor's sister greeted me with "sabah el kheir" and asked how she could help me. I was taken in by her simple straightforwardness. It was rare to see a woman working in those days, but her manner demanded respect. Her black hair was pulled back into a ponytail, and she was wearing a simple white collared shirt, one that could have almost been mistaken for a man's shirt. She was young, perhaps in her early twenties, her clear skin and bright eyes marking her youth. I pulled the fabric I had bought out of the bag to give my hands something to do and stumbled through an explanation of the suit I wanted. Her gaze never faltered as I spoke, and I finally sputtered into saying I wanted the same suit as my friend's.

She wrote down something on a small piece of paper and pinned it to the fabric, then came around the counter and ordered me to stand with feet apart and arms outstretched. She proceeded to pull the measuring tape across each part of my body, from my neck to my torso, along the length of my arms, down the height of my legs. I kept my body still, allowed her to do her job in silence. Each time she measured, she wrote the numbers down. When she finished, she returned to her place behind the counter and pinned the paper to the fabric.

"come back in two weeks," she said as she picked up the bundle of fabric and placed it on top of a pile on the shelf behind her. "shokran," I said and kept my mouth open, hoping I would think of something besides thank you to say. But before I could gather a thought, the door opened with another customer, a middle-aged woman carrying a pile of white and black fabrics that she could barely balance. I held the door open for her and lifted the pile of material from her arms to unload it on the counter. The woman thanked me, and I muttered "afwan" in response and left.

The young woman lingered in my mind as I waited to return to the tailor. She hadn't even smiled at me, but something about her manner, her lack of self-consciousness, her complete disinterest in making an impression, had captured me. I thought of her as I worked on one of the office projects; her face came back to me when I was in the middle of a meeting. It had only been ten days since I dropped off the fabric, but I could no longer wait.

When I opened the door to the tailor this time, it was a man who stood behind the counter. He looked to be in his mid-thirties, with a full head of curly black hair and a straight face. He looked up with eyes that seemed to know exactly why I was there.

"misa'a el noor," he greeted me, and added nothing, waiting for me to speak.

I stumbled through a sentence about having left fabric for a suit. He asked for my name and then turned to look behind him at the piled shelves.

"one minute," he said, and then stepped through a side curtain.

I counted to ten to steady my heartbeat. When he came back, he said it wasn't ready, that I had dropped it off less than two weeks ago, a slight edge to his tone as if accusing a child of not doing his multiplication tables correctly. I apologized and left.

I waited another two weeks before gathering the courage to return. When I entered the small shop, she was standing behind the counter, and I'm certain I saw her lips curve into a smile.

"misa'a el kheir, ustaz farid," she said, and added, "you took some time before you returned."

A knot of panic hit my stomach, and I wondered if her brother had told her about my last fumbling entrance into the shop. "asef," I apologized, and added something about being busy at work.

She pointed her gaze directly at me, and I knew she didn't believe me. "you must have an important job," she responded as if to humor me.

I attempted to explain my work, and she let me continue until I ran out of breath.

"would you like your suit?" she asked as if picking it up was an option.

I nodded, by this point all my words having been depleted. She handed me the bundle and gestured to where I could try it on in a small, curtained-off section in the back corner. When I came out, I stood still while she walked around me, tugged a sleeve, and bent down to straighten the pant legs and ensure they were the same length.

"it looks good," she said, "but the sleeves need to be about two centimeters shorter. we'll adjust them."

"shokran," I said, afraid to say anymore at this point.

When I reemerged after changing out of the suit, I handed it back to her refolded.

"you can pick it up in two days," she said, again marking the instructions on a piece of paper that she pinned to the bundle. She looked up. "and this time, don't be late," she added, her lips twitching into a smirk.

"of course not," I responded, adding another apology as I left.

Outside, I wiped my sweaty hands against my pants and took several long breaths to calm my rapidly pounding heart.

After I went back to pick up the suit, I returned several times that year, and I had three suits made, five pairs of pants, and two jackets. I became known as the best-dressed man, and I was almost penniless. But each time I returned to the tailor, I lingered a few extra minutes and Zeinab and I spoke. That slight upturn of her lip became a smile and eventually a laugh when I attempted a joke. She started calling me the king since I had told her I was named after King Farouk. "and where will the king wear this suit?" she would ask. Every two weeks, I made my way to the tailor, to pick up an article of clothing, to drop off more material, or to have something adjusted.

After a few months, I ventured to bring a flower with me—just one bright yellow daisy. When I offered it to her, she looked almost frightened, and quickly I explained that it was to replace the one in the vase, that I had noticed it was wilting the last time I was there, and indeed the vase was sitting on the corner of the counter empty. Zeinab took the flower and placed it in the vase, then turned her attention to getting the pants I had come to pick up.

I rarely saw her brother. He usually stayed in the back, as if he were a nocturnal animal more accustomed to dark spaces. When I did see him, he reminded me of a wild dog, his hair always unkempt and his gait unsteady. When I came in and he was there, he would extend his glance at me and let it settle for too long, until I had to find a distraction, something to force his gaze away.

After a year, I approached my eldest brother. He lived in our parents' old apartment in the center of Maadi. When he married, he had followed tradition and moved in with his wife. Now, as the eldest, he had inherited the apartment. When my other brother, Khalil, married Mervat and started his own family, he also rented a place in Maadi.

I sat in the living room with Morcos. Little had changed since my parents' passing. The richly upholstered furniture that had been considered luxurious in the past remained in the room. I presented what I wanted, my face turning red as I described Zeinab and tried to utter my feelings toward her. My brother sat quietly until I was finished, leaning back in his chair, arms folded.

"what is her name?" he asked.

This is what I had feared, what I had pushed down into the recesses of my mind each time I entered the tailor's shop. It was Zeinab, the woman, who attracted me. I had erased religion, as if we could rub out the way it was stamped on each of us, written on our ID cards, embedded in our names.

"her name is zeinab," I said, not lifting my gaze.

I didn't have to look up to feel the rigid tension of my brother's body.

The burden of our history descended over the room as heavy as the blocks of limestone used to build the pyramids. Under the weight of the past—from the Muslim conquest of the seventh century, to the taxes imposed under threat of conversion, to the loss of language, to the burned churches—the room fell, threatening to sink us into the mud from which we all came.

My brother sat upright, his back erect, a ruler with exact measurements. When he spoke, he looked steadily at me.

"mesh momken," he said, his tone even and tight as he asserted the impossibility of my request. He paused a second as if allowing me to respond. But the only answer I offered was the blood draining from my face. "this is not a woman for marriage," he continued. "if you want to play a little, go ahead. but you will not marry a muslim woman. we are better than that. did you forget who you are when you went to amreeka? i didn't send you there so you could return and throw away your future and break the family. if you marry her, your name will be removed. you will not be from us. forget this matter and i'll find you a good wife."

I wanted to respond, to refuse his words, to claim this woman as the one I wanted. But my throat felt parched, my tongue stuck to the roof of my mouth, shutting off all words from escaping. My brother got up with one last word, "khalas," putting an end to the discussion. I never returned to the tailor to pick up the last suit.

* ⁂ *

In the end, Farid let his eldest brother choose. He found a woman from a good family, one who would take care of her home and her children and maintain the family's status. Farid knew that his wife fulfilled her duties. She gave him three children—Maha, Sonya, and Fathy—and she ran the household efficiently, but sometimes, he would search for a look in her eyes, wanting her to see him as more than a duty to fulfill. He shook his shoulders as if to shrug off his romantic illusions.

Farid made sure each of his children went to college, and that his daughters married men who were educated and successful. Once they married, Farid bought each of them an apartment in Heliopolis, one of the best neighborhoods. Their homes were well furnished. His grandchildren attended the best French schools, and he knew that they too would inherit his success. It was his son he worried about. Fathy was the youngest, arriving after they had relinquished hope for a son. Farid saw how his wife and daughters spoiled him, turning him into a frivolous man. Already, he was in his thirties and still hadn't settled down. Farid found Fathy a good job in a foreign company, but he hadn't received a promotion since he started. Every time Farid tried to open the conversation about marriage, it seemed that Fathy suddenly remembered he had an appointment. When Farid complained to his wife, she brought him a cup of tea and assured him that their son would find his way, that he just needed a little more time.

The last time Fathy came over, Farid tried to guide him toward the importance of family. "you must build your legacy," he said as he accepted tea from his wife. "look at our family, this is what matters."

Fathy watched his father as he took the first sip of tea, careful to test its temperature as it approached his lips. "i'll get married, inshallah," Fathy responded, "but first i want to see the world, travel a bit."

As if his son's words had unlocked a box, Farid stiffened his posture and began to speak: "don't think of amreeka. in amreeka, we would have been scattered like watermelon seeds. amreeka is not what it seems to be. i spent a year and a half there. it's a land of isolated people. you go to work alone, you eat alone, you live alone. children leave their parents. parents abandon their children. there is no family in amreeka. you're like a branch cut off from the tree. there's nothing to nurture you. for a year and a half, i lived alone in that country."

Fathy attempted to shift the conversation, asking how Layla and Hafez were doing, but the mere mention of their names only made his father's voice rise. "hafez shouldn't have gone. i tried to tell him, but he didn't hear me. he thought he could have more in amreeka. in nasser's time, many things were not available, but there was not such discrepancy between rich and poor. when we were equal, people wanted less, felt less deprived. but amreeka enticed us with its movies, and watching the wealthy made us hungry. hafez was doing well, working hard, acquiring a reputation. there was no reason for him to leave. the only purpose for amreeka is to make money. this was the promise that we saw in all the movies they exported to our country. he would have become a millionaire if he had stayed, and in amreeka he has not become one. so, what has he achieved? he lost everything. one sister there; one brother here. he shifted the ground beneath him, and his castle cracked to a pile of stone. in egypt, you can be king, but in amreeka, you are always a peasant."

The apartment in Mohandessein expanded each Friday. Farid's wife, Ghada, situated his favorite chair in the center of the living room facing the couch. He sat, the bulk of his frame filling the seat, waiting. The calls to prayer were louder on Friday, the holy day for Muslims. Through myriad microphones, the chants intoned through the city. They were a reminder to stop and give worship, although most continued about their business, the calls having become a ritual that merged with daily routines. Farid's two daughters arrived shortly after the Dhur call to prayer. Maha, the eldest, and Sonya, the younger, had inherited their mother's smooth, dark hair and their father's brown eyes. Their entrance carried the confidence of their lives, and behind them their husbands and children followed. One by one, they approached to greet Farid, leaning over to kiss him on both cheeks.

The home rose and fell with the voices of three generations. For a few minutes, his five granddaughters succeeded in sitting politely next to each other on the couch across from him. They sat according to their ages—from the eldest, with a sweet round face, to the youngest, with long, wavy brown hair.

Farid surveyed them as if they were his subjects and passed his questions over each of them—about school, piano lessons, obeying their parents. Once his questions concluded, they knew they could remove themselves from the adult world and enter into their playing. Their high tones pulsated through the apartment, an accompaniment to the adult conversations. Farid's daughters took their turn speaking with him, checking on his health. Then they entered into the kitchen to offer their assistance to their mother and began the chatter of their lives. Both daughters had jobs, one as a teacher in a French school and the other as a manager in a bank. But their kitchen conversation circled around taking care of husbands, children, home, hair, clothes, sustaining the status of their lives. Their mother taught them how to hold their place within this social structure.

Farid's sons-in-law presented their greetings and offered him a drink, perhaps a scotch from the bottles they had given him over the years, purchased from the duty-free shops on their travels. He nodded with approval, accepting both the drink and their role in his family. One was a doctor and the other was a dentist. His daughters had done well. He enjoyed hearing about their success, their trials in the world from which he was now retired, and they reclined into the comfort of their seats, their limbs stretching to take the space provided. One lengthened his legs forward and crossed his ankles, leaned back into the comfort of the couch. The other sat up in the high-back chair, reached his arm holding the drink over the edge as if waiting for his glass to be replenished.

They were at ease in Farid's empire. And they listened like students, knowing there was something to be learned here. After each took a turn to update him on their success, he distributed his advice. His words had weight. He had had a strong career and achieved a rare position in the ranks of the ministry as a Copt. As dinner approached with platters arriving on the table, he ended his monologue as he always did—"you can succeed here. there is no need for amreeka."

There was one empty seat as they sat down, waiting for Farid's son to arrive. His knock on the door came after everyone was already at the table, and his entrance was greeted with jokes about timing his arrival to the exact moment of dinner. Everyone joined the laughter except for Farid, who gave his son a grim look, not even turning as Fathy bent to kiss his cheek. Despite being in his thirties, Fathy still looked like a young boy, endlessly youthful, and he was the only child to have inherited the thickness of his father's eyebrows and his soft, pouty lips.

Fathy took his place at the table and proceeded to tease his nieces, making them giggle until his mother lightly told him to stop so they wouldn't choke on their food. He kept the mood light, making jokes until his father finally allowed a smile to slip over his lips.

Dinner continued with Farid at the head of the table. His daughters served him, and his wife kept a careful eye on his plate, catered to his needs. His grandchildren called him "geddo."

He held the firmness of the decision he made forty years ago. Around the table, an abundance of voices rose in unison. He knew that in America, his children would have spread out across the expanse of the country, returning only for the brief visit of a holiday. Here, they gathered at his request, and he could see his accomplishments laid out before him. The kingdom he created held them all.

Farid's Return

Farid returned a year and a half after he left. Some in the family had expected that he would remain in America, that the enticement would be too strong to resist, that like our cousin Misha he would disappear into the vast continent that no one could outline. But there he was, walking out of the gate and into the airport where I waited. He was a little thinner, his back slightly stooped, but I couldn't tell whether it was from the bag he was carrying or another weight. His smile opened when he saw me, and we greeted one another surrounded by others equally joyous at their reunions.

"alhamdulillah, you came back," I said, "amreeka did not steal you from us." I spoke lightheartedly, thinking he would respond with some laughter, throwing a joke back, but he only mumbled back "alhamdulillah" as if he had been spared a great catastrophe. We collected his two suitcases, which later we discovered carried only what he had taken with him. He brought no presents, as if he wanted nothing to trace him back to where he had been.

When we stepped out of the airport, the heavy afternoon air hit our nostrils with a combination of dust and diesel. I kept walking but stopped to look back when I realized Farid had not followed me. He stood still while people walked around him as if he were a marker in the road.

"yala," I called out, "your aunt fayza has prepared a meal for a king and we're all hungry."

Farid registered my words and followed.

It was midafternoon, the traffic heavier as everyone made their way home from work eager for their afternoon meal and rest. Farid seemed to settle into his seat with no need to speak. I tried to draw him out.

"so was amreeka to your liking?"

He looked at me, becoming aware that my question required an answer. "it's a good place to learn. but not to live."

I plowed him with more questions about the women, the food, the houses, but he had little to offer, as if he had been in a barren land for the last year and a half.

As the airport retreated behind us, Farid's shoulders relaxed and he began to talk, asking about each member of the family, and I relayed the news—who married, who was born, who was ill.

After a pause, I said, "you know everyone works for the government now. there are almost no private companies. the government has taken them over."

Farid nodded.

"what will you do now?" I asked.

"build a family," he responded without hesitation

For the rest of the drive, Farid opened his window and looked out as if he were watching a movie. When we neared home, he asked, "what did my aunt cook?"

I laughed. "she has been cooking for a week, changing her mind each day about what you would want to eat. she has made kofta, lamb, rice, molekhia, and she even fried some taamia in case you have a craving for the old food. you'll eat for days."

Hafez and Layla's Departure

My brother-in-law Hafez sat in the front seat next to me, and his wife, my sister Layla, sat in the back with the two carry-on bags. As soon as the car doors closed, it seemed the air had been sucked out of the car, leaving us with a limited supply of oxygen, allowing only shallow breaths. For the first ten minutes, silence shrouded us, and we moved as if suspended in time. We drove through the darkness of early morning. Once we crossed the Airport Bridge, I turned the handle to open the window, attempting to release the tightness I was feeling in my chest.

"the air is beautiful so early in the morning," I suggested.

Hafez kept his eyes fixed ahead, and Layla nodded, exhaling with an almost imperceptible hum in response.

I tried again, finding it hard to hold the tension in the car. "the flight leaves at six?" I asked, although I already knew.

This elicited a movement from Hafez as he reached into his pocket to pull out the ticket and squint to look at it in the darkness.

"yes, six," he said, and I could see the tilt of Layla's head in the back seat as if she were waiting for a different answer.

"six hours to london, then a three-hour layover, then seven more hours to boston," Hafez responded with his rehearsed answer. Layla leaned back into the seat and turned her face to the window. Her departure would leave me and Hala. I was the eldest and Hala the youngest, and Layla was the one between us. With her leaving, it felt as if the rope of our connection might break, but I hoped it might only fray a little. For now, I only wanted to comfort her anxiety.

"inshallah, it will be a good flight. i heard they give you good food on these planes. and you can even get a drink," I said, shifting my body in the seat.

There was no response. I moved my head to catch Hafez through the corner of my eye. He sat like a wax statue without a single muscle moving. He had relinquished everything—the apartment, the car, the furniture. When Layla pleaded to keep some things in storage, he refused, as if he did not want anything to pull him back. Leaving something behind meant the possibility of not succeeding, of returning as a failure. When Layla pleaded, he only said, "we will buy new things." And that seemed to calm her, perhaps imagining the mansions, large cars, and glittering clothes she saw in the movies.

"yes, everything will be good," I heard Layla say from the back seat. She sat up straighter, as if she had made a decision. "life in amreeka will be good," she added, and I could hear her erasing the hesitation in her voice.

Hafez pushed his back against the seat, and I closed the window.

As the airport lights flickered in the distance, more cars appeared on the road. *where are they all going?* I wondered. *how many were travelling for pleasure, how many for a dream?* I maneuvered into the airport traffic and up to the entrance.

"i'll park and meet you inside," I said.

Hafez got out and opened the door to retrieve the handbags as Layla stepped out of the other door. Before they reached the trunk, the rest of the family had arrived to help, and their four suitcases were carried away by other hands, the momentum taking them through the doors and into the neon-lit chaos of the airport.

Everyone had come to say goodbye. I was still young then, in my late twenties, and maybe I didn't understand what it all meant. Misha's departure had been almost fifteen years ago, and his memory had faded for those of us who were young at the time he left. Now, only two people were leaving, and there were so many of us still here. We were like a force of energy, and, even so early in the morning, our laughter rang against the ceiling of the airport. We talked and joked as if it were any other family gathering. But when they called for boarding the plane, we each took our turn to kiss them farewell. Our father tried to hold his dignity, but after he hugged Layla, he turned his face away to hide his tears. Those of us who were younger tried to lighten the mood with a joke, but our faces bloated with the tears we held in. Our mother held Layla and wouldn't let go, until my father pulled her away.

It was when Hafez's parents went to say farewell that we all stepped back. To lose a son is no small thing. They were not too old at the time, but already you could see the stoop of their backs bending into their bodies. His father was not accustomed to any touch of affection, and his arms tapped his son's body like wooden sticks. They pulled from each other quickly, fearful of what might happen if they held on. His mother engulfed him as if she could take him back into her womb. He embraced her and assured her with a mumble of words, so she could release him. It was my aunt Afaf who finally let them go, waving her hands toward the plane and saying, "yala, yala, the plane will rise." And we watched as their steps turned toward the sky.

Hafez and Layla – 1969

Layla's cousin Misha had been gone for fifteen years. He received the phone call that his mother died peacefully in her sleep six years after his father's passing. When his uncle Malek called him, Misha only said, "yes, yes, thank you," and nothing else. After that, his uncle called him when there was news—a cousin got married, someone gave birth to a son, a daughter. Each time, Misha repeated his words—"yes, thank you"—as if they were the only language he knew. His uncle tried to draw him out, asking about Dunya, about his job, but Misha only added "everything is fine," as if lives could be lived without details. And when he said to Misha, "we would like to see you," Misha only responded with "the distance is far." Those early letters describing the luxury of life in America stopped. The family couldn't understand how he was raising Dunya alone. Rumors spread that he had remarried, that he had found an American woman with blond hair and that she made Dunya look like an American, that he now lived in a big mansion and drove a Mercedes, that he didn't return because he had become better than everyone.

There was a chair in his mother's living room that had come to be known as Misha's chair. It was a simple wooden chair where Misha usually sat. When guests came over, Misha always insisted that they take the more comfortable couch and cushioned chairs, claiming he preferred this wooden seat. It didn't match the rest of the furniture, but it remained where it had been placed next to the couch and against the window. No one sat in it after Misha left. It was as if his presence still lingered there. After his mother died, when Malek took over the apartment, the chair was no longer there. When someone asked about it, Malek kept his gaze on the ground and said, "it's over, there is no misha."

Hafez was born the eldest of his four siblings, followed by his brother, Walid, his sister, Magda, and his youngest brother, Kamel. Their grandfather, Suleiman, had lived his life in Cairo beholden to his brother Salim, who kept him employed at the bakery despite his ineptitude. The salary he made was only enough for survival. Salim told him that if he wanted more, he would have to find his own way—perhaps out of stinginess or perhaps hoping to motivate him. But Suleiman settled into his job, keeping track of the inventory and managing the other employees' schedules, content with his low status. Hafez's father, Moussa, inherited his father's complacency and settled into his life, finding employment as a ticket collector on the train. He travelled back and forth to Alexandria, to Menya, and other places in the country, stamping tickets and asking no more from life than the predictability of each train's destination.

Hafez grew up in Old Cairo, in the same house that his grandfather had managed to build with his meager income. It was in one of the poorest neighborhoods, where the houses crumbled and the streets remained unpaved. Until he was eight years old, Hafez knew nothing beyond the place where he lived and the school he attended. His days repeated a pattern except for Sundays, when the family attended the liturgy at the Hanging Church in Coptic Cairo nearby. During the liturgy, Hafez liked to look up at the ceiling with its wooden beams, intended to resemble the inside of Noah's ark. The church was suspended above the original ruins of an old Roman fortress, and he imagined that it might rise with everyone in it, and, like Noah's ark, save the people from their sins. At the end of the liturgy, each person was handed the round orban stamped with a cross. It was the only time Hafez was given food that he did not have to share, and he lingered over the taste of the bread, tearing off one bite at a time, savoring the soft sustenance with its flavor of flour and holiness. At home, his mother, Sabah, did her best, but there was never enough for the children as they sprouted tall with increasing appetites. They grew up eating fuul and taamia, both made with fava beans, along with feteer, the round flaky bread, and a few vegetables—the food of the poor. Only on Christmas and Easter did they taste some meat.

This was Hafez's life until he turned eight and told his great-uncle Salim that he wanted a job. Salim planted his gaze on the young boy with a steady force. It was Friday morning, a day with no school. Hafez had left early, having already outlined his mission. It took an hour and a half to walk to the bakery. He knew that his great-uncle kept the habit of going there early each day. From the time he had started the bakery, he arrived first to open its doors for business, and he was the last to leave and pull down the shutters. Salim's eyes remained on Hafez as he stood in the small office at the back of the store.

"and what kind of job do you want exactly?" Despite being in his late sixties, Salim still stood tall, his face etched with the years of his work.

The previous week, Hafez had gone to the bakery before school and stood across the street, watching. Now he had his answer prepared. He had noticed people on their way to work turn and look longingly through the window of the bakery, their steps hesitant for just a moment before they looked at their watches and hurried, tucking in their hunger.

"i can stand in front of the store with a few loaves of bread and sell it to people passing by, so it can be quicker for them to buy something."

Salim's thick eyebrows raised, and his heavy staring almost made Hafez lower his eyes, but he held himself tall and stiff.

"you are not your father's son," Salim said. "be here tomorrow at the same time. i will give you ten percent of what you sell."

* ⁂ *

When Hafez tries to remember how he gathered the bravery he needed to make this request of his uncle, he returns to the day he accompanied his mother to deliver some curtains she had made for someone her sister knew. His mother could sew well, and occasionally her sister brought her various things to make, because she lived in a tall building and knew her neighbors. Usually, her sister would drop off the material from the customer and pick up the finished work to deliver it. Hafez's father had given his approval to have his wife do the sewing, but he had insisted that she not enter other people's homes alone. This time, her sister was ill, and the woman needed the curtains immediately. When Hafez returned home from school, his mother rushed him and told him they had to do an errand. She shushed his questions and just told him to hurry.

They took a taxi that drove them out of Old Cairo through downtown and beyond, where the air smelled like apricots. The taxi came to a stop in front of a six-story building in Zamalek, and Hafez's mother warned him to remain silent as if he were not there.

Once they entered the apartment, Hafez stood by his mother's side and obeyed her instructions to be invisible. But he couldn't have spoken, because he didn't have words to explain where he found himself. It felt like the earth was cracking open beneath his feet. His mother stood in the living room as the woman who had opened the door for them sat on the couch and invited them to also sit, but his mother stuttered through, saying they had little time. While she proceeded to show the woman the curtains she had made and ensure that they met with her approval, Hafez looked around at the white upholstered furniture of the room, the glass-topped table in the dining area, and the carved piano in the corner, and he felt the breeze that entered through the balcony carrying the faint aroma of jasmine. From where he stood, he could see into the corner of the kitchen. On the counter, there was a platter with two chickens and another piled with grape leaves. Even when they ate chicken on the holidays, for the five of them, there would only be one. He did not hear the conversation between his mother and the woman. For the first time, he saw his own poverty.

Perhaps it was that moment that planted the seed of ambition in him. He knew that he did not want to follow in the footsteps of his father and remain in Old Cairo to raise children whose stomachs never knew the fullness of nourishment.

Once he started working at his uncle's bakery, his eyes and ears grew bigger. He understood that in this country, your birth determined your future. Perhaps one day, he could open his own store, but he wanted to reach beyond four walls and the status of a storekeeper. To be someone who deserved the respect of others, to have enough money so that he never had to fear hunger again, to be able to feed his children, to assure them of a solid future. His days became a rhythm of school and work. He spent evenings studying late into the night, preparing for each exam as if his life were staked on it. In the last year of high school, he achieved grades high enough to admit him to medical school at Cairo University, the top program. Instead, he chose architecture. He preferred to deal with solid structures rather than the fragility of the human body.

Hafez hoped that his success would motivate his brother Walid, but he had little aptitude for studying and, after barely graduating from secondary school, he became an upholsterer, learning the trade once it was clear his marks would not admit him to college. He married Noura, a distant cousin on their mother's side, and refurnished the bedroom he grew up in, moving his wife into the family home. Hafez's sister, Magda, grew up a quiet, obedient girl, and it seemed her destiny would inevitably lead to marriage and a husband. His youngest brother, Kamel, went about his business alone, each day going to school and each evening struggling with his homework.

Hafez was five years old when Kamel was born. His mother had grown tired of caring for children, and his father repeated his steps each day, unaware of his children's needs. Kamel and Hafez grew close. Each night, Hafez checked on his brother as he fell asleep, and each morning, he wished him a good day. When Kamel started school, Hafez sat with him as he did his homework, helping him to figure out shortcuts for his math problems and to study for his tests. In the summer, they spent half their time in the street, kicking around a deflated ball with the other kids. Hafez taught his brother how to play soccer, and when Kamel became the better player, Hafez felt only pride in his accomplishment.

When Kamel was nine years old, he wanted to learn to ride a bike. He asked his father to get him one, but the only answer he received was, "if you want to go somewhere, use your legs." Hafez watched him sit on the balcony and look down at the kids who rode bicycles on the street. Hafez found a shop that fixed bikes and managed to convince the owners to hire him to run errands in exchange for an old bike and lessons on how to fix it. It took a couple of months, but one day he came home with the bike, a little rusty but in working condition. He called to Kamel, who was already on the balcony. When he looked down and saw Hafez holding the bike, his eyes grew round, and Hafez could almost feel the intake of his surprised breath. He dashed down, and Hafez assured him the bike was his. It took the rest of the day and the next until he stopped wobbling and found his balance.

In his last year of college, Hafez moved out of his family's home. The apartment he rented was three floors up, the steps narrow and steep. The landlord was glad to find anyone willing to take it, so the rent was cheap. Hafez told his parents that he needed to be closer to the university, and he told himself that he wanted to give his family more space. The small house in Old Cairo was barely enough to hold them all. The truth was he wanted to escape the house, with its marked poverty, to step as far away from it as he could, to believe that his destiny lay in richer places. Once he succeeded, he promised himself, he would help his family, give them more than what his father could.

Hafez was at the top of his class and was working two jobs along with studying. His family had no connections that could lift him up, and his father could offer nothing, so he worked to earn the money for his books and supplies. When he had even an extra pound, he gave it to his mother, without his father's knowledge.

Layla's cousin Farid was his classmate in the Engineering College. He recognized his name and approached him. They had not seen each other since primary school, when their families used to gather together, but their relationship stretched back to their grandfathers in the village of Kom Ombo. Salim was Farid's grandfather, whose hard work had travelled down the generations and placed Farid's family in a firm upper-class position, whereas Hafez's grandfather, Suleiman, with his lack of ambition, had placed Hafez's family firmly in the lap of poverty.

The first time I saw Layla, I was spending the evening at Farid's house to study together. She was in her last year of high school. When I saw her laughing with her friends, I was caught by her open smile. It seemed that happiness had settled in her, her face bright and joyous, so different from the faces of my family. Layla had a lightness to her, as if she were partly floating. I felt that she owned happiness and that perhaps if I were with her, I might come closer to it. She would be my guide up the ladder, so I could become a man of status, not bound by my years in Old Cairo, this neighborhood of donkeys and mud streets and dirt, where the smell of garbage wafts in through the open balcony. I waited until my career was established and I could offer more. Two years after I graduated, I proposed, and I was accepted.

* ⁂ *

THE EARTH SEEMS TO CRACKLE AT THE BEGINNING OF THAT SUMMER, AN ENERGY IN THE AIR THAT MAKES PEOPLE WALK A LITTLE FASTER, LINGER OVER THEIR TEA A LITTLE LONGER, AND TALK A LITTLE LOUDER. RADIO CAIRO PILES ON THE PROPAGANDA AGAINST ISRAEL AND ANTICIPATES ITS IMMINENT DEFEAT AT THE HANDS OF THE EGYPTIAN ARMY. AHMED AL-SAID, THE RADIO ANNOUNCER ON THE VOICE OF THE ARABS, PREDICTS, "WE'RE GOING TO SHOVE ISRAEL INTO THE SEA." SONGS BY ABDEL HALIM HAFEZ ALREADY CELEBRATE VICTORY. BANNERS SUPPORTING THE ARMY MULTIPLY IN THE STREETS.

ON THE MORNING OF JUNE 5, 1967, THE RADIOS TURN ON IN ONE HOME AFTER THE OTHER, ANNOUNCING THE WAR AND EGYPT'S TRIUMPH OVER THE ENEMY. AHMED AL-SAID'S PRONOUNCEMENTS OF VICTORY COME ON THE RADIO, RECOUNTING THE NUMBER OF ISRAELI PLANES SHOT DOWN.

THE TRUTH IS THAT IN THE FIRST THREE HOURS, ISRAELI PLANES MANAGE TO DESTROY OVER HALF OF EGYPT'S AIRCRAFT AS WELL AS THE RUNWAYS THAT WOULD HAVE ALLOWED THEM TO TAKE OFF. THEY FLY IN SILENCE UNDER THE EGYPTIAN RADAR, THEIR PURPOSE UNDETECTED UNTIL IT IS TOO LATE. THEN THEY PROCEED TO DESTROY THE SYRIAN AND JORDANIAN AIR FORCE. THE WAR IS LOST IN THE FIRST SIX HOURS, BUT THE TRUTH DOES NOT EMERGE UNTIL SIX DAYS LATER.

* ⁂ *

On the morning of June 5, Layla and Hafez woke to the sharp ring of their phone.

Layla's mother's voice screeched on the other end, "turn on the radio, turn on the radio, el akhbar, did you hear the news?"

Layla's groggy voice answered, "what is there, ya mama?"

"harb," she said. "we entered a war," her voice lingering on the last word like an extended note.

Hearing the words coming through the phone, Hafez rose out of bed and left the room to find the radio. Layla and Hafez had been married for less than a year, and, like most newlyweds, they went out most nights. The previous evening, they had gone to eat at the Nile Hilton, sipping their drinks as the sun descended slowly over the water, oblivious to the Israeli forces gathering to stage their attack.

Hafez stood in his pajamas in the middle of the dining room and fiddled with the radio to get the right channel. He heard Layla assuring her mother that she would call her back in a few minutes. The newscaster's voice was dry and hoarse, his words sounding like gravel, although he was announcing victory.

That evening, they gathered at Layla's parents' apartment along with the rest of the family. Fayza and Wassef greeted their daughter and Hafez with deep hugs. Layla's brother, Fanous, and her younger sister, Hala, were there along with Wassef's sister, Afaf. Other family members arrived, and Fayza and Wassef ushered them all in with subdued tones. Misha and Farid were in America, but still the family was full, and a few grandchildren had already sprouted. They sat on chairs, on couches, on the floor. Fayza made Turkish coffee and offered no one sugar. They closed the shutters and curtains and sat in silence as if in the ritual of a funeral.

The town crier walked down the streets announcing the curfew and commanding everyone to turn off their lights. The family settled in a circle on the living room floor in pitch darkness. Layla sat between her mother and Hafez, holding each of their hands. Fanous and Hala sat next to each other. No one spoke. Even the younger children seemed to sense the urgency of the situation, and they sat still. Their bodies stiffened when they heard the planes droning in the sky. After a while, the sound subsided, but they remained where they were, falling asleep against each other's shoulders.

The ritual continued for six nights, and no one left the house, fearful of becoming a random target. During the day, the men debated what was happening. Wassef insisted they would win the war, regain the Palestinian homeland, while Morcos insisted that whatever happened, Egypt would be the loser. "we should not be fighting for someone else's home—let them fight their own battles." On the radio, Abdel Halim's voice sang songs of victory. Hafez remained silent, and no one asked him to speak. His brother Kamel had been drafted into the army and was somewhere in the Sinai. Each day, he dialed his parents' number to see if there was any news, but their answer was always nothing.

After six days, the sense of defeat settled on the nation like a shroud. Every step moved as if treading on quicksand. The air held still, voices sounded hollow, and the weight of loss fell heavily on each doorstep. There was no news of Kamel. Soldiers began to return, silent and stooped. Hafez made myriad phone calls, trying to gather something about his brother's whereabouts, but each phone call was passed on to another office with nothing offered. When Hafez's sister told him that she had heard that a young man in their brother's regiment had returned home, Hafez headed to his house without announcing his visit.

The family lived in Garden City, in one of the buildings tucked around the corner from the Nile. Hafez was unfamiliar with the area as he tried to follow the spiraling streets. Several times he asked for directions, but in attempting to follow them, he often found himself back where he had started. Finally, he entered a small grocery store to ask. The owner sat on a stool behind the counter, his heavy body precariously balanced on the seat. "misa'a el kheir," greeted Hafez, and the man responded with "misa'a el noor." The man wasn't sure of the location of the street Hafez needed, and he called over his son, a young boy perhaps only eleven or twelve who delivered groceries to people in the neighborhood. The boy tried to explain, but Hafez couldn't focus on the intricacies of his directions. Exasperated, he offered the boy ten piasters to take him there, and the boy stood up straighter and responded with "aywa, ya pasha." Hafez followed the boy, who seemed to float rather than walk on solid ground as he led him directly to the correct building. "shokran," said Hafez, and he gave the boy what he had promised. The boy wrapped his fist around the coin and ran off.

* ⁂ *

Hafez stands in front of the building, his feet cemented to the ground. He tries to resist the fear that hums through his body, the sense of certainty about what he will learn if he steps inside, but he knows, as the eldest of his siblings, it is his duty, that he will have to serve as messenger. He walks in, greets the doorman with "salaam alaikum," waits for his response of "wa alaikum el salaam," and then asks for the correct apartment.

He remains focused on each step as he makes his way up the three flights. Already, he feels lightheaded. He stops in front of the door, releases a breath and a silent prayer. He knocks twice, listens, but hears no sound emanating from the apartment. Another two knocks. Now he hears the shuffle of footsteps, the question of "meen?" The woman who answers the door holds a dish towel in her hand. She is short with a rounded figure, and her hair is pulled into a bun, black with streaks of gray that reveal her older age. Her face is smooth, and there is a shine in her eyes that tells Hafez he has found the right apartment. He apologizes for the intrusion, introduces himself, and explains his mission.

"etfadel, etfadel," the woman welcomes him in, immediately understanding.

Only days before, the same creases of anxiety indented her face as she waited for news of her son. She offers Hafez a seat in the living room and says, "just one minute" as she goes to another room. Hafez hears her hushed tone as she wakes her son from his afternoon rest— "sami, sami, get up. there is someone here"—and then the shifting of blankets and the movement of limbs muffle the rest of the words.

A young man enters the room, his right arm in a sling. Hafez can tell that he is not much older than twenty, but he has the physique of someone in the military and his face reveals an age beyond his years.

Hafez can no longer proceed with the preliminary greetings. He stands to shake the young man's hand and immediately speaks. "you were with my brother," he says. "his name is kamel—kamel boutros." Hafez pauses as if saying his brother's name demanded a payment he couldn't afford to make. "we haven't heard anything of him." Once the words are released, Hafez finds that he has run out of breath, and he sits down, feeling the words he has spoken like rocks lodged in his throat.

The young man sits on the edge of the couch and shakes his head as if to wave away the question he is being asked. The word "kamel"—meaning "whole," "complete"—trips on his tongue. "i don't remember," the young man says. "there were many of us."

Hafez lets the silent pause sit between them. The young man's gaze reaches beyond Hafez, through the door to some other place that bears no resemblance to this living room with the mother who stands nearby still holding the kitchen towel.

The man turns his eyes toward Hafez. "his name?" he asks.

"kamel boutros." This time Hafez says it mechanically, draining all emotion from it.

The young man looks toward his mother and says, "water, ya mama."

She bustles to the kitchen and returns with a glass of water. She hands it to him and stands nearby as if waiting for another order. Turning to Hafez, she says, "from the day he returned, he's always thirsty. i don't understand."

The young man drinks half the glass in a single gulp and places it on the table. He takes a breath, and his chest seems to settle. "the sound, the sound was hard, they were shooting bullets at us, constantly, and sometimes a mine would explode, but sometimes there was an explosion and we didn't know where it came from. that is what happened and we all fell, scattered on the earth. when we rose up, we couldn't see or walk."

"haram," his mother says. "his arm was broken."

The young man continues as if his mother has not spoken. "some couldn't rise, an arm or leg shattered. and some remained in the ground. kamel—I looked for him. he was my friend. but it was not possible for him to get up."

A few moments pass, each one a heartbeat in the silence of the room.

Hafez gets up, places his hand on the young man's shoulder, and leaves.

* ⁂ *

Hafez had guided Kamel through his childhood, but it was Kamel who comforted Hafez when their father said that he was a fool to choose architecture when his grades could admit him to medical school. Kamel told him to follow his dream, that their father would come around once Hafez succeeded. And it was Kamel who encouraged him to propose to Layla despite his concern that their family status would not be acceptable. Kamel had a wisdom beyond his years, as if he had seen the world before and knew its secrets. With Kamel gone, Hafez felt as if he had lost his whole family.

* ⁂ *

“what do you mean we go?”

Hafez sat at the small square table in the kitchen as Layla was preparing breakfast. He looked at her as she faced the stove, stirring the basterma into the eggs. It was Friday morning, the beginning of a day when he didn’t have to go to work and when she always made his favorite breakfast. Her dark-brown hair was loose, falling to below her shoulders. When he had met her, her hair reached her waist, but after their marriage, she had cut it, saying she didn’t want to look so young now that she was a married woman.

Layla faced Hafez, still young but having refashioned herself as a wife. He knew how close she was to her family, how they gathered together for each occasion and how they spoke each day. Her elder brother, Fanous, who always knew how to lighten the mood, and her younger sister, Hala, whose preoccupation with the latest fashions and trends kept them all entertained. And her parents, who had embraced him into the family, never bringing up his background, looking only at the successful man he had become. Hafez had taken Layla’s family as his own, happy to sit among them and to be owned. Now he had to offer a reason for leaving that he did not fully understand.

“there are opportunities,” he began, “our lives can be better. and the country, the country is gone.”

The radio played in the background, Umm Kulthum’s voice entering their kitchen with the words “ebka fa’enta al-amal,” entreating Nasser to stay, affirming hope in his leadership. As the song lingered, Hafez refrained the words, “there is no hope.”

Layla turned back to the stove, stirred the eggs one more time and placed them on a plate along with the Syrian bread and the feta cheese. She brought it over to Hafez and sat across from him. The plate remained between them, hovering as if waiting for its destiny to be announced.

“the country is here, ya hafez,” she said, placing her hand on his. “your brother is gone, but we are all here and life must keep moving.”

Hafez pulled his hand away and reached for his fork but then placed it back on the plate. “everything is owned by the government, and only the work i do for them is acknowledged. i can't get credit for my work at the private companies. i can't even sign my own drawings. my visions are rising out of the ground, and i can't claim them."

Hafez's words whirled around them like a sandstorm. Even before they could settle, he continued, "because i work for the government, i'm not allowed to work for anyone else. there is no possibility of advancing. the notion of socialism and equality is driving the country, and an individual's desire to rise remains curbed, held in check by government policies. the government says each man will get his turn in order; the one hired on monday will receive his promotion before the one hired on tuesday regardless of who does the better job."

Layla tried to avoid looking directly at Hafez. "i know," she said, "but it can't be that the answer is to leave."

"i want the master's degree, and here it's impossible. each year, they give the scholarship to study abroad to someone else with a lower rank than me. they will never give it to someone who is a christian." He coughed out the last words as if they had gathered phlegm in his chest.

I looked at the man I married. My parents did not pressure me; they asked if I wanted to accept the proposal. They said I was young and pretty, so there would surely be other suitors. But I had already noticed Hafez, seen him when he came with my cousin Farid. And I saw how he walked with a strong steady pattern. His pace was exact, each stride the same length, and the intensity of his dark eyes told me that he would create his own success. I knew he came from poverty. My older cousin Morcos took me aside and cautioned me against marrying into Hafez's family. "from poverty comes poverty," he said. But I felt that Hafez and the life he would build was my destiny.

I had never thought much about my future. Our lives were comfortable. I attended an English language school and did well. When I was young, our lives rotated around family. One Friday we gathered at the house of my eldest uncle, Sa'ad; the next at my uncle Malek's house; and the next at our home. I grew up cradled among my aunts and uncles and cousins. My elder brother, Fanous, watched out for me, walked me to school, helped me with my homework. And my younger sister, Hala, looked up to me, imitated my clothes and followed me around from the time she could walk. I never thought beyond these days, never imagined a future for myself that existed beyond these boundaries of family. Until I saw Hafez, I couldn't see myself as anything other than a daughter and sister.

When I first met Hafez, I was only in my last year of high school, and I still wore my hair in two long braids. By the time I was twenty, I was engaged, and by twenty-one, I was married. But Hafez encouraged me to continue my education, not to settle simply for housewifely duties. I went from my parents' home to my husband, but Hafez gave me room to grow.

* ⁂ *

Layla looked at Hafez, knew the weight of his words. Each year, he applied for the scholarship that would allow him to go to America to complete a graduate degree in architecture, and each year he was rejected. She had seen the hardness forming in him, like a stone lodged in his shoulder.

Layla recognized Hafez's ambition, and sometimes she wondered if he chose her out of desire or because of her family's status. Now, even she was not enough, and his ambition stretched further than she could have predicted.

Hafez's voice broke her thoughts. "if i could be successful here, i will be successful in amreeka too. i will build a good life for us. and we can come back, every year if you want." He sounded almost pleading.

Layla had always imagined that her life would remain within the confines of her own country, her children growing up within the circle of their family, retracing the path of each generation before them.

She faltered, "i don't know, ya hafez. amreeka is so far away."

Hafez straightened his back. The food remained on the plate, the fork still clean. He decided to speak his thoughts aloud: "i don't want to raise a son in this country." He looked directly at her, forcing her gaze to meet his. "we will raise him and then this country will take him and throw him away like they threw away my brother."

Hafez and Layla continued their daily lives, but each time they were at home together, they felt the presence of the words that had been spoken between them. Their conversation crawled into the corners of their apartment and tried to remain out of sight. The rooms grew quieter, as if preparing for the final outcome.

* ⁂ *

After the '67 war, the country was held prisoner to the ongoing military maneuvers between Egypt and Israel. All resources went to the military. As early as six, Layla's phone would ring, and she would listen to her mother's eager voice telling her she heard sugar was available at the government market in Mohandessein, pushing Layla to quickly get dressed and run out the door. Usually, a crowd had already gathered, men still in pajamas and women with curlers in their hair, following the news of the sugar. Other times, a neighbor would knock on her door and in a frantic voice announce that there was rice at the Maadi market, and they would rush in the hopes of finding it still there. The military became the highest priority, and people could barely find enough to live. Everything was scarce, and no one imagined that things would improve.

In April of 1968, word spread that the Virgin Mary had appeared at St. Mary's Coptic Church in Zeitoun. After the initial sighting, crowds began to gather every evening in the hope of catching a glimpse of the ghostly figure said to appear above the dome of the church. Chairs were set up to accommodate them. Fayza insisted they go, but her husband refused, saying it was only the hysteria of a nation in pain looking for comfort. In the end, she went, taking Layla and Hala with her. They sat among thousands, and when darkness filled the sky, a hush fell over the crowd as every pair of eyes turned upward to the dome. Someone would stand and stretch their arm to point, saying, "there she is," and the crowd would surge up to see, only to be deflated by the emptiness of the sky. Layla sat next to her mother, hopeful each time the crowd rose, scanning the sky for the figure that could bless them. Hala leaned against her mother's shoulder, tired from the late night and frustrated with the futility of each hope that brought them to their feet. Layla leaned back in her chair and looked up to the giant dome of the church outlined by the dark sky. Her vision floated around the dome, and from behind it a shine caught her eye, a white light moving, its shape not human but still distinct, and she followed it as it floated above the dome until it disappeared behind the church. She turned to her mother and sister, about to ask if they saw it, when her mother said, "nothing will happen tonight, let's go." Layla tucked the vision inside her mind and said nothing.

* ⁂ *

Three months after their conversation, Hafez was sitting on a chair in the living room, reading the newspaper, and Layla was on the couch working on some needlepoint. Without looking up, she said, "i'm pregnant." And it was understood.

* ⁂ *

It didn't take long for their paperwork to go through. Their application to emigrate was swept along by the Immigration and Nationality Act of 1965 that repealed the quota system of 1924, opening America's doors to immigrants from non-European nations. The act gave preference to those with professional degrees and their family members, attracting the workers needed to help establish the country as a world leader.

They were not the only ones applying to emigrate. Like a sharp wind that pushes at your back, the war seemed to direct everyone to departure. The air seemed to carry conversations of immigration like a contagious virus, affecting everyone who came in contact with it and spreading among the educated, who heard that they would be given preference, that applications were being approved quickly, that a door was opening to a place filled with hope, that they could leave behind the sandstorm clogging their lungs.

* ⁂ *

"You're an architect" was the first thing the interviewer said to Hafez, almost before he had fully taken his seat for the immigration interview.

"Yes," Hafez responded, releasing a slight cough to clear his voice.

"What exactly do you do?" the man behind the desk asked.

Hafez thought the man looked to be in his early forties. He was slim, no sign of extra weight, and his light hair was perfectly shaped to his head as if it could have been a custom-made wig. No gray hairs, no wrinkles. *did people in amreeka not age?* he wondered. *was their youth permanently intact?*

Hafez described some of the projects he had worked on. Arriving at certain words, his voice halted, trying to translate from Arabic to English, to dig out the correct pronunciation from his memory. The man nodded, took notes, but seemed to not really be listening, as if what he was writing was unrelated to the interview. Hafez began to lose his voice as he received no acknowledgment from his listener. Finally, the man looked up, and, without responding to anything Hafez had told him, he turned to Layla and asked why she was applying to go to America.

Layla placed her hands in her lap, holding them together as if they might flutter away. "I will support my husband," she said. The words came easily, her English learned and practiced through her years at the British school she had attended.

Without giving any indication that the interview had come to an end, the man stood up and put out his arm, forcing Hafez and Layla to quickly rise and shake his hand.

* ⁂ *

They decided it was best to tell Layla's family that this was a temporary trip, that they would return once Hafez received his degree. The memory of Misha had been tucked beneath the mattresses they slept on, and no one wanted to pull at its frayed edges. The lie settled awkwardly as they passed it around like a deck of cards.

Hafez liquidated all their assets. He poured them through a sieve unfiltered, until everything was gone. Their apartment, their furniture, their bank accounts, their accumulated objects. Layla suggested they store items at her parents' house, that perhaps they should keep a bank account open, but once their path had been marked, Hafez refused to leave anything that might tug them back. Behind Layla's request he knew were the questions *what if it doesn't work? what if they didn't make it?* By eliminating everything they owned, Hafez erased the question.

They were allowed two suitcases each, and they had to choose wisely. What items held enough value to take up that precious space? Hafez packed his best architectural drawings, Layla took three pairs of patent leather shoes, Hafez folded his two best suits, Layla found space for the embroidered tablecloth her mother had made, Hafez put a small Arabic-English dictionary in the outer pocket of his suitcase, Layla placed a pouch with her jewelry in the bottom of her handbag. Layla was twenty-five and Hafez was twenty-nine as they packed their lives into the four suitcases.

Layla wanted to take an extra suitcase, but Hafez refused, insisting they would only take what was permitted. He didn't want to encounter any difficulties in the airport. In the end, Layla gathered a few things. They were almost random—a small wooden bird that caught her attention when she was shopping in the Khan el Khalili market. The man she bought it from said his son had carved it. Layla liked the rough quality of the bird that made it seem more real than if it had been polished and smooth. There was a pair of high-heeled shoes that seemed too frivolous to take, a large tablecloth she had started crocheting once she was engaged that was too bulky, a dress her mother had made for her when she finished high school that was already too small, and other things that she rescued without reason. She wrapped each one, put them in a box, and gave the box to her sister. "hold them for me," she said, "i'll come back to get them." And her sister took them as a safekeeping.

Layla's mother, Fayza, stood in the front pew of the church, dressed in a blue gown that sparkled with its sequins. At almost sixty, she was still an attractive woman and could make an impression. But her makeup was heavy that day, trying to hide the sorrow beneath her eyes at the celebration of her younger daughter's wedding. It was absence that made her tug at the handkerchief in her hand. When she asked Layla and Hafez to come, they said they couldn't, that it was too expensive, and Hafez couldn't leave work.

Fayza followed the path set for her, from childhood to marriage to motherhood, and she has lived content with her life. That contentment was founded on the presumption that others would follow the same path, that her children would marry and that one day she would be a grandmother, her home filled with the voices and play of the next generation, that she would see her life continue in the line of her offspring. But she has not even touched the face of her grandchildren. She only sees the grainy photographs that are sent too rarely and hears the reels of tape that arrive, tainted by the recording device. Fayza plays them over and over, the voices entering her home, but instead of bringing joy, her sorrow releases as she hears the voices of grandchildren she has never known and a daughter whose own remembrance recedes every day, until she wakes up with a start in the middle of the night unable to recall the image of her own child's face. Now the wedding of one daughter is celebrated without the presence of the other. Only the shadow of absence stands where Layla should have been.

Fayza's husband, Wassef, stood next to her, a man who was too tall for himself, who often hunched his shoulders and held his gaze perpetually downward. He inhaled his wife's sorrow, but he never had hope that Hafez and Layla would be here. Fayza had cajoled on the phone numerous times, and he heard her pleading voice—"just two days, come to the wedding and then go back"—but the only response from the end of the line was "i'm sorry, ya mama," over and over like a mantra that doesn't heal but only seeps deeper into the wound. Wassef tried to comfort his wife with the reminder of who was still present—their son, Fanous, and her nephews Morcos, Khalil, and Farid—but he knew nothing could compensate a mother for the absence of a daughter.

Fayza heaved a breath through her body, and Wassef placed his arm over her shoulder, bent to her ear and whispered "be happy for hala's sake." A tiny movement of her lips responded to him, and she tucked her sorrow in as the wedding began.

What Wassef didn't want to tell her was that he had seen Hala scour each of Layla's letters, reading and rereading the transparent blue paper that over the years arrived less frequently and with more English words sprinkled through the Arabic twists of sound. He saw the curtain that shadowed Hala's eyes when talk of America entered any conversation. He knew it was only a matter of time until more absence would enter their lives.

* ⁂ *

Layla gave birth three months after their arrival—a daughter, not a son as they had anticipated. When Layla was told that it was a girl, her body tightened, a panicked knot of fear that they shouldn't have left. A daughter would remain safe from the military, negating the decision they had made. She held her tiny infant in her arms, the head full of silky brown hair and the large green eyes staring, innocent of the upheaval that had impacted her life even as she was in her mother's womb. Hafez entered the hospital room and sat on a chair by the bed.

"it's a girl," Layla said, the word forming tears in her eyes.

"she's like the moon, beautiful like her mother," Hafez said, reaching to brush his hand over his daughter's hair. The child's breath weaved around them, tying them into a family. "there will be other children," Hafez said, "and when we have a boy, he will be safe here."

Their son was born eight years later, finally affirming their decision. By the time he was born, they had been granted citizenship. Their Egyptian passports were pushed to the bottom drawers along with most of what they had carried with them.

Life took over—finding jobs, buying a house, putting the kids in school, the swirling of days until this place became a home.

Layla stood in the middle of the home goods department of Jordan Marsh. In front of her on a shelf were two porcelain figurines that she had placed side by side, so she could compare them. One was a young woman dressed in a flaring blue skirt, holding a yellow parasol; the other was a young child with its hand outstretched, holding a bird. Whenever she had enough money, she came to the store to look at these figurines, and slowly she had accumulated several that sat on an étagère in her foyer, displaying the collection. Layla decorated her house in the ornate style of British-colonized Egypt. Silky upholstery, elaborate wooden side tables, ceramic knickknacks—all reminders of older homes in Egypt. The décor was discordant with the style of their New England Cape Cod house. This transplanting of home arrived intact with them, tucked into the lining of their suitcases. In their new house, Layla created a familiar world, and the specificity of location dissipated. After a few moments, she reached for the young child with the bird and went to make her purchase.

When she arrived home, eager to show Hafez the new figurine, she was greeted by his voice on the phone.

"aywa, i'm thankful, very thankful, i'll see you tomorrow at ten. i'll bring hundred-dollar bills. of course, of course. shokran. thank you."

Hafez hung up and turned to face Layla. "that was sharif, a friend of girgis's. he's going to egypt, leaving tomorrow night. i'll see him in the morning."

Layla nodded. Each time Hafez heard of someone going to Egypt, he gave them an envelope to pass on to his family. It was cash in dollars, bills that he knew would multiply once exchanged for pounds. The money would help to pay for the household expenses, his nephew's education, his parents' medicine. Perhaps a suit for his father, a necklace for his mother. He sought out every opportunity to send money to his family. And each time he did this, the weight of his burden lifted slightly.

After seventeen years, Hafez and Layla returned for a visit to Egypt. Each year, one of them would raise the possibility of a trip. And each time, an obstacle would present itself—Hafez was starting a new job and couldn't take that much time off, they were still saving for a down payment for a house, they needed to buy a new car, they wanted to build a deck. And each year, these needs appeared more urgent than returning to visit family. Until the calls from their siblings became more frequent, itemizing their parents' frailties, and it was no longer possible to deny the passing of time. They accumulated their vacations, so they could each take off three weeks. The suitcases sat open in the living room, waiting for the presents that Layla bought during her lunch hour at Filene's Basement—the clothes, the perfume, the chocolates overflowed from the open cavities until they would ask one of their children to sit on the suitcase as they zipped it up. They arrived in Egypt with their overstuffed luggage; their daughter, Amal, who was sixteen; and their son, Yusef, who was eight years old.

A few days after they arrived, Layla's sister asked if she wanted the box. She had kept it in her closet, secure all these years waiting for its owner's return.

Layla's face showed no recognition when her sister asked. "a box?" she questioned. "i don't even remember what i put in it. mish mohem," she said, discarding its importance.

And the box stayed in its corner, small particles of dust circling it.

Magda and Lutfi's Departure

The last time I saw Hafez's sister, Magda, was at her wedding. It was held at the Hanging Church in Coptic Cairo. A small wedding followed by a reception with food made by family members. Magda looked beautiful with her hair up in a chignon but also restless, as if she were rushing to get to another appointment. So, a month later, when she asked me for a ride to the airport, I was not surprised. The night before, they invited me over to the house. Magda wanted me to look at the suitcases, to make sure they would be accepted. People thought I had a certain knowledge about airport procedure. I was asked for advice about the best suitcase to purchase, the items that should be packed, and to estimate the weight of a suitcase by lifting it to see if it would pass the scales at the airport. I complied and tried to offer some helpful response to these requests. The truth was that I had never flown, had never actually left Egypt. My excursions only led me as far as the Red Sea in the Sinai and the Mediterranean in Alexandria, all by car or train. My family sat on the sandy beaches and swam in the waters that circled the country. I felt no need to go further, or perhaps the truth was I was afraid that if I stepped beyond the borders of my own country, I might not be able to return.

The gathering at the house in Old Cairo lacked the festive air of other farewells I had attended. Magda's father, Moussa, sat on the couch, his mouth set in closure. Her mother, Sabah, moved from kitchen to dining room, bringing out plates of food as she prepared each of them. There was a small platter of chicken that I knew represented an expensive luxury for the family. Alongside, there was a plate of fried potatoes that Sabah kept refilling. Magda's older brother Walid was not there, but his wife and son sat stiffly on the chairs. Magda and Lutfi sat next to each other, the plate of potatoes resting between them. The family had lost their eldest son to America and their youngest son to the war, and now their daughter too was leaving.

Shortly after I arrived, Walid entered with a wrapped package that he placed on the table, untying the ribbon that held it together to reveal a tray of basboosa. The glistening sweetness of the dessert looked out of place among the somber faces. When a piece was urged on me, I accepted and took a bite, the sharpness of the sugar stinging my taste buds.

Walid situated himself on a chair between his parents and Magda. His body seemed to move like a block of wood all in a single piece. After Hafez left, he had taken on the role of eldest son, and, as his parents aged, the head of the household. His fate was sealed. He couldn't deviate from the path where he had been placed, and the demand of that role had stiffened his body. Walid attempted some conversation, asking me about the family. Once a sufficient amount of time had passed, I left, assuring Magda and Lutfi that I would be there in the morning to take them to the airport.

By the time I arrived, the two of them were already standing outside. Next to them stood Walid, all three of them wrapped in the silence of morning. With my best effort, I pulled a smile to my face to alleviate the morbid portrait that stood in front of me. "sabah el kheir, sabah el kheir," I intoned almost in song to greet them with a morning of good luck. I could see the easing of breath in both Magda and Lutfi, but Walid stood in stillness. They piled the luggage into the trunk and back seat. Before they entered the car, they turned to look up to the balcony, where I could see Magda's parents, Walid's wife, and Walid's infant son, Amin. Magda and Lutfi waved up to them. Magda opened her mouth, but no words emerged.

The car bumped its way through the unpaved roads of Old Cairo, jolting us up and down. "it's like we are on a roller coaster," I said, but my joke didn't elicit any laughter. Once we were on Salah Salem Street, the ride became smoother. Magda and Lutfi had carried the glum mood of their departure into the car, and I felt a need to alleviate the heaviness.

"boston is a beautiful city," I attempted. Receiving no response, I continued, "they have a park in the middle of the city with boats that look like swans."

"like swans," Magda echoed from the back seat.

"yes," I said, brightening at the response, "you can take a ride on them and see the city around you."

"is it a big city, ya fanous?" asked Magda.

"yes, at least as big as cairo. layla says hafez has to drive for an hour to get to work."

Lutfi chimed in. "they can't drive like we do here."

I chuckled. "no, that is amreeka. everything is orderly. they stop at the lights and everyone stays in their lane. in amreeka you have to obey the rules."

Lutfi leaned back in his seat. Magda's union to this man had been arranged quickly. Perhaps he loved Magda or perhaps he only wanted to get to America. Perhaps his family convinced him that this marriage, which would lead him to the Golden Land, was a stroke of luck and he would be a fool to reject it.

From the back, I heard Magda's voice enter the conversation more fully. "layla told me that she goes shopping every week, that the stores there are all as big as omar effendi and some bigger. you can spend hours in them."

"yes," I responded, "amreeka has everything." In my own mind, I wondered if all these things were necessary. This desire for so much had been born from Nasser's regime, when all the doors had closed. The imported products that came in under the British disappeared as Nasser implemented his socialist regime and tried to build the country up from the inside. But you can't expect compliance from people who are being required to give up what they had. Among the middle and upper classes, Nasser only embedded the desire for what was lost, and America siphoned off those who could contribute to its growth, with its ongoing promises of luxury displayed on the large screens of American movies.

The ride continued with each of us sharing what we had heard from Hafez or Layla about the city they were about to enter, and by the time we arrived at the airport, it seemed the cloak of their mourning had lifted. The three of us stood at the gate surrounded by several other families embracing those about to leave. I wondered if these families were losing their first ones. With each departure, the number of people going to the airport decreased. Was it the monotony of repetition? Was it the painful weight of each farewell? We waited in silence, having run out of words. Finally, the flight was called, and it was only me who was there to bid them farewell on their journey.

Magda and Lutfi – 1974

When Hafez left, his family's home became a tomb. His father's shoulders stooped, and his mother's eyes filmed over, blurring her vision. Walid sharpened his bones like a machete that could strike through stone. After Kamel died in the war, the years that followed held them all captive. Each day felt like they were walking through sand. The country was holding its breath, conserving its resources, and everyone was forced to sacrifice, accept the scarcity imposed on them in order to feed the army that would one day avenge the country's pride, although it could never bring back the ones that were lost.

In the first year, the family received letters from Hafez. He told them he had found work and Layla had a job. They were hoping to buy a house soon. But Magda could find nothing in those letters that said if he was happy, if he was glad he had left, if he felt their absence as they felt his. After just six months, he began sending money home. Small amounts at first, but it made a difference in their lives. Magda was able to buy a second pair of shoes, instead of waiting on the street while the man resewed the pair that tore from being worn each day. His mother was able to get glasses, so she could remove the film from over her eyes, although she rarely wore them. Walid refused the money, wanting to tear the green bills and let them fall from the balcony to be stepped on by the feet that walked along the muddy roads of the neighborhood.

Walid worked long hours as an upholsterer, and his hands became jagged with scars. When he returned home in the evening, he collapsed on the bed until his wife went to wake him, so he could eat. When he was young, he was always laughing, playing outside, his shirt untucked and his hair disheveled from kicking around the plastic bottle he and his friends used to play soccer in the streets. He brought laughter into the house, and even his father smiled when he came home out of breath, rambling on about his adventures. While Walid relayed his stories, Hafez would sit silently at the table, eating his food as if it were a duty he had to fulfill. For him, life was school and everything was an assignment.

Once Hafez immigrated, his silence sat at the table with his family every night. Even after he had left the house and was married, he would arrive every week with an offering for his mother. Fresh loaves of bread unlike the day-old ones they usually bought, a few kilos of eggplant, fresh chickens ready to be cooked. Although he had moved from the house, they felt his presence with the gifts he brought. Now he entered their home only with the money he sent through acquaintances visiting Egypt. Someone would knock on the door unexpected, announce their mission, and hand whoever answered the door an unmarked envelope, as if they were exchanging illicit information. They rarely came in, claiming another appointment, and Magda wondered if being accustomed to the wealth of America they preferred not to spend more time in the poverty of Old Cairo.

Life continued with its daily needs. People went to work, struggled to make ends meet, and tried to find some joy in their lives. In 1970, Nasser died, mourned by millions who crowded the street at his funeral. Sadat became president and opened up the country. New products came in with the move toward capitalism, but nothing changed for Hafez's family.

The weight of Hafez's absence settled on his parents. Moussa had often criticized him when he was young, reprimanding him even for the ghost of disobedience, but once Hafez entered college, his father almost never spoke to him and left him to his own peace. Hafez worked so much that his family rarely saw him, and most days, he came in late, after they were asleep. Perhaps he was preparing his family for his permanent absence. But sometimes the other children heard their father talking to someone, and all he spoke of was his son Hafez who was at Cairo University, studying to be an architect. His shoulders straightened, and the pride of his words carried through his voice. "my son the architect," he said, as if in his hands he held the diamonds of Africa. After the immigration, their father swallowed his voice, and when Walid or Magda mentioned Hafez's name, his glare quieted them, and everyone retreated into the silence.

Sabah's eyes brightened a little each time a letter arrived, and she would ask Magda to read it to her when Moussa was not there. Sabah would guide Magda to the front room that was used only for guests and shut the balcony doors, enclosing the room like a cave, and sit next to her daughter on the couch to look over her shoulder as she read the words. She insisted on being able to see them, tilting Magda's hands, even though she couldn't decipher them. Magda would read, and "slower," her mother would say. Then she would ask her to read it again, and by the third time, Magda could see her mother's lips moving, anticipating the words, already memorized in her mind. Magda wondered if she recited them as she did her housework, a mantra to sustain her. Each time Magda read a letter, her mother would say, "that is my son," and Walid and Magda receded, as if through his absence Hafez had become larger, filling the house so there was no room for the rest of them.

When Hafez left, Walid was already married and working. He and his wife had settled into the room that he had shared with Hafez. Two years after their marriage, his wife gave birth to a son. After that, no more children came. Over the years, Walid's face darkened, and his eyes sunk deeper. His son, Amin, grew up in the house, imbibing absence and lost dreams.

* ⁂ *

When Walid found himself alone, he walked through the house, composing the words he wished he could say to his elder brother. *you abandoned your family. a son's place is by his parents, to care for them in their old age. but you followed the smell of wealth to amreeka and neglected your duties. our parents glorified you as the chosen child. you had your college degree, a good job, the title of architect. i saw you come home wearing creased pants and pressed white shirts, sitting like a guest in our house.*

After Hafez left, his mother's tears flooded the living room, and neither Magda nor Walid could console her sorrow. They knew she had lost her firstborn. Walid sat next to her and reached to kiss her hand, to tell her he would remain by her side. But she waved away his gesture like a fly and filled absence with grief.

Walid recalled how when he was growing up, his father's anger had lashed out like a whip against his back. The words "you should be like your brother" had slapped his face. He knew that even though Hafez left, he remained among them. Each guest who entered their home asked for news of him. It was only in front of others that their father was willing to speak about his eldest. With his eyesight dimming, he would ask Walid to read the most recent letter to guests. Hafez's accomplishments rattled from the thin airmail paper—his job, his house, his car, everything he now owned. The words congealed in Walid's mouth, and when he finished, he folded the letter carefully. The father, whose inability to provide sufficiently for his family marked itself on each of his children when three pounds a month couldn't feed them, now found refuge in his son's success. He held up the money Hafez sent home as a trophy of his own success as a father.

Hafez's mother's refrain rang out along with her husband's when guests came by—"my son in amreeka," she said. And Walid felt her words negate her other children as if she had birthed only one child. When she called him, she slipped and began to say Hafez's name. "ya haf-walid," she said, catching herself halfway through. Sometimes, it slipped off her tongue whole, as if she were trying to call up Hafez's presence, with his name layered over Walid's. In his thoughts, Walid wanted to shout at his brother, *you left us behind with a myth but no son-brother-uncle to help carry the family*.

Magda was in college when Hafez left. After his departure, she turned her faith to studying. She enrolled in the Faculty of Commerce at Cairo University and stayed focused on achieving the necessary grades to continue to the next year. The family no longer heard her voice in the house. Each day she came home and settled at the same table Hafez had used to complete his architectural drawings. By the same dim light, she held her eyes steady over each of her assignments as if memorizing even the shape of the paper on which they were written. She kept her eyes downcast at home as if she could diminish her presence and remain unnoticed. Before she left for school each morning, she'd check her one pair of shoes to see if she would have to stop by the cobbler to get them fixed again while she waited in stockinged feet on the sidewalk. Her father gave her enough for bus fare and books. Walid was not sure if his generosity was genuine or if Hafez demanded he use some of the money he sent for her education. He wondered if Hafez had whispered words in her ears before he left, promises of America if she studied hard.

THE AFTERNOON OF OCTOBER 6, 1973, RINGS LIKE AN ALARM, WAKING PEOPLE FROM THE NUMBNESS OF THEIR LIVES. AN ELECTRIC SHOCK BUZZES IN THEIR EARS TO ANNOUNCE THE NEWS THAT EGYPT AND SYRIA HAVE ATTACKED ISRAEL ON YOM KIPPUR. THE TWO COUNTRIES SEND THEIR SOLDIERS OVER THE BORDER TO THE SINAI AND THE GOLAN HEIGHTS, TERRITORIES THAT ISRAEL GAINED DURING THE '67 WAR. THE ARAB MILITARY ATTACKS WHILE ISRAELIS HONOR THIS DAY OF ATONEMENT, REFRAINING FROM FOOD AND DRINK AND IMMERSING THEMSELVES IN PRAYER AND REPENTANCE. THE STEALTH OF THE EGYPTIAN ARMY CATCHES ISRAEL AT ITS MOST VULNERABLE, AND THIS TIME THE NEWS ON EGYPTIAN RADIO ANNOUNCES THE VICTORY ACCURATELY.

FOR TWENTY DAYS, THE COUNTRY CROUCHES IN ANTICIPATION, FEARFUL THAT ONCE AGAIN THEY WILL BE TRICKED INTO THE DEFEAT OF '67. BUT WHEN IT IS OVER, THEY WAKE TO THE CLAIM OF VICTORY, ALTHOUGH TRUNCATED BY THE INTERFERENCE OF THE COLONIAL NATIONS.

Walid came out of the train station on the afternoon of October 6 and felt the electricity in the air. It was normally quiet at this time, just edging past four in the afternoon, when most people had already returned home for their midday meal. He heard the words being slapped back and forth in the air. Approaching a kiosk where several men were standing, he greeted them with "misa'a el kheir." The men paused for a moment to take him in. No one responded back with the appropriate greeting.

"did you hear," one of them said, "we entered a war."

"what does that mean?" asked Walid, uncertain if he had heard correctly.

The words tumbled out of the men in a symphony of discordant sounds. He hurried his footsteps back to the house, assured that at least by now everyone would be home and taking their afternoon rest. When he arrived, he heard his mother's whispered tears and the radio announcer's hurried voice. Only his sister was sleeping soundly.

"ya ibni, alhamdulillah, that you've come home. another war. what will we do?" His mother emerged as soon as she heard him enter.

He sat next to her and put his arm around her. "i'm here, ya mama, don't be afraid. we don't have anyone in the war this time."

When Magda awoke, they told her that they would be remaining at home. Although the fighting was distant, a sense of danger shrouded the city. They spent the rest of the day with the radio voices a constant hum in the house and the shadow of '67 following them, Kamel's footsteps like a ghost among them.

* ⁂ *

Four months after the war ended, Magda received a letter from Hafez. It was the first letter he had sent only to her. Walid handed it to her when she came home from work. Magda had finished college, attending the business school at Cairo University and finding a job at the National Bank of Egypt. She was earning a salary, and each month, she gave most of it to her father, keeping only a couple of pounds for herself. Neither of them spoke as she handed him the bills. He held his head straight and looked past her into the distance. Magda glanced toward the floor and quickly folded the money into his palm as if they were only passing each other in a hallway. She knew that the money she gave him was more than what he earned in a month.

Walid said nothing as he handed her the letter. She thought he might have opened it, but the thin blue envelope was still sealed, its contents intact as if they could remain buried in their paper tomb. Now she wondered if her brother didn't open the letter because he already knew what it held. What she wouldn't find out until years later is that two months earlier, Walid had received an identical letter.

my dearest sister,

i send my greetings to you and to my parents and to my brother. inshallah, you are all well. we are fine here. we have been here for five years and, alhamdulillah, we took the citizenship. the american law allows us to bring our brothers and sisters, so now i can do the paperwork and send for you. there will only be more wars. there is no future in egypt. it would be better for you to get married before you come.

your loving brother

Magda turned the thin paper over, looking for something more. *did he miss me? did he think i would be happy in amreeka? did he think it was right for me to leave our parents?* She refolded the letter and put it away. The house felt smaller and the air heavy, until it was too much effort to breathe. After dinner, Magda said she wanted to go to the evening service at the Hanging Church. They lived so close to the churches of Coptic Cairo that no one minded if she went alone.

The churches cloistered around one another, forming a village that resounded with church bells and the smell of incense. Magda made her way down the uneven stairs leading to the homes, stores, and churches of Old Cairo. There were doors on the narrow alleyway that opened into people's houses.

Her father's cousin and his family lived here when they first arrived from Kom Ombo. They went to visit them once, but Magda only remembered the darkness of the space and its smallness. A table sat in the middle of the room as soon as you entered. It was where the family ate and where the sons, Bashir and Halim, did their homework, hovering under the gas lamp. She never saw the back rooms, but she imagined there was no light as you retreated into the apartment. The family left after two years when the father found a job selling tickets at the bus station, and they rented an apartment in Helwan.

Magda walked up the church stairs, making the sign of the cross as soon as she entered. A few older women in black dresses and with kerchiefs over their hair were scattered among the pews. Some were sitting, their heads lowered and their bodies swaying in rhythm to their prayers. Two women were kneeling, muttering into the wooden pews, and one woman was standing, her hands outstretched, her furrowed brow revealing the pleading agony she was offering the Lord.

Magda slipped into one of the pews toward the back of the church, fearful of disturbing the other women. As she sat down, she realized she had no prayer to offer. Her life had been as consistent as her one pair of shoes. She was taught to obey at home and at school, and one day, she was expected to marry and have children. Her college education enabled her to earn a living and increase her status for marriage. Now her brother offered another path, but one that she knew would tip the balance of their family. When Hafez left, there were still two of them. They could take care of their parents as they aged, and the scale still weighed in their favor. But if she accepted Hafez's offer, only Walid would remain.

Magda had never stretched her imagination beyond the life she inherited. It was Hafez who looked through the walls of their existence, who caught dreams with the same precision that he made his architect's drawings. People assumed she was quiet, obedient, but the truth was she grew with fear lodged in her throat. Each day, she heard her father's anger lash out at one of her brothers. It took only his interpretation of a look or tone of voice for him to accuse them of disrespect. Her mother cowered, kept her voice only a whisper in the house, and Magda learned invisibility from her.

Only Hafez offered her some attention. In secondary school, when she was struggling with math, he would come home from a long day of work and sit next to her to help her decipher the numbers. On those late evenings, he convinced her to study harder, to go to college. Now he was opening another door. Magda closed her eyes, tried to imagine herself in America, but no image came. They didn't own a television and there was not enough money to go to the movies, so she couldn't conjure up an image of this land of wealth. She didn't know how to place herself in the frame. But here, she knew her role would be to take care of her parents, to marry, and to stop working once she had children. That's where she ended. She enjoyed her job at the bank: going in each morning, making her way out of Old Cairo to downtown, where the city felt alive and vibrant; being greeted as Miss Magda; having others come in to hand her a file, their postures deferential; being able to sit behind a desk; making decisions that affected something larger than herself. But after marriage, she would be relegated to wife, housekeeper, and mother, no different from her own mother. And life would stand still, eternally rotating on the same axis.

After the letter came, the house seemed defeated. On the roof, the chickens stopped their constant squawking, and the house fell quiet as if sinking deeper into its foundation.

* ⁂ *

When Walid received the letter from Hafez, he slipped it into his pocket and carried it with him for three days. One day, after work, he stopped at a café, ordered a Turkish coffee, and opened the letter.

my dearest brother,

i send my greetings to you and to my sister and to our parents. inshallah you are all well and the war has not impacted you. i am afraid for you and for your son. we have received citizenship and now i can bring you here. when you come and get settled, together we can send for our sister and parents. once i hear from you, i will begin the paperwork for your immigration.

your dear brother

Walid wanted to tear the blue aerogram, scatter its fragile paper with all the anger that erupted at reading his brother's words. *was he living in a film, an american film with the sun shining every day and gold under his feet? had he forgotten our lives? my parents, already in their late sixties and settled in their lives, how could they live in amreeka?* Walid saw his father's wizened face, made older than his years by the constant labor that earned him little and the frustration of being unable to provide for his family. He had seen his eyes when he turned away after Magda gave him her salary, the defeat that embedded itself deeper into the grooves on his face and made his cheeks sink. And he noticed how his mother had sewn herself an invisible cloak to wrap around her loneliness. He knew that she always favored Hafez. He was her eldest son, and she had put her hopes in him, proud to be called Um Hafez after his birth. Once he left, no one made that reference to her. A mother does not have children so they will leave her.

Walid wrote back to his brother, told him not to bother with the paperwork. That his place would remain here with their parents.

A month after Walid sent his response, the letter for Magda arrived. Walid knew she was considering, her eyes looking beyond her vision. She sat with the family, but it was as if she were already gone. Her mother had to ask her twice if she wanted more food, and her father had to ask more loudly for her to bring him his tea. The glitter of America had already caught her fancy. And he understood. She had grown up in this house, with its enclosed walls, its poverty, and she knew she was not likely to make a marriage much above their station. The possibility of America opened her suppressed desires, and, once unlocked, they couldn't be closed again.

Walid never told his wife about the letter. Noura was a simple woman whose family came from the same village as his grandfather. When it was time for him to marry, his father had suggested this young woman. Walid trusted his judgement and wanted to please him. They were all part of the same extended family, and they accepted the proposal. The move to the city was viewed as an advance in the village, giving the family status for having a daughter living in Cairo. But his wife kept her simple village ways, and Walid couldn't imagine that she could become an American.

* ⁂ *

Magda stood at the altar of the Hanging Church, her white dress trailing to the floor, next to the man who would be her husband. The priest intoned the ancient ceremony of marriage, the chanting of the liturgy cloaking them like the golden robes that had been placed over their shoulders. They stood with heads bowed to receive the crowns, accepting the prayer that tied them together for their remaining days as the priest recited the words "crown them with glory and honor, oh father."

Magda's parents sat in the front row along with Walid, his wife, and their son. Each face held a mask that erased all emotion. They stood and sat and responded to the priest's "ameen," repeating the motions programed into their bodies.

Walid told me that he had made subtle inquiries at work and learned that someone had a cousin who was looking to get married. He comes from a middle-class family, he explained, adding that he was someone who would normally be above our family's reach for marriage. I never knew what my brother said, what promises were made, or what was whispered about me.

The family arrived on Friday afternoon. My mother ushered them into the front room that had been thoroughly cleaned and prepared. Walid had gone all the way to the pastry store in Garden City to purchase a full tray of konafa. I lowered my eyes as I met each member of Lutfi's family and shook hands with his parents. But when he approached me, I stood with my arms at my side and only nodded toward the floor as if the words of greeting had been stamped beneath my feet.

We sat down, and the first awkward moments were eased when my mother began serving the tea and offering each person a piece of konafa. Plates and cups were passed with questions of how many spoons of sugar and thanks being exchanged. The sounds of sipping tea and eating followed, fork against plate punctuated by a woman's voice yelling for her child from the street, a man selling peanuts calling out to entice customers, and the tumble of cars against the uneven road. These were the sounds of Old Cairo, and I felt self-conscious as they entered the apartment. My father should have been the one to open the conversation, but it was Walid who spoke first, beginning by asking about the well-being of the family. Lutfi joined the conversation, offering his credentials like an employee seeking a job. He said he was an accountant working at a company with a good position. I glanced over as he spoke, noticing that he was tall and handsome, his features drawn with precision. He had a quick smile and seemed at ease in his body; he owned himself in a way I couldn't imagine.

I watched Lutfi's father take a final sip of his tea and sit back in his chair. He cleared his throat and began to explain that they had two younger sons, one in medical school and one still in high school, also hoping to become a doctor. Their profession would make it difficult to leave the country, and so they served as insurance that the parents would be taken care of as they aged. With three sons, he said they could afford to have one go to America. Lutfi would be expected to help his brothers as they completed their education, so they were willing to relinquish him.

I remained quiet until Lutfi's mother asked about my job and if I planned to work in America. I answered carefully, avoiding any certainty and repeating "as god wills it." Lutfi and I said nothing to each other. Only once as others were talking, we exchanged a silent look.

When the proposal arrived, I accepted, recognizing that Lutfi and I had been brought together by our desire for America.

The house became a tomb guarded by Walid. No one knew the demons that plagued him, that made him lash out at his son over some simple error—dropping a fork at dinner, taking too long to purchase bread from the bakery, forgetting to close the balcony door. The son was molded into obedience like a plant whose branches are bent each day to grow at a prescribed angle.

Every evening, Amin struggled with math equations and the syntax of Arabic. At first, his father tried to help him, guide him through the steps of each problem, but Walid would grow frustrated with his own sense of inadequacy, leaving him alone at the darkening table. "if your uncle or aunt were here, they could help you," he snapped as he left the room.

Once Amin entered high school, his father would lecture him at every evening meal. Before Amin could swallow the last morsel of food, Walid began his rendition of the words his own parents had uttered against him, as he reminded his son of his uncle's nightly study habits and the success those earned him. The comparisons and reprimands slapped across Amin's back, and his body folded in on itself as his father's words raged against the walls of the small house. In the last year of high school, Walid locked his son in his room each night with nothing but his schoolbooks and forced him into a cave of studying. His wife pleaded with him to bring Amin a plate of food, but he pushed his hand against her shoulder and her feet stumbled backwards.

The son retreated into the same room where his uncle had spent his nights. He stared out the small window into the street where the house sat. People circled their steps around the patches of water that rose and clogged the road; others kept their path straight, stepping into whatever debris they encountered. Amin did enough studying to just barely pass his exams and proceed from one year to the next. Mostly, he thought of his uncle, who had transformed their lives by his success and disappearance. America seemed a monster that swallowed people whole. He watched his family piece together their existence, made of leftovers and scraps.

One afternoon, Amin looked out the window to see a man and his young son walking, the man dressed in a gray galabiya and the boy in trousers already edging up his ankles and a slightly crumpled white shirt. The boy looked to be about five years old, just on the verge of stepping out of childhood. The man pulled at his son's arm, urging him to walk faster, but the boy only stumbled when his father pulled harder. And each time the father turned to his son to urge him along, the boy seemed to deflate, his body shrinking and his face turning red with an effort he couldn't muster. Another tug and another stumble, and the father turned to his son, his frustration about to unleash, but as his eyes looked down to confront the boy, he hesitated slightly, took one step, and then scooped up the boy in his arms to carry him the rest of their way.

Amin managed to do well enough on his Thanaweya Amma exams to be accepted into the Faculty of Economics at the University of Helwan. His father received the news, saying, "you could not gain admittance to cairo university or even ain shams, but at least there will be a college degree in your hands."

* ⁂ *

Walid tried to pick up the responsibility of eldest son that Hafez left behind. He assumed that his sister would stand beside him, but when she received Hafez's letter, he saw the look of desire in her eyes and did not try to dissuade her. The '73 war had scared them, and Hafez's pull was too strong to resist. Walid fulfilled his duty as her elder brother and found a good husband for her. They married, and, within a month, the family waved to them as they drove to the airport, Magda wearing a new pair of shoes to take her to America.

* ⁂ *

Magda opened her closet door and knelt down to pull out a pair of brown pumps. Then she opened the shoebox next to her and pulled out a new pair of short-heeled black pumps and put them in place of the other ones. It was an annual ritual for her, this replacing of one pair of shoes for the other. The result was that there were always three pairs of shoes in her closet. In the winter, it was one pair of pumps, one pair of boots, and one pair of casual shoes. In the summer, it was one pair of dress shoes, one pair of flats, and one pair of sandals. Each year, she replaced them and donated the old ones to a charitable organization that offered free items to those who needed them. When Lutfi had first suggested she take them to Goodwill, she refused. "i don't want anyone to pay money for these shoes. if you don't have enough money, you will not spend what you have on shoes."

Even with the house that she and Lutfi had bought, the banking jobs they had both acquired, and the surplus food in their refrigerator, Magda did not want to forget. She saw the way Hafez had folded up his past neatly and placed it in an iron-clad box that he had permanently buried. He went to work, established a comfortable life for his family, saved money diligently, and sent money to their brother at every opportunity. But Magda did not want to release the memories, especially of those years between '67 and '73 when they had survived on the fringes with what little they could acquire. She let them flutter around her like a tablecloth hovering momentarily before settling on the surface.

But even as memories trespassed into her days, the necessity of building a life took over, and the calls to her brother in Egypt went from once a month, to only on holidays, to her sometimes forgetting and negating the promise she had made to herself to call another day.

Lutfi and Magda did not consummate their marriage until they arrived in America. It was in America that Magda understood that she had married a kind man, one who would be gentle with her. His touch awakened pleasure that she did not know was possible. And she was grateful to America for giving her this husband who exceeded her dreams.

Lutfi helped her to find joy in their new country. Each weekend, he led them to a new place of exploration. They went to Hampton Beach, to Gloucester, to Nantucket, to Martha's Vineyard. Lutfi had a childlike quality to him, a joy in the simplest of daily things, and slowly Magda caught some of that joy.

After Walid buried his parents, he sat next to his wife, settling into an acceptance of the daily monotony of the days. Each Christmas and Easter, a phone call entered their house with its distinct long-distance ring like a forgotten guest, and the voices from America raised the volume of their existence. Wishes for a good holiday and inquiries about each person's health became a matter of heightened importance. The conversation raised the family's spirits, and even after the receiver returned to its cradle, they spoke of the words that had passed back and forth through the lines that stretched across the ocean between them. But after a short while, their breaths became shallow, feeling betrayed by the inquiries that arrived only twice a year, and their complete isolation settled back on them with a greater heaviness.

Amin's resentment toward those who brought joy only to take it back with the click of the receiver grew over the years without his awareness.

He was only an infant when his uncle left and five when his aunt departed. When he thought of them, their features smudged across the back of his eyelids. He couldn't recall a word either of them had spoken to him, but he watched his father take on each obligation they left behind: caring for his grandparents, fixing the cracks in the walls of the house, upgrading the plumbing in the bathrooms.

Amin finished college, acquired a job as a teller at a small bank, and after a few years, he married Samira, a young woman from the neighborhood whom he had glimpsed from time to time. She often sat on the balcony, drinking a cup of tea and watching the comings and goings of the street. She was a plain young woman, hair pulled back into a bun and no makeup to create an illusion.

Amin and Samira moved into a small apartment in Shobra after they married. Their lives blended into the landscape of the neighborhood, and they managed their days with the usual pattern of work, food, family, and sleep. The absence of other things crumbled beneath their feet like the loose gravel of the streets.

* ⁂ *

Walid's health began deteriorating in his early fifties. It started with various aches. One day, he complained his arm hurt, another day he was limping, and another his back kept him from standing straight. Slowly, his body began to distort, unable to keep all its parts aligned and steady. Amin took him to one doctor after the other, but their diagnoses were like a man searching for a needle with his eyes closed. One said his heart was beating too fast and his body couldn't keep up, and another said his muscles were weak and he needed to eat liver every day. His wife cooked liver until the smell of it seeped into the corners of the house and no one could escape it.

The day Walid fell down at work and couldn't get back up, Amin was called, and he went to gather his father's crumpled body from the floor and bring him home. For a few weeks, Walid would attempt to raise himself from the bed where he had been placed and stand upright. Sometimes he made it as far as the bathroom; other times, he gathered his steps to the living room and stood leaning against the doorway. His wife would wrap him in her arms and kiss his forehead three times, saying, "look at my husband, strong and good thanks to god," muttering her words like an incantation over him.

But there was no magic to her words, and his deterioration appeared inevitable. His condition worsened, even as his wife fulfilled her duties tirelessly, watching over him like a hawk as if her vigilance could keep away whatever was harming him. Within two years, he became restricted to the house, the only exposure to the outside world coming when he sat on the balcony and watched the movement below him.

Walid held on to the tail end of life, his last days tightened by illness. When he passed on and the phone calls from America came, the voices echoing surprise at his father's death, Amin responded flatly, saying he had been sick for some time and they should have known.

* ⁂ *

It wasn't until after his father's death that he discovered that his uncle Hafez and aunt Magda had been sending money on a regular basis. More money began to arrive from America. Unexpected knocks on the door brought visitors who had been given the task of delivering envelopes heavy with bills. At first, Amin kept the envelopes in a drawer unopened, their seals tight. But when his mother's health dwindled and each doctor prescribed more pills, he had little choice but to peel across the seal and release the bills.

* ⁂ *

Amin walked with his father's footsteps, an almost imperceptible stoop of the shoulders, a steady awkwardness to each step, a methodical tediousness to the movements of his body. Each day he rose from his bed, a sunken mattress marked by the indentation of his small frame. Like his father, he was a short man, slim, with a boy's body despite his age. He attended to his duties with the willpower of obligation. His father's words repeated like a mantra in his mind: "our obligation is to our family. each child must take care of his parents as they took care of him. a good son does not abandon his family." The lesson ingrained itself into his body and marked his life's destiny.

He rode the metro from his home in Shobra to the Ramses station to another train that took him to the house in Old Cairo. Each morning, he unlocked the blue iron door and climbed the steps to find his mother dressed in her long black galabiya, the sign of her mourning wrapped around her floundering frame. Two years since his father's death, and he knew she would continue to wear black until her own passing. She greeted him with a kiss on both cheeks and shuffled her weight to the tiny kitchen to boil water for his tea.

"what do you need mother?" he inquired as he did every morning.

"there is nothing; there is nothing my son. i don't need anything."

He surveyed the small sitting area, taking note of the number of loaves of bread on the table. "i will get bread and a half kilo of roomy cheese. do you want white cheese? and i will get some fuul. anything else?"

"as you see fit my son," she answered as she brought in his tea in a glass cup, her hand quivering while setting it on the small round table. "how many spoons of sugar?" she asked.

"three," he responded as he did each morning, her question only an excuse for conversation.

She settled her weight on one of the chairs, the folds of black material tucking around her body. "how is samira doing?"

"thanks be to god," he responded.

"and all is good with the pregnancy?" she continued.

"yes, alhamdulillah."

"god be with her." His mother executed the blessing. "and may your child be clever like your uncle."

"yes, and where is he now?" His tone bitter like the sour cabbage his grandmother used to pickle.

Amin watched his mother's frame lean over to retrieve the cheese from the refrigerator that stood almost in the middle of the living room since there was no space for it in the kitchen. He could barely recall her appearance in her youth; as a young boy, he had taken little notice of her physique or her face. Now he wished he could call up her image as a young woman. But he only knew his mother as she was now, with the slide of her slippered feet across the floor, the effort of lifting each foot and carrying the weight of her body too much of a burden.

Her presence held him to this house, gave structure to his days as he came to check on her and purchase what she needed daily. Each holiday, he brought his family with him to occupy her, to give her the task of preparing food so there was something for her to anticipate. Life was finite, he knew this much. And those who didn't die left for America. They were the ones who lived forever. Death from a distance means nothing. You hang up the phone after you are informed and find no difference in your life. A real death should leave a tangible void—the face you used to look at no longer available for your gaze, the voice that spoke to you each day replaced by silence.

When Magda got pregnant, she and Lutfi began to anticipate the birth of their first child and their family growing. In the second month of her pregnancy, when Magda noticed some bleeding, they rushed to the hospital and were told it was a miscarriage. The doctor assured them that it was nothing to cause concern and that they could start trying again soon. The second time, Magda took extra precautions, made sure she rested each day after work. Lutfi took over the cooking and the cleaning. Layla visited every couple of days, chatted with her about anything to keep her mind occupied and away from dangerous thoughts. But Magda's body stiffened, and she lay still, awaiting only what she knew was inevitable. At the beginning of the third month, the ultrasound showed that the fetus was no longer viable. The doctor explained with words that did not settle clearly—"inflammation, scarring, permanent damage"—and she and Lutfi understood that there would be no children in their lives.

Magda withdrew into a quiet depression. The children her body had relinquished lodged inside her, and she mourned their loss. For a while, Lutfi allowed her the space to grieve. Then slowly, he began to urge her to take a walk, to go out to eat. Every few days, he came home with a video of a funny movie, insisting they watch it together. When some time had passed, he broached the subject, assuring her that he did not mind not having children, that the two of them were enough. And he reminded her that they had Hafez and Layla's children to care for as aunt and uncle. Magda remained quiet to his assurance. She felt fortunate that fate had led her to this man. It was not so much the desire to be a mother as an assumption she had lived with like poverty, marriage, and remaining in Egypt. Her life had taken turns that she couldn't have anticipated. Slowly, she covered the memory of each unborn life and returned to find a husband who welcomed her.

She invited Layla and Hafez over, bought presents for each of their children, and opened her home to them. On the weekends, she and Lutfi took the children to the Franklin Park Zoo, to Canobie Lake Park, and to Hampton Beach. Their parents were relieved to drop them off at her house so they could have some quiet time. Magda became the trusted aunt, drawing the children toward her. She told Yusef stories about his father in Egypt, and she taught Amal how to put henna in her hair. Magda and Lutfi filled their house with their niece and nephew. And Magda found that this was enough, that her life had the fullness of love she had craved.

Hala and Nessim's Departure

Hala and Nessim's flight left at a reasonable hour in the morning, but with all the usual chaos at the airport, they still needed to get there early. When I arrived at their apartment in Zamalek, everything was in a state of disorder. Cups and glasses littered the living room table along with open bottles of wine, and in their bedroom, the suitcases lay on the bed gaping open, waiting to be fed. Neither my sister Hala nor her husband looked like they had slept; darkness circled their eyes, giving them a haunted look, and their movements all seemed misdirected. Hala tried to orchestrate, shouting to Nessim a list of items to pull out of drawers and closets, to be folded or crumpled into the suitcases.

Last night, there had been a farewell party with family and friends filling the apartment, drinking and joking, with food catered from the Four Seasons Hotel. I came over for a short while, and the laughter rang to the ceiling. It didn't feel like a going-away, but simply an interlude after which we would all resume our lives.

The next morning, I found Salima in her room, almost forgotten. She had dressed herself and was attempting to stuff an abacus into the suitcase on her bed.

"i'm not sure that will work," I said.

"but i love it and i want to take it with me. mama said i couldn't take it. but maybe if i can find a space."

I looked at the assortment of shoes and clothes folded and layered into the suitcase. Salima was eight years old, and I knew she would quickly outgrow every one of those items. I asked her to point to her least favorite outfit, and she gestured toward a green dress with a high ruffled collar, a white wool sweater, and a pair of shiny black shoes.

"i don't like these," she said. "they're itchy and the shoes hurt my feet, but mama says they're pretty, so we have to take them."

I plucked out the three items. Salima nodded, and together we tucked the colorful abacus into the bottom of the suitcase.

"this will be a secret between us," I said, putting my finger over my mouth.

I tried to make myself useful by gathering the cups in the living room and taking them to the kitchen to wash them. I poured the remaining wine into the sink and wiped the tables. The kitchen was in upheaval, and I ended up dumping most things into the garbage. Inside the refrigerator sat the remains of food—half a chocolate cake, a platter of cheese, the fried eggplant our mother had made because it was Nessim's favorite, and other partially eaten dishes. It was too much to clean up, and I imagined how each item would mold and shrink, transforming into new substance.

Hala and Nessim were in the living room, weighing suitcases on a bathroom scale. They kept removing items, so the luggage could reach the required weight, leaving behind an assorted pile of clothing that was likely to remain where it was for some time to come.

We managed to fit everything into the car, with Salima and Hala in the back seat, along with two suitcases. It was Friday, with most people at prayer, so the roads were not as congested, and we were able to move at a good speed to make up for the time lost. Hala seemed to wake up once we were on our way.

"fanous," she said, "the housekeeper is coming on tuesday next week, and she will clean up and take out the garbage." She reached over to hand me a set of keys. "can you please go check after she goes and let me know if everything has been done?"

She spoke as if they were simply going on vacation for a few weeks, perhaps to the Mediterranean Sea in Alexandria, and would be returning to pick up their lives where they had left off. Nessim sat silently in obedience. He had lost his job, and now, without title or status, he already seemed bereft, a man with nothing to claim, nothing to ground him. I looked down at his polished Italian shoes and wondered how long they would last in America.

We believed that it was Hala who pushed Nessim to go, that she wanted a more glamorous life like the one she watched in those foreign movies and the one her sister described in her letters. For some, those films were enough to cure them of their longing, but for others, they only incited their desire.

In the back seat, Salima sat quietly leaning against the window. She had been kept awake by the noise of the previous evening, and her tiredness made her small body shrink into the seat.

At the airport, family and friends were waiting to say farewell. It appeared to be a continuation of the evening before, with a few jokes bantered about. When the call to board came, they said goodbye to each person with a quick hug and two kisses as if we would be seeing them again in a few days. As they made their way to the plane, those of us left behind felt the space opening to reveal the presence of absence.

Hala and Nessim – 1984

After Layla left, her family continued on with their lives. The space of her absence opened a wound that they kept trying to heal. Hala and Layla were eight years apart. From the time she could walk, Hala looked up to her sister, following her around, imitating her actions. Whatever Layla did, Hala wanted to do the same. In secret, she would try on her sister's clothes and apply her makeup, and, despite being found out and being reprimanded, she continued. For her, Layla was like a mountain she had to climb.

Hala was fifteen when Layla left, and she thought her sister would be back by the time she finished high school, that she would return and slip back into the family as if her absence had only been a shopping excursion to downtown. At first, the reasons they gave had substance. Hafez was working on his degree, then Layla finally became pregnant again, and they wanted to wait until the baby came. For a while, it was money—the cost of the tickets, paying off bills. But then the reasons became as thin as the blue aerogram letters. They were worried about another war, their son was young so they worried he would get sick, Hafez didn't want to jeopardize his chances of getting a promotion.

Nasser died in 1970, and millions crowded the streets at his funeral. Hala's family didn't understand how people could still worship him after the devastation of the '67 war and what it had done. Sadat took over and there was some hope, but his Open-Door Economic Policy only made everything more expensive, so people could afford even less. The Muslim Brotherhood gained more power, and those who were Coptic began to fear for their place in the country. Everything took a turn to become more conservative. You couldn't find the novels of Ihsan Abdel Quddous; the romance stories that young girls like Layla had grown up reading were now considered taboo. The deaths of Abdel Halim Hafez and Umm Kulthum felt ominous, and the country seemed to be closing in on all sides.

* ⁂ *

I knew that college was my best chance for finding a husband. When I got ready each day, I took my time, making sure my clothes accentuated my figure, my hair was styled in the latest fashion, and my makeup just right. I kept my eyes open. I stayed away from the men who looked too eager, knowing they were looking for a woman who would replace their mother. And I kept my distance from the ones who kept their gaze downward, knowing they didn't have the confidence to succeed. In my third year, I noticed Nessim. He was one of my classmates in the School of Economics. Nessim came to the university sporting European leather shoes and souvenir pens with London landmarks. I liked the way he slid into his seat with an easy confidence, the way he was not afraid to argue with the professor. He was taller than most Egyptian men, and his stature made others respect him. His gaze was neither arrogant nor fearful, but somehow when he settled his dark eyes on someone, they stopped to listen. I learned he had gone to British schools and that his English was fluent.

I noted his movements, arranging to be in his line of vision. It didn't take long for me to maneuver myself so that he would notice me. But, once I caught his attention, I knew to float further from him, so he would believe he was the one doing the pursuing. He began to sit next to me in class and would ask to borrow a pen or make a comment about the class material. I replied politely, but I didn't pursue the conversation. One day, he asked if I understood a particular point the professor was making that was unclear to him. When I said yes and proceeded to explain it, he requested that we study together, complimenting me on my grasp of the subject. I agreed, and that is how it began. We were married one month after we graduated from college.

On the day of Hala's wedding, it was Fanous's wife, Salwa, who stood next to her. The letters that Hala and her mother had sent and the phone calls they had made with pleading requests did not make Layla materialize for the wedding. No one remembered the reason why Layla and Hafez were unable to attend; they only knew that their places in the church pews remained empty.

Just a few months after she married Nessim, Hala became pregnant. The pregnancy was unplanned, and Hala was reluctant to accept it. Marriage freed her from being under her parents' watch and from the restrictions that came with being a woman. She wanted to go out, to take pleasure in what the city had to offer, and, at her urging, she and Nessim went to the Opera, to concerts, to films. The city expanded for Hala, opening its treasures of pleasure and amusement. She enjoyed having money to purchase new clothes, to dress herself up into a new role. At twenty-two, she was not ready to turn into the women she saw around her, their bodies blown out, with pregnancy transforming them into permanent maternal figures.

One morning as Nessim was immersed in reading the newspaper, she told him that she wasn't sure she wanted to go through with it.

The words startled Nessim, and while he was generally willing to go along with Hala's wishes, this time he blurted out, "but it's not right."

"but what's right for me?" Hala responded as if she had already prepared the words. "i'm only twenty-two. i don't want to be a mother yet."

Nessim looked at his wife. It's true that she was young, but motherhood would mature her. Still, he knew an argument was not likely to solve the problem. He flattened his hand across the newspaper lying on the table in front of him. "let's make an appointment and talk to the doctor," he said.

* ⁂ *

The doctor leaned back in his chair, his graying hair and moustache along with his white coat giving him the appearance of intelligence and authority. He nodded as Hala made her request.

"of course," he said, seeming to agree, "you're young and not ready." Then he bent toward her across the desk and proceeded to explain the details of the procedure Hala had requested, exactly what was involved and the things that could go wrong, including the possibility of becoming infertile.

Hala's body stiffened as if each of the doctor's descriptions were attaching to her body. By the end of the conversation, she had changed her mind.

What Hala never knew is that Nessim had gone to speak to the doctor before their appointment and asked him to convince her not to go through with the abortion. It was perhaps the only assertive action Nessim would make during their marriage.

The actual birth of the child was difficult, putting Hala in labor for close to twenty-four hours. In the end, she was too exhausted to push and they rushed her in for a C-section, marking the entrance of the child with a large scar that would permanently tug at Hala's skin. When the child finally emerged, they named her Salima, grateful that she had arrived whole.

* ⁂ *

Two weeks before Salima's first birthday, the phone rang after Hala had put her daughter to sleep. She picked it up quickly, afraid it would wake the baby. Her mother's wails came through on the other end of the line, but she couldn't decipher the words. Then she heard the static of movement and Fanous's voice enter the phone.

"our father, ya hala. he collapsed. i have to go to the hospital. come now because of mama."

"tayeb," Hala barely answered and let the phone slip out of her hand. Nessim picked it up, and she heard his voice speaking as she stepped out the door.

Hala found her mother sitting in the middle of the living room floor, her body swaying as tears flowed to curtain her face. Hala placed herself next to Fayza and wrapped her arms around her. "he fell, he fell from me," she said, her eyes looking into nothing. And Hala imagined the scene she described. Her father returning home, placing his keys on the table and falling, breaking like a vase. All she could say was "ya mama." Fanous left to go to the hospital as soon as she arrived. Hala and her mother remained where they were as if they were another fixture of the room.

Nessim arrived a short while later after dropping off Salima with his parents. He gathered Hala and her mother up and took them to the hospital. By the time they arrived, Wassef was in surgery and Fanous was in the waiting room. A swirl of noise surrounded Fanous, with doctors and nurses moving about, the hospital humming with movement, but he sat shrouded in silence when Hala and her mother joined him to wait.

"layla, did you call layla," Hala asked Fanous.

"it's the middle of the night where she is now," Fanous said.

Fanous was the joyful one in the family, his easy smile softening every moment of tension. But as Hala saw him sitting in the dim waiting room, he looked drained and empty of all joy.

"we'll call her when he comes out of the surgery, bel salama," Fanous said.

Fayza closed her eyes and leaned on Fanous's words.

Wassef survived the operation, and when they were given permission to see him, they surrounded his bed. Fayza sat at his side, her tears streaming.

"woman, why are you crying? did you want to get rid of me?" Wassef's joke released the breath they had all been holding.

Fanous called Layla, and she heard the news of her father's attack and his recovery in one breath. She called the following day to ask about him, and then a few days later, and then one more time the next week. The calls lasted no more than five minutes, so Hala couldn't tell her of the hours they had spent in the hospital, each of them taking turns watching him sleep, keeping their eyes on the heart monitor, calling the nurse if they sensed any hesitation, those first days they feared they might lose him. But when Layla called, Hala only said he's doing well.

Fayza prayed daily, her lips always in the movement of worship. She prayed to the Virgin Mary, vowed to fast in exchange for her husband's health. And she kept her promise, fasting for three weeks in August every year, her offering for his recovery.

After Wassef regained his health, Hala became restless. She wanted to escape this predictability of life and death. She thought of Layla on the other end of the phone line and sometimes wished she were there instead of sitting by her father's hospital bed. She grew tired of the way her mother slipped Layla's name into hers, forgetting her absence and calling Hala by her sister's name.

Nessim had a good job, and Sadat's open market allowed those who had the money to purchase imported goods—soap, nuts, chocolate—but Hala wanted more. The restrictions of Nasser's regime had lifted, but now people could taste America on their lips.

Every day, Hala heard about someone who was leaving. They were usually going to America, but sometimes those who had gone to French schools went to Canada or France, their education having already set them in that direction. But America was the pinnacle, the place where everyone believed your problems became dust beneath your feet.

When Layla and Hafez came for their visit, Layla brought presents for everyone. She gave Hala a perfume bottle in the shape of a woman wearing a long yellow dress, the skirt flowing out. The bottle twisted open at the woman's waist. When Hala opened it, it smelled like an English landscape garden, the kind she had seen in pictures of Versailles.

* ⁂ *

Despite Nessim's status and wealth, his desires were simply fulfilled. His contentment focused on his job, home, and family. To immigrate, Hala had to create his discontent. Every time he uttered the smallest complaint, she caught it and remolded it into an insurmountable obstacle, whether it was difficulty catching a cab, an employee who made a simple mistake, or the lack of fresh produce in the market. Slowly, she burrowed the sense of unease into her husband.

Nessim came home carrying a package wrapped in brown paper. As he entered, he handed it to Hala, saying, "this is all i could find, two kilos. i went to three fish markets."

"but we need at least three kilos," Hala said, taking the package and weighing it with her hand as if she could increase its weight by holding it.

"i know." Nessim sat down as if to relieve himself of the effort of his journey. "but there is apparently a shortage of shrimp and that cost twenty-five pounds a kilo."

Hala gasped at the price and went on, "they take advantage of us at every turn. who can afford twenty-five pounds? Soon we'll all have to live on fuul and taamia."

* ⁂ *

ON OCTOBER 6, 1981, TELEVISIONS BROADCAST THE VICTORY CELEBRATION FOR THE EGYPTIAN ARMY'S CROSSING THE SUEZ AND RECAPTURING THE SINAI PENINSULA IN THE WAR OF 1973. WHEN THE SOLDIERS JUMP OUT OF THE MILITARY VEHICLE, SADAT STANDS READY TO RECEIVE THEIR SALUTE. ONE SOLDIER RETRIEVES THREE HAND GRENADES FROM UNDER HIS HELMET AND THROWS THEM. THE LAST ONE EXPLODES, FOLLOWED BY THE ERUPTION OF BULLETS FROM OTHER SOLDIERS. THE MILITARY PROTECTING SADAT REMAIN FROZEN FOR FORTY-FIVE SECONDS BEFORE THEY BEGIN FIRING BACK AT THE SOLDIERS SHOOTING THEIR BULLETS. CHAIRS ARE THROWN ABOUT TO SHIELD THE PRESIDENT, CREATING AN AWKWARD SCULPTURE OF INTERTWINED LIMBS. ABOVE, THE PLANES CONTINUE THEIR CELEBRATORY TURNS AND TWISTS.

THOSE WHO HAVE THEIR TELEVISIONS TURNED ON AS THEY CLEAN OR COOK OR TALK STOP MID-MOVEMENT AND TURN TO SEE THE CHAOS OF THE SCENE ON THEIR SCREENS. FOR TWO HOURS, THE NATION STANDS SUSPENDED, WAITING FOR NEWS AFTER SADAT IS AIRLIFTED TO THE MAADI MILITARY HOSPITAL.

THEORIES ABOUT THE MOTIVATION BEHIND THE ASSASSINATION BOUNCE FROM ONE TO THE NEXT: THE PEACE TREATY HE SIGNED THAT MADE EGYPT THE FIRST ARAB COUNTRY TO ACKNOWLEDGE THE EXISTENCE OF ISRAEL, THE ROUNDING UP OF THOSE WHO EXPRESSED CRITICISM OF HIS LEADERSHIP, THE MASSIVE ARRESTS THAT SENT A TREMOR OF FEAR THROUGH THE COUNTRY. SADAT'S PARANOIA STRETCHED TO ANYONE HE SUSPECTED OF OBSTRUCTING HIS PLANS, AND EVEN THE POPE OF THE COPTIC CHURCH HAD BEEN EXILED TO THE DESERT.

SOME REJOICE THAT SADAT IS GONE, BUT OTHERS KNOW THAT THE FUTURE WILL ONLY CONTINUE THE SAME PATTERN—AND THEY ARE PROVEN CORRECT AS VICE PRESIDENT MUBARAK TAKES OVER THE COUNTRY.

* ⁂ *

It was because of Sadat that Hala's mother could make her Christmas baklava with pistachios. He had switched the country's alliance from the Soviet Union and opened the doors to the forbidden fruits of the West. Nessim worked for an American company that had been able to set up business because of Sadat's Open-Door Economic Policy. Although Mubarak promised to continue in Sadat's footsteps, trepidation knocked at the door of each foreign company, and the smaller ones decided it was better to dissolve and cut their losses than be confiscated by the new government. Nessim found himself unemployed and sitting with empty pockets in his apartment.

Hala let him remain undisturbed. She stopped complaining about the price of shrimp or the dirt filling the streets or the difficulty of finding good chocolate. Without telling Nessim, Hala asked her sister to begin the paperwork for their immigration. She knew that America allowed immigrants to bring their siblings. They called it family reunification.

After two weeks of looking for work, Nessim sat at the table eating the afternoon meal with his wife and daughter. Salima was almost eight years old, but he had paid little attention, playing the role of the father as he had learned it. He looked at her black hair, the bangs that aligned on her forehead, and her deep-brown eyes. He praised her when she did well in school, and he rarely had to reprimand her, as she did what she was told. He observed her as she ate the stuffed pepper on her plate and realized he knew little about this child whose entrance into the world he had ensured. What life could he offer her in the future of this country?

After Salima went to do her homework, Nessim asked Hala to sit before going to wash the dishes. She placed the dish with the remaining peppers that she was carrying back on the table and sat down facing her husband. A car honked outside followed by another in response, and then the street retreated into the silence of the afternoon. Hala looked at Nessim, whose eyes seemed fixated on the remains of their meal.

"nessim," she said barely above a whisper and reached her hand toward him. He looked up and lifted his posture into the chair before their hands could touch.

"i found a job today," he said, keeping his gaze directed above Hala.

"mabrouk!" she said, "this is great news." She leaned forward in preparation to hug him.

"no," he said before she could reach him, and she retreated back. "the work is for the government and the salary is a third of what i was making."

He looked up to meet Hala's eyes. They both knew what this meant. They would have to find a cheaper apartment, Salima would no longer be able to attend the prestigious English school, and their lives would fall into the stupor of sustaining their existence.

Hala considered the man she had married—his handsome features, his naive kindness, and the earnestness with which he moved through the world. She couldn't imagine him going each day to perform the meaningless work of a government job, bowing down to superiors who had gotten to their positions only because of their connections.

"nessim." She said his name as if she were summoning him and paused until he settled his gaze on her. "i told my sister to begin the immigration papers for us."

* * *

The night before their departure, over fifty people came to wish them farewell. They drank, ate, talked like at any other gathering. Salima ran around the apartment laughing with her cousins, her face flush with the energy of the evening. The party lingered, and Hala and Nessim barely managed to get a few hours of sleep. The next morning, Nessim weighed the suitcases and said they were too heavy. Hala opened each one and pulled out a jacket, a skirt, a pair of pants, whatever caught her hand, and she let the clothing fall about the room until the weight of each suitcase settled into what they were permitted to take.

The beds were left unmade, the covers twisted into the pattern of their last few hours of sleep. The refrigerator still held intact the kilo of the sharp roomi cheese and the package of Syrian bread Hala had purchased, thinking she would make sandwiches to take to the airport. But there had been no time. Fanous arrived at five, urging them to leave so they could make the seven o'clock flight. The apartment was left in a state of suspension, as if waiting for them to return from a day's outing, reluctant to acknowledge the permanence of their decision. The living room curtains stayed open, the windows reflecting the towering city.

For the first few months, they stayed with Layla and Hafez. Arriving at the beginning of summer, the days extended like a vacation in Alexandria. Layla and Hafez took time off work to show them around the city—a walk along Newbury Street to gaze at the fashion boutiques; a stroll in the Boston Commons; a ride on the swan boats; a trip to Harvard University, where they looked up at the brick buildings and told Salima that someday she would go there. Hala said Boston was like a city of magic. One Saturday, they drove to Cape Cod and spent the day on the beach—Amal, Yusef, and Salima laughing as they entered the ocean and floated their bodies on the water. It was this moment that Salima would hold most clearly in her mind over the years. When the laughter of her parents reached her as she swam with her cousins and the world felt in harmony, before America intruded into their lives.

Salima slept on a foldout cot in Amal's room. She had trouble sleeping those first few weeks, and as she lay in her makeshift bed, she could hear her uncle's voice rising from the living room with occasional interjections from her father. She wondered at their conversation; she couldn't imagine that they talked about clothes and food like her mother and aunt. Sometimes she caught words like "apartment," "savings," and "jobs," but she didn't know how to put them together. The days felt like her summer vacation, and somehow in her mind, she expected that in September she would be returning to her old school and her home.

On the first day of school, Salima's mother and aunt walked with her to the entrance and left her with a teacher who was standing outside the building to greet students. After they left, the teacher ushered Salima into the building and took her to a classroom, where she gestured inside and said, "This is your classroom." But nothing here felt like it belonged to her, and she knew that neither this classroom nor this school nor these other students would ever be hers. She walked in, the classroom only holding a few children, most of them sitting in front. Their glances toward her came sideways, and no one said anything. She went to a desk in the middle of the room and sat down, slipping the red bag that her parents had bought for her right before they left under the desk. It was the one she had been coveting since third grade, the one with gold locks that snapped open and closed that the older students carried. But already she had noticed that the students here carried backpacks that they flung over their shoulder, and she knew that tomorrow she would bury the red bag beneath her bed, where it would gather the dust and the ghosts of her dreams.

The rest of that first school day whirled around her. She stood when the teacher introduced her then sat back down. The teacher struggled with her name, and Salima had to say it aloud. It was the only word she spoke that day. During recess, the boys ignored her, but some of the girls came and surrounded her. They bounced questions toward her, but her ears couldn't catch the sounds and make meaning. She stood silent until they walked away, shrugging their shoulders. The English words did not have the same rhythm as the words her teachers at the British school had spoken. Here the sounds tumbled out of people's mouths like pebbles bouncing on the ground. She couldn't distinguish where each word began and ended to create meaning. For those first months, she withdrew into her own silence, creating a curtain to shield her from the harsh gravel of sounds she couldn't decipher.

After a few months, her parents purchased a house just a few streets away from her aunt and uncle. Salima had her own room with a real bed, a dresser, and a desk, but the space expanded and echoed with each of her footsteps. She learned to stay still, sitting at the desk or lying on the bed, so she would not hear the sounds of her movement echoing back to her.

Once they moved into the new house, Hala was no longer at home when Salima returned from school each day. Instead, Salima wore a string around her neck with the house key attached. At the end of the school day, she walked home and pulled the string out from under her shirt and unlocked the door. She entered into quietness, put her books in her room, retrieved a large bag of potato chips from the kitchen, and settled herself on the couch. For a few hours, sound entered the house through the television set that sat heavy on a table in the living room. She watched *Lost in Space*, *I Dream of*

Jeannie, *Bewitched*, the shows with magic appealing to her the most, allowing her to be in worlds where you could create what you needed from the power of your imagination. Slowly she began to understand the words the characters spoke, and the language around her gained meaning. She did her homework rather than returning it blank and she completed the tests she was given, but she kept her silence during recess and the other children forgot about her.

* ⁂ *

When Salima left for college, her parents renovated the house, expanding its walls, extending the rooms, and creating new spaces beyond its original boundaries. The house stretched and breathed itself into a new form. Hala surveyed the expansion, giving attention to each detail—the doorknobs, the color of the granite, the wood of the kitchen cabinets. She dreamed her new house into existence, and in each room, something sparkled, tempting you to enter. After a year, the house resembled a Zamalek villa, a leftover from Hala's imagination. She had looked at those villas, her eyes stretching to see beyond the stone walls that surrounded them, to glimpse the life people lived there. It was the ambassadors, the expatriates, the elite who inhabited those homes, while the rest cramped themselves into apartments, raised their children in two-bedroom flats with no gardens. No tea and cake served on the balcony; only watermelon seeds spit into the fist of your hand.

* ⁂ *

Hala sat at Layla's kitchen table. The window looked out to the front yard with the tall pine that Layla and Hafez had planted when they bought a potted Christmas tree the same year they purchased their home. In the apartment, they had settled for an artificial tree that popped out of its box already assembled and decorated. After that first year, they reverted to purchasing trees they discarded on the sidewalk like their neighbors. The only difference was their tree lingered until January 7, a commemoration of the Christmas celebrated in Egypt. After all the other trees had been unceremoniously deposited outside, lining the sidewalk, theirs made an appearance later in January, a lonely remnant of a holiday celebrated in another country.

The afternoon sun came in, and Hala turned her back slightly to the window to avoid its glare. It was Saturday, and Hafez and Nessim had gone to the hardware store to purchase some wood for expanding the back deck. Layla placed the tray of konafa she had made that morning on the table and proceeded to cut each of them a piece. The shredded dough filled with hazelnuts, almonds, and raisins glistened with the syrup that Layla had poured over it.

Layla took a bite and said, "do you remember when it was so hard to find the nuts in egypt and how expensive they were?"

Hala let the sweetness of the first bite linger in her mouth. "you left during nasser's time. but sadat brought us nuts and other things—we weren't isolated anymore."

Layla placed her fork on the plate and looked toward the window as she said, "but still you wanted to come here."

Hala swallowed the konafa, feeling the taste of the hazelnuts tingle on her tongue. "we didn't know what was going to happen after sadat's assassination. we were scared that we would return to nasser's regime, that we would have nothing. and there are things that became worse. the population increased, the buses became crowded, and the streets filled with garbage." Hala's voice trailed off as she remembered the last time she took the metro. She had to stand, and a man came up behind her and stroked her back. It was too crowded to move, and her throat closed up, unable to utter a sound. She got off two stops early and walked the rest of the way. "we wanted to build something good for salima," she added.

Layla turned to her younger sister. The years between them and the years spent apart made them feel more like acquaintances than siblings. At times, Hala's obsession with fashion made her seem superficial, and Layla wondered if the reason her sister followed her to America was to have more material possessions. But when Hala spoke about her daughter, something changed. She looked at her daughter as if she might lose her at a moment's notice. And Layla saw that she often reached out to touch Salima as if to make sure she was really there.

"yes, it's all for the kids now. this is for them," Layla responded.

It was rare that they talked about the past—easier to remain in the present, balanced between past and future.

* ⁂ *

Fayza slept soundly, her breath heavy, each exhale inflating her body. Most nights her mind remained a blank slate as if purposely erasing any images that might intrude into her dreams. Her husband was still with her, but he had grown weaker, his tall physique like a slender sugarcane bending into the wind. After the surgery, he tried to return to work, but within a few weeks it was clear that he couldn't continue to run the grocery store. Fanous was already an established engineer and couldn't take it on. Wassef sold it to a stranger who knew nothing of the years it had taken for him to build it, creating it from his own imagination.

Tonight, Fayza's mind entered a dream of moving in space. She attempted to find her footing, to determine place, but she could grasp nothing to balance her. She didn't know who she was, where she belonged, or what belonged to her. Her brain fluttered as it tried to remember what she had, and there was nothing. Her husband woke, disturbed by her moaning. He placed his hand gently on her and called her name. Fayza's body pulled out of sleep, and when he asked if she was alright, she blinked her eyes and said, "i could not remember . . . i could not remember that i have daughters."

* ⁂ *

The large square room with desks was divided by partitions, turning it into an urban corn maze. Voices escalated upward toward the ceiling and buzzed along with the fluorescent lights. The windows on one side let in light that settled thinly on the carpeted floor, unable to reach those who worked in the room each day.

Nessim sat at one of those partitioned desks, a pile of folders on the left corner. He picked one up at a time, opened it, double-checked the math that someone else had already done, and if it was correct, he used the stamp he had been given to imprint "Approved" at the bottom of the first page in the folder. It was not often that he found an error, but when he did, for a moment, he felt the rush of achievement, although he did not know what exactly he had accomplished. He would redo the additions and subtractions to create a new sheet with perfectly scripted numbers. The files that were approved were picked up by a young man, perhaps still in high school, who pushed a shopping cart from desk to desk to gather them up. There were times when, for a moment, Nessim forgot where he was and was tempted to ask the young man to bring him a cup of tea. It was what he had done in his office in Egypt. There was a man who sat all day waiting for an order, and if he was called upon, he would arrive with a glass cup of sweet tea with a sprig of mint, allowing Nessim and his coworkers to rest for a minute, to lean back and inhale the sweet liquid sharpened by the taste of mint, to chat with each other, to look out at the city rising around them before continuing their work. But here such breaks were scheduled precisely, and Nessim knew the young man would not be inclined to get him a cup of tea, nor would he know how to add the mint. He only knew the job he had been given, to pick up the folders and take them to their new destination.

The partitioned room was mostly filled with men. Nessim spoke to few people, remained at his desk while overhearing the conversations of others, which ranged from sports to politics. Occasionally, someone would ask about his weekend, but he had nothing to offer, so he only said "good." Eventually, he understood that he needed to ask the question back and that he would receive the same answer. It was a game like ping-pong, but not the way it was done in Egypt, where the answers weren't direct repetitions but rather variations on a theme. "sabah el kheir" was answered with "sabah el noor," moving from luck to light, whereas here a "Good morning" simply elicited another "Good morning" in response. It was due to a lack of imagination that Nessim blamed on the music he heard from the radio, repetitions of beats over and over as if drilling through the ground, not the way Umm Kulthum could take a word and repeat it so its meaning twirled and came back with new insight.

It had taken a while for Nessim to find work. His experience as an accountant did not appear to carry much weight, and at each place he left his resume, he could almost hear the pages flutter into the wastebasket when he walked out the door. As he wandered the streets of Boston, he tried to retrace the thoughts that led to the decision to leave everything, even his beloved Cadillac now locked up in a garage.

In his dreams, he stepped out of the door and began walking, the landscape consisting of dried cracked dirt that he followed until it cleared into a simple road, and when he made a turn, he was on Fourth of July Street in Zamalek, the crush of traffic and people serenading him. A young boy stopped his peanut cart next to him and enticed him to purchase a bag. Nessim reached into his pocket for a coin, but when he pulled out his hand, it was empty, and he woke with a start to find himself in Layla and Hafez's spare room. The dream returned in myriad ways. He was driving on an American suburban street, and when he made a turn, he found himself in front of their old apartment building in Zamalek. Even after they bought a house, the dreams continued.

* ⁂ *

Nessim's father waited and assured his wife that they would retrieve their only child. His wife was a small whisper of a bird, ten years younger than her husband. Only a few months after Hala and Nessim left, she began to deteriorate and eventually became bedridden. Her husband, a man who stood more than a foot above her, doted on her and took care of her until he guided her soul out of her body.

When his wife died, his son still did not return, and he stood alone in the church, his siblings having already passed on and their children scattered to Canada and Australia. Now Nessim's father lived alone, his eyesight receding, and there were no more relatives to check on him. In the morning, he drank tea with milk, dipping his bread in the liquid; in the afternoon, he went to the same kiosk a few steps from his apartment to purchase a bowl of fuul to eat with bread; and in the evening, he had a small bowl of yogurt. This was his daily pattern of nourishment. Sometimes in the evening, he talked to his wife and laughed until he remembered she was gone. He had shrunk to the existence of his life alone, spending each day in laughter with his wife for a little while, his diminishing eyesight allowing him to believe in her continued presence.

* ⁂ *

Hala stayed at home for the first few months, focused on decorating their house, learning how to cook the packaged food in the supermarket, and taking care of Salima. When an entry-level position opened up at the company where Nessim worked, Hala applied and, like Nessim, she was given a cubicle with a desk and the job of moving files from place to place. It was a monotonous job of pulling out files, adding things, and then releasing them to their next destination. The room was full of women, and if the manager was not around, there was a steady chatter. Mostly, she listened, and although some tried to bring her into their conversations, she had little to offer to the talk of their American lives that still felt distant to her.

During her lunch hour, she explored the shops, discovering the higher-end stores of Boston, like Bonwit Teller, where the saleswomen doted on her, making suggestions for how to put together an outfit, telling her which colors went well with her complexion, and offering more conversation than the women with whom she worked. She went to Filenes, where the makeup clerks lured her with the promise of a free gift with her purchase. On most days, Hala, whose desire to come to this country had filled every fiber of her body, came home with shopping bags from Bonwit Teller, Lord & Taylor, Bloomingdale's, or Macy's. Salima watched the brightness of her mother's face as she showed her and her father the items she had bought, holding each one up and repeating the words of the saleswoman to prove the value of her purchase. But once the clothes had found their place in closets and drawers, Salima noted how her mother's mouth curved downward across her face.

Their lives moved from their split-level home to their car to their partitioned offices. Only when they gathered with other Egyptians did the space enlarge, as they spilled from the dining room to the living room to the deck, expanding the house with their movements. The sound of Arabic swung through the rooms, and voices deepened with the call-and-response of the language.

Kareem's Departure

When the phone call came from my cousin Kareem, my hands trembled as I heard his request. Kareem was Aunt Afaf's only son, born when she was already forty years old. No one had considered that he might leave. The exodus from Egypt had slowed down. America was taking less immigrants, the application for a visa had become too expensive, and the country had fallen into a kind of apathy that kept people from striving for anything better.

"but how did you get accepted to amreeka?" I asked over the phone.

"not amreeka. i'm going to canada," Kareem responded.

"canada . . ." I let the sound of the word linger as my mind called up mountains of snow, the whistle of a cold wind, and Kareem lost in the fog of a winter night. "the world is cold there," I said quietly.

"that's why i'm going in the summer, so i can acclimate before the winter comes," Kareem replied with the usual touch of irony in his voice.

I wrote down the day and time of the flight. Just before hanging up, I whispered, "are you sure?"

The pause lingered over the phone line until Kareem said yes.

When I arrived, I couldn't bear to go up the stairs and see Kareem's mother. I didn't want to witness this farewell between a mother and a son who had been each other's comfort for so many years since the passing of Kareem's father. I had told Kareem what time I would arrive and said I would wait outside, making the excuse of how difficult it was to find a parking spot in Doqqi.

Even as I stood in the morning air, the weight of what was happening in the apartment above me fell heavily. When Kareem came out, one suitcase in each hand, I rushed to help him, and the shuffle of luggage allowed each of us to tuck in our emotions.

It was just the two of us in those early hours. We moved through the darkness of the city, its shapes silhouetted against the shadows. When we reached downtown, a few sprinkles of light cleared our path until we approached Heliopolis and made our way toward the airport. We passed by El Qubba Palace, used as a presidential residence by King Fuad, followed by King Farouk, followed by Nasser.

Neither of us said much until we had crossed over the 6th of October Bridge and were making our way to Salah Salem Street.

I tried to lighten the heaviness of the dark landscape and the mood, making jokes about how he would no longer have to put up with the family trying to find him a wife. But the jokes sifted into the night, and Kareem could muster no more than a slight twitch of his lips in response. My words failed to reach him, as if he were already gone even before he got on the plane. Kareem was Afaf's son, and Afaf was my father's sister. Once my parents married, Afaf entered our family, became part of us, and her son was the same as one of our cousins. Kareem was the quietest of all of us. He kept things in as if holding them in a container with a sealed lid. When the rest of us would argue and push our words against each other, he would only say "maalesh" and retreat.

"which part of canada?" I asked.

"montreal. maybe my french will help me," he answered.

Kareem was educated in Jesuit schools and fed the French language until he had been forced into fluency. "yes, you have a point. and for sure the food in montreal will be better than in amreeka."

Kareem laughed, adding, "at least the cheese will be good."

As the airport drew closer, I couldn't help but ask, "and your mother?"

"she gave me her blessing," answered Kareem.

When we arrived, Kareem asked me to just drop him off. He had insisted that no one come to the airport, so he would not leave with doubts stamped on his cheeks. He wanted to walk in alone.

Kareem – 1998

Each day, Kareem came home defeated. For five years after he graduated from the Faculty of Tourism at Helwan University, he looked for work and found little. There was a small job here and there, but they never lasted. He carried the weight of the city on his shoulders. For his mother, he put on a smile and gave a wave of his hand to say something better would come. But in the evenings, he sat on the chair that faced the balcony, the white curtains fluttering with the breeze. He looked through them to the buildings across the street and the sky above covered in a haze of clouds, and he saw nowhere that he could go. He thought of his uncle Wassef's daughters, Layla and Hala, who had immigrated a long time ago. Things weren't bad when they left, but who could've known what was to come.

Kareem was a happy child, always with a group of friends around him. He would skip through the door to announce that he and his friends were going on some adventure, his voice ringing in the house. When his father, Munir, came home and told him to be quiet, it was always with a smile, and Kareem knew he didn't really mind. In the summers after their late supper, Kareem and his father would sit on the balcony, and their words caught in the curtains. Afaf could hear Munir talking and Kareem asking him questions. She didn't want to intrude, so she stepped into the kitchen or bedroom and let their voices carry through the night.

Afaf had never expected to have a child. She married in her late thirties, by which time everyone assumed her opportunities had passed. They blamed her father, who had encouraged her to study, seeing no difference between men and women. It frustrated Afaf's mother, the way he took an interest in her schoolwork, sat with her to go over math problems each night. "you have a good brain," he would tell her. "you can see more than what is in front of you." Perhaps his encouragement came out of the disappointment in his son, Wassef, who never attended college. Although her brother had opened a grocery store and was successful, Afaf knew that for her father an education mattered more.

Afaf studied hard to please her father and received good marks. When she graduated from the College of Commerce at Cairo University, she found a good job at Banque Misr. She worked at the Mohandessein branch, only a couple of kilometers away. At first, the men who worked there tried to flirt with her. They thought a woman who left the house each day and worked among men was available. It didn't take them long to realize that she was serious. Every time someone bothered her, she went to the manager's office and, loud enough for everyone to hear, she put blame on the man who had annoyed her. Maybe the manager grew tired of hearing the complaints and told the men to leave her alone, or maybe they just gave up, but she was left to do her job, and, after a while, they seemed to forget she was a woman.

When Afaf's sister was born, her mother took no chances. She dressed her in pink frilly dresses and shiny leather shoes. And that's who she became, putting attention on her appearance. Every time there was a wedding or a party, she purchased expensive material to make her dress. Everyone complimented her, remarking on her beauty and good taste. Afaf's parents wanted Afaf to marry first because she was the older sister. But no one came. So, when her sister had a good proposal, they accepted. And Afaf stayed at home.

* ⁂ *

It was a Tuesday, and I was running late on my way back from work. I had decided to walk home, but it was April and the khamsin winds with their dust were at their height. By the time I came through the door, I was disheveled, my hair wild, my skin dusty, and my clothes wrinkled. I walked in, apologizing for being late and explaining about the metro not coming, and I was almost at the end of my monologue before I realized there was someone else sitting in my parents' living room. I stopped talking and apologized again, this time for intruding, and was about to go to my room, but my father gestured for me to join them. I sat down on the chair opposite my mother and caught her disapproving glare. My father introduced me to the man in our living room, saying he was a colleague's son. The man was plain-looking, a little chubby, his hair thin, but his face looked open and clear. He sat a bit stiffly at the edge of the chair, his hands folded in his lap as if he were afraid to let them loose. Something about the suit he was wearing made it seem borrowed, as if it were unaccustomed to covering his frame. The seams of the shoulders were a bit off, and the length of the sleeves a touch above his wrist, as if the suit had been made for a shorter, stockier man. I looked at his shoes; they had been resewn, perhaps more than once, but they were neatly polished. I assumed he was here to deliver something to my father, so I leaned back in my chair, took off my shoes and pulled my legs up under me, and ignored my mother's extended stare.

"this is munir," my father said. "he is an assistant manager at the national bank of egypt."

I mentioned the bank where I worked in response, and we began a conversation about our jobs that digressed into other areas, until we were sharing stories of riding the metro. At one point, my mother got up to get the tea. She tried to gesture that I should join her, but I purposely ignored her attempt. I was not much of a hostess and preferred to stay in the conversation.

After Munir left, I put the evening out of my mind and continued with my daily routine. It was only a few days later, on Friday morning, when my father asked me to join him on the balcony. It was the customary time for prayers, and most people were at the mosque. The streets seemed to be taking a breath, a quiet exhale that laid a blanket over the morning. My father settled into one chair, placing his glass cup of tea on the small table. Each morning, he drank his dark tea with a sprig of mint. "it's like breathing the earth," he would say regarding his insistence on the mint. I sat in the other chair, holding a demitasse of Turkish coffee. I liked the strong brew, the way the thickness of the liquid touched your lips and settled on your tongue before being swallowed. I allowed myself a spoon of sugar, just enough to take off the edge of bitterness.

"how is work?" my father asked.

He shifted his weight and attempted to cross his legs, but then uncrossed them again. My father was not a man who engaged in much conversation. He left that to my mother and preferred the silence of daily action. I chatted a bit in response and then paused, letting the quiet settle between us until he was ready to speak again. The hum of the morning began, people's feet moving toward mosques for prayers, the beating of a rug being dusted, the voice of a child calling out to a friend.

"ya afaf, munir has requested your hand in marriage."

The words from my father popped out like marbles and bounced on the tiled floor. Munir had left my mind after that meeting, although sometimes on the metro, I would find myself remembering something he said or the way he had openly laughed at a joke I made. I remained quiet in front of my father until he broke the silence.

"how would you like me to respond to him?" he asked.

I looked up from where the words had rolled to see my father's face. He was giving me the choice even though he had the right to decide for me. I could imagine that he and my mother must've argued, so he could be allowed to offer me this decision. My mother would have said that no daughter gets to choose. That this first proposal I had received at the late age of thirty-eight must be accepted, that there would be no other possibilities for husbands in my future.

I turned to my father. "what is your opinion?"

He picked up his tea and took three sips, keeping his eyes over the street. We could hear a few birds calling their morning song. My father replaced his glass on the table and turned his gaze to me.

"he is a good man, simple. what you see is him. i told him that if he married you, he would have to let you be as you are. and he understood."

* ⁂ *

Afaf's father's words were true. Afaf continued to work, and Munir let her be, making no demands. She cooked and kept a good home, but he didn't act like he expected anything. They enjoyed each other's companionship, whether they spent the evening in conversation or sat in silence as they drank their afternoon tea. Munir had come from a modest background, growing up in Shobra, but he had worked steadily to receive his education and get the job at the bank. He had resisted his parents' urging to marry, reluctant to find himself with someone who would expect more than he could offer. He didn't enjoy large social gatherings, and he knew he couldn't offer romance. Afaf learned to see his quiet love that came through small gestures. In the morning, he made her a cup of coffee, learning exactly how she liked it. In the evening, after dinner, he stood beside her in the kitchen to clean up. And even when she told him to sit and rest, he stayed. He enjoyed a good game of backgammon, but instead of going out to the coffee shops and playing with the other men, he stayed at home, and they played together. The dice rang against the board, and their laughter echoed when one of them made an unexpected move.

They never talked about having children. Afaf was close to forty, and Munir was a few years older. It was almost three months into the pregnancy before Afaf realized it. Kareem arrived unexpectedly, a gift in the middle of their lives. He filled their home, making them a family.

In the morning and evening, Afaf and Munir still shared their quiet moments, but Kareem pulled them out of their routine. They took him to the pyramids, where Munir and Kareem climbed up on a camel, with Kareem holding on to his father and squealing half in fear and half in delight as the camel raised its hind legs, making them lean forward, and then its front legs, threatening to make them tumble backward. They took a trip to Marsa Matruh, so Kareem could see the Mediterranean Sea. Kareem was eight at the time, and Munir taught him how to swim, holding his hands gently under his back so he could learn to trust the water to hold him up. When Kareem started school, he came home and regaled his parents with stories of his classmates and teachers—the boy who always asked the teacher to repeat the instructions because he wanted to put off doing the work, the teacher who wore his shirt inside out every day, and the principal who insisted they all clap when he entered the classroom. Their laughter tumbled out at Kareem's descriptions, as they felt their world expand with his stories.

When Kareem was twelve, Munir came home one day, shaken. His face ashen and his clothes dirty. When Afaf opened the door, he was swaying, and she had to help him. He crumpled into the chair.

"what happened?" she asked.

"just something small," he said. "a car hit me, but there is nothing. everything is fine."

"where? how?" she asked, insisting on more details.

"in my side, my right side, but there is nothing. i'm fine," he insisted.

Afaf let him rest and brought him soup and a shot of whiskey, which he used to say could cure anything. The next day was Friday, and he spent the day resting. But then he insisted on going back to work, saying he was fine. Afaf believed him, but sometimes she would catch him leaning against a door or a chair, as if he couldn't keep his balance. Or, after dinner, he would linger at the table a little longer, and she would see him rubbing his side. She asked him to go see the doctor, but he said it wasn't necessary.

Munir comes home from work exactly two weeks after the accident, says he's tired, doesn't want any food, and gets into bed. When Afaf goes in to check on him, she thinks he's asleep. She lays her hand on his forehead, and he's gone.

After Munir died, Afaf watched Kareem withdraw and spend days in silence. Later, he would yell about the slightest thing. He knew he had lost something, and he didn't know what to do with the empty space. Afaf tried to be there for him, but she knew that one person can't replace another. She didn't want to make another change in his life, so she refused to move back in with her parents and insisted that she and Kareem were family enough.

Each holiday, Layla and Hala wrote to Afaf, telling her about the new things they had bought and their houses that were like the villas in Zamalek. *maybe that is happiness*, she thought. Afaf looked around her small apartment in Doqqi, with its balcony overlooking Tahrir Street, leading all the way to Tahrir Square. Here, she had what she needed, but she knew that Kareem saw nothing for himself. Maybe there was something for him in this other country. America had stretched its long arm into their lives. Every Thursday, people rushed home to watch the next episode of *Dallas*, mesmerized by the lives of these wealthy Americans with their mansions and numerous cars. They imagined that all you needed to do was to step on American soil and all this wealth would be yours. But the censors left out the dramatic turns with the affairs and bedroom close-ups. People could guess at what was happening between the truncated scenes, but they never imagined that such immoral acts could enter their lives if they were there. Luxury is what they learned to crave from what entered their homes on these screens. Once one person emigrated, the seed was planted, and you couldn't dig it out.

* ⁂ *

Kareem became frustrated by the closed doors that slammed in his face at every attempt. His degree from the Faculty of Tourism at Helwan University carried little weight. When he took the Thanaweya Amma exams, his scores were not high enough for Cairo University or even Ain Shams, so he settled for Helwan. Sometimes he wondered if he purposely didn't study hard enough, if he set himself up for failure, if perhaps he never wanted to succeed in this country. After he graduated, he couldn't find a job, at least not without an underhanded connection, and his middle-class status did not open any doors.

His father had worked at the bank his whole life, earning enough to meet the family's needs. He was a man of steady routine, although Kareem wondered if he wanted more adventure. He recalled his father's story about how one summer when he was still in college, he and three of his friends pooled their money together and came up with enough for a trip to Italy. They took a boat from Alexandria to Rome, where they wandered for a week. They made it their goal to see every fountain, keeping the Trevi Fountain for last. His father told him how he threw a coin over his shoulder, having heard the legend that this would ensure that he would return to this grandiose city. Then the friends took a train to Florence and spent another week there, walking the cobblestone streets, visiting the museums and cathedrals. Kareem's father described how when they stepped out of the famous Florence Cathedral, he saw a man in the center of the Piazza del Duomo, singing opera. Munir couldn't understand the words, but he stood mesmerized by this voice that raised itself with astounding harmony, making music dance on the cobblestones.

Kareem was only a young boy when his father told him these stories. When Munir would sometimes stop mid-sentence, Kareem felt like his father had returned to Italy, that he was no longer across from him sitting on their little balcony. His father would return with a heavy sigh and say, "those were days of the past." Other times, his voice would falter in the middle of a story, and he would laugh a little as if someone had just whispered a joke in his ear, then remembering Kareem was there, he would say, "when you get older, i'll tell you the rest of the story."

Kareem knew his mother loved him with her whole heart. She listened to every thought he had, supported every wish he made, and kept them a family. Their house became the center, and cousins, aunts, and uncles came over, carrying food and the problems plaguing them, knowing that Afaf would heal them with wisdom, a cup of tea, a bowl of koshari. She became the family matriarch. Kareem never felt alone except when he stepped out on the balcony, and that's where he found his father's spirit, always there waiting for him. Sometimes, he'd linger, hear his father's voice, but then the awareness of his absence severed the wound, and Kareem would step back into the warmth and fullness of his mother's home.

Kareem's mother urged him to pursue whatever career he wanted, never pressuring him into medicine or engineering. He chose tourism, but this was no longer the Egypt of his parent's childhood. It was the 1990s, and there were sixty million people in the country, twelve million of them in Cairo. Only the rich could move forward.

With the Gulf War, more Muslim women began wearing the veil. Kareem would walk into a shop or a café and find that the woman who had been working there for years with her hair loose was now wearing a headscarf. Along the streets, those not veiled became the minority, until the assumption was that the unveiled were all Christian. The veil became an emblem of national identity, and once again Christians became suspect.

When Kareem graduated from the Faculty of Tourism, the Gulf War had ended, but the damage was already done. Tourists were wary of coming to Egypt. The country was viewed as part of a dangerous region, and tourists were not risk-takers. Kareem had hoped to get a job with one of the Nile cruise boats that travelled between Luxor and Aswan, stopping at the ancient monuments. He wanted to reveal the mysteries of the Valley of the Kings and Queens, unearthing secrets that had remained beneath the earth for all these years. But those jobs only came through personal connections. The jobs he got were sporadic, mostly giving tours of the Giza pyramids, where tourists seemed more interested in taking pictures to prove they had been there than learning anything. No one wanted to know the names of the pharaohs who built the pyramids or the objects they buried with them for the afterlife. They were more eager for camel rides, which required Kareem to make the usual underhanded arrangements with someone who offered them, assuring his group that this man would charge them an honest price, when in reality they were being overcharged and he received a cut.

This was not how he had imagined his life. He thought studying tourism would allow him to travel, to be in constant motion, but he had not gone beyond the boundaries of his birth country. After three years with his life at a standstill, he started entering the immigration lottery for the US, but he didn't tell anyone. For the past five years, Kareem had watched his older cousin enter the lottery. For those years, his cousin's life teetered between struggle and hope. Then, one day, his cousin announced that he and his family were immigrating to Canada.

Kareem decided he didn't want to continue gambling his life on the lottery, waiting year after year with his hopes pinned on the chance that his name would be drawn out of a hat. Everything felt stagnant, each day carrying the weight of the one before it, continuing the same pattern. From his cousin, he learned that applying for immigration to Canada was cheaper and quicker. He filled out the application but hesitated to submit it, knowing he couldn't make that step without his mother's approval.

* ⁂ *

AT 8:45 ON THE MORNING OF NOVEMBER 17, 1997, SIX GUNMEN CONCEAL THEMSELVES INSIDE THE TEMPLE OF HATSHEPSUT. THEY SHOOT THE TWO POLICE OFFICERS WHO GUARD THE ANCIENT TEMPLE. THE ATTACK BEGINS AS THE TOURISTS WALK FROM THEIR BUS TOWARD THE TEMPLE, BUILT 3,500 YEARS AGO TO HONOR QUEEN HATSHEPSUT, WHO RULED FROM AROUND 1478 BC TO 1458 BC, THE ONLY WOMAN TO REIGN AS PHARAOH OF EGYPT. THERE IS NO ONE TO STOP THE GUNMEN AS THEY FIRE AT THE TOURISTS. IN THE SPAN OF A HALF HOUR, FIFTY-EIGHT TOURISTS FROM SWITZERLAND, GERMANY, JAPAN, GREAT BRITAIN, BULGARIA, FRANCE, AND COLOMBIA ARE KILLED ALONG WITH FOUR EGYPTIANS.

THE EGYPTIAN NEWSPAPERS REPORT THE ATTACK AND ITS IMPACT ON TOURISM. IT COMES ONLY TWO MONTHS AFTER THE ATTACK AT THE EGYPTIAN MUSEUM THAT KILLED NINE PEOPLE. THE THREE-BILLION-DOLLAR INDUSTRY THAT BRINGS ALMOST FOUR MILLION TOURISTS EACH YEAR IS AT RISK OF DISSOLVING. ONE MAN WHO SELLS MINIATURE STATUES OF THE TEMPLE IS INTERVIEWED, SAYING, "HOW WILL WE EAT NOW? IT IS THE TOURISTS WHO WERE FEEDING US."

* ⁂ *

Two days after the attack, Kareem approached his mother.

Afaf knew that Kareem had heard the stories of how Layla and Hala and their husbands had left, and he read the letters they sent, describing how well they were doing. Perhaps her son's destiny was in this other country, or maybe he was looking for a way to erase the past, to release his loss. So, she let him go.

"don't worry about me," she said. "i will be fine. i know how to live alone. go and see your future."

* ⁂ *

After she stepped out of her building, Afaf felt the unexpected chill in the air. The first few days of January had been unusually warm. She had expected today to be the same and put only a light sweater over her dress, but the air carried an icy coolness that surprised her. She hesitated, thinking she should go back to put on a heavier jacket. But there was so much to do to prepare for the holiday that she shrugged her shoulders and hoped it would become warmer as the day continued.

She walked to the corner of Tahrir Street to catch a taxi. The cars flew by one after the other, a stream of black, white, and gray speeding to their destinations. She put out her hand each time she caught sight of a taxi. Usually, they were already carrying a passenger and they sped by. The ones that were empty slowed as they approached, but once they noted her age and appearance, they picked up their speed and passed her. She stood in the chill of the air, knowing the drivers saw an old woman and assumed she would pay too little. When you entered the cab, the meters were never turned on, and the drivers negotiated the price. They had an uncanny ability for detecting those customers willing to pay the most. Afaf's hands began to stiffen as the air became crisp. She pulled her sweater tighter around her body, shook her head at the cars passing by as if to reprimand them.

Finally, a taxi slowed as it approached her and came to a stop. She stepped into the back seat. The driver glanced toward her as she settled herself in and pulled the door shut.

"sabah el kheir, ya sitt," he greeted her. "where can i take you today?"

She asked him to go to the Metro supermarket on Syria Street.

"ay khedma," he replied politely, offering his service.

She settled into the seat, and as she looked around the taxi, she noticed a small cross beneath the dashboard and felt relieved.

When they arrived, he accepted the amount she offered without question and thanked her. Inside the supermarket, she made her way through the aisles. This was one of the larger stores that attracted the wealthy and the foreign. She didn't come here often, preferring the intimacy of the small grocer down the street from her home run by the same man for over thirty years. She had known him as a boy when it was his father who sat behind the counter, and she had watched him grow up in the store. He had been responsible for gathering the items each customer wanted. Climbing ladders to reach the towels and napkins on the high shelves, gathering cans from their various corners, and wrapping cheese and luncheon meat ordered by each person who came into the store. Now, after his father's passing, he was the one who sat behind the cash register, and his son took on his original role. But in the foreign-inspired Metro supermarket, customers moved through the aisles gathering their own products. Yet, she had to admit, some things were better. The lentils and rice she put in her cart were cleaner, less likely to have the small stones she had to filter out before cooking. But it was mostly the chocolate that had brought her here. They carried imported chocolate, although at a high price. The Egyptian chocolate sold at other places melted like plastic—no flavor, only the tight texture of sticky gelatin in your mouth.

She wanted those who came to her home to enjoy the taste of food. Her house was the gathering place where everyone gravitated. She was eighty years old, still independent, coming and going on her own, cooking, crocheting, taking care of others. She had lived through King Fuad and King Farouk, the revolution with Nasser, then Sadat, then Mubarak. Now, she had become the matriarch of this family dispersed across the oceans, trying to hold everyone together, threaded under her watchful care.

She made her way through the aisles, gathered each item, sighed at the price as she placed it in her cart. Flour and sugar for the kahek and ghorayeba; chocolate for the petit fours; rice and meat for stuffing the grape leaves; and for herself, a small container of black olives that had caught her eye, their round fullness enticing her. She paid for her purchases, gathered the two bags, their weight surprisingly heavy as she lifted them. The sugar and rice in one bag and the flour in the other stretched her arms tight as she stepped out of the store.

She stood on Syria Street, once again hoping to catch a taxi, but the area was too congested to get a driver to stop. So she gathered her bags and walked another block. Every taxi that passed appeared full, and the rare empty one took a quick glance at her and kept going. She walked a few more blocks to the corner of Syria Street and Gameat Al-Dewal Al-Arabeya, the chill in the air increasing and the sun covered by the polluted sky offering no warmth. She put the bags down, stretched her arm out every time she saw a taxi, but after ten minutes she gave up, picked up the bags and started walking. It was about a kilometer to her apartment and easier to keep walking than to stand, waiting for something that would never arrive. It was colder than when she had left, but she hoped the walk would warm her.

She kept her steps steady, watching where the sidewalks were uneven and broken. Her mind went back to the first time she had walked to the store alone when she was eight years old, her mother entrusting her to run an errand for her. It was 1939 and her family was living in the house in Maadi, facing the Nile. The streets were quiet and empty then. There were barely two million people living in Cairo, and they spread themselves out among Maadi, Giza, and downtown; there was plenty of room to live, to breathe. The foreigners and wealthy Egyptians inhabited the island of Zamalek, while the middle and lower classes had the rest of Cairo. Afaf had been sent to the market by her mother to buy flour. It was early January, and her mother and her aunts had been in a baking frenzy for Christmas. Each day, her aunts arrived in the morning, their faces flushed as if ready to enter into battle. The kitchen smelled of butter and sugar, and each morning, she woke to find a new pile of kahek, ghorayeba, and petit fours that appeared overnight as if by magic. She was shooed out of the kitchen when she tried to trespass on their activities. But she would always be sent off with a cookie. She was still considered too young to abide by the Coptic fasting, so they would use her as their taster, and she would oblige, unaware of the nuances of their questions about the ratio of butter to flour, only knowing each cookie melted into sweetness inside her mouth and filled her with something that felt like music.

In the middle of a Thursday afternoon as the women were rolling and kneading, her mother opened the cupboard to realize there was no more flour. They couldn't leave what they were already in the middle of, so her mother told her to run quick to the market and purchase two kilos before they ran out. Imbued with the seriousness of her task, Afaf ran the two blocks with the coins held tight in her fist. When she arrived out of breath, she saw the lines of people, and, uncertain of where to go, she edged around, trying to catch a glimpse of flour. But she couldn't see enough to decipher the merchandise exchanging hands. Her eyes fell on two women standing together, and she approached them to ask for help. They pointed her to the correct line, and as she ran off, they shouted after her, "don't forget to bargain or they'll take advantage of you. you're so young." The words stung Afaf's ears as she wiggled her way into the correct line.

Now the coldness seemed to increase, but by the time she was halfway there, she was sweating, the trickle of heat moving from her neck down her back. Yet, she still felt the cold seeping through her bones. She kept walking, the bags seeming to attach themselves to her arms, until they felt like an extension of her body. The cars whizzed by her, adding to the pollution of the air until she could feel the smog clogging her throat. She felt a trickle of sweat along the ridge of her nose, and her mind returned to her wedding day. Her sister had arrived ready with paints and brushes to transform her into the expected beautiful bride. She succumbed, and her sister made her up with rouge and lipstick and eyeshadow and mascara, decorating her with an expert hand. After her sister left, she looked at herself in the mirror and saw a face she did not recognize, made up to look like a young bride, an act of deception. She grabbed a tissue and began wiping off the rouge, the mascara, smearing them together, ruining her sister's work. She washed her face and looked again in the mirror, and for one moment of vanity, she thought she looked beautiful.

By the time she reached her building, her head felt light and airy. She made her way up the three flights of stairs, stopping at the end of each one to take a breath, but she was afraid to put the bags down, as if releasing them would make her unable to carry the weight again. She dropped the bags once she entered the apartment, letting them settle on the floor where they fell, and she went to her bedroom, lay on the bed with her clothes and shoes on until a light, fitful sleep allowed her some rest.

When she awoke, the evening had settled, and even the sounds of car horns had subsided, blending into the sunset. She lifted her body and sat at the edge of the bed. The sweat had seeped into her skin and left a thin layer of stickiness. But her hands still felt cold. She walked to the bathroom and turned on the hot water in the sink. She heard the gas ignite in the water tank. She threw some of the cool water on her face, letting it drip to her neck before she reached for a small towel to dry herself. Then she placed her hands under the water that had warmed, so the heat could penetrate her skin. It took a few minutes until finally it felt that the warmth entered her.

She went to the kitchen to make herself a cup of tea, and by the time the water boiled and she poured it into the glass cup, the phone was ringing. She recognized the off rhythm that told her it was an overseas call. Carrying the glass cup, she quickened her steps to the living room and picked up the phone as she set down the tea and sat in the corner chair.

"ezayek, ya mama?" Her son's voice travelled through the distance connected by these telephone wires. Every Saturday, he called her at the same time, offering her this predictability to assure her of his safety and his remembrance of her.

"alhamdulillah," she responded.

"your voice, your voice is tired—is everything ok?"

"yes," she answered, "i closed my eyes, just five minutes."

And as if to ensure she was not hiding something, he asked about her brother, her sister, his great-uncles, the list of elders in the family.

"they're all well," she said. "everything is the same."

Except it wasn't. Her son was in Canada, living in a town she couldn't pronounce, where he said it snows for half the year. The gathering of the family continued to shrink. Now her son was married and expecting his first child, and she wondered if she would ever hold the child in her arms. The family had dispersed among the vast continents. As Christmas approached, she was reluctant to count the ones remaining who would gather at her home. Chairs sat empty, as if awaiting the arrival of those who were gone. She wondered if they felt the absence of what they had left behind.

She spoke with Kareem for about a half hour, and after she replaced the receiver, she returned to bed.

* ⁂ *

Kareem's cousin Atef met him at the Montreal airport. When Kareem scanned the people waiting for passengers, his gaze ran over him until Atef yelled out his name. As Kareem approached his cousin, he saw that he looked crumpled and older.

Kareem stayed with Atef and his family, but he did not want to impose. From the first day, he started looking for work. His cousin advised him to begin with hotels, and they drove from one to the other where Kareem left the resume that he had so carefully written and printed before leaving Egypt. It was on standard Egyptian paper, measuring 8.26 × 11.69 inches, unlike the Canadian standard of 8.5 × 11 inches—just a little off, just enough to mark it as not quite right. On his resume, like all other Egyptians, he listed the schools he had attended from kindergarten through college. In Egypt, people knew the value of the early schools, evaluating a candidate based on whether they had attended a French, British, American, German, or public school. At each hotel, the person who accepted his resume smiled and said they would be in touch. After two weeks, nothing came, and when he called to inquire, he was told that he didn't have Canadian experience.

"what is this business with canadian experience?" Kareem said in frustration after another day of rejections. "what is the difference between work here and there? experience and training are the same. they don't even want to give you a chance."

Kareem's cousin looked at him with the sorrow of a parent having to explain to their child that the world is not always fair and just.

After another week, Kareem started working at a grocery store owned by someone his cousin knew through the Coptic church. He hoped it would give him the elusive Canadian experience. When he talked to his mother, he told her he was working at a shop that sold gifts and souvenirs to tourists just to get his foot in the door. He didn't want to stretch the lie too far, but he couldn't bring himself to tell her the truth.

He stood behind the counter, repeating the words of service he had been taught: "Will that be all?" "Seven dollars and twenty-one cents please." "Have a nice day." His body memorized the motions for scanning all the items, placing them in the thin plastic bags, and handing them to the customer. The people who came in blended into one another for Kareem. He could distinguish nothing memorable about them. One would offer a cheery "Good morning," another, complete silence. For the first six months, he worked the night shift, and he would return to his cousin's house to sleep through the day. Time stretched into a continuous cycle of work and sleep. Canada froze him, framing him with his foreign looks, his accent, and his lack of Canadian experience. It became neither a place nor a location, as he almost never saw it in daylight. After those six months, he switched to a day shift when another new immigrant seeking Canadian experience arrived to take the night shift. Kareem resumed his job search, this time focusing on smaller hotels outside of the city.

He was hired as a hotel clerk to work behind the front desk, checking people in and out, replacing their lost keys, answering their phone calls when they requested extra towels, blankets, and soap. His conversations with his coworkers remained on the surface. A "Good morning," a "How are you?" a "How was your shift?"—all with the predictable answer of "Fine," as if life could be lived in one note. He felt a barrier around himself, unable to enter into this society. When he called his mother on the Saturday after he started, he told her he was working at an elegant Montreal hotel and that his job was something like a manager. As the words translated from English to Arabic, it did not seem like too much of a lie.

The job enabled him to rent his own apartment. He found something close to the hotel, which put him an hour away from his cousin. They saw each other on Sundays at the Coptic church. It was the one place where he actually spoke to people. After the liturgy, they all gathered in the church hall to drink coffee and eat the food offered, grateful for the nourishment, since most of them had fasted to receive communion, but more grateful for the companionship that relieved their isolation and reminded them of who they were. Kareem got to know a few other young men who, like him, had arrived alone seeking some success in their lives. For a few hours, he could breathe in enough air and hear his own voice again.

Aside from those few hours each Sunday, he found himself frozen in isolation. After two years, his mother began urging him to get married. But who would be willing to share this still life? After those phone conversations, he would look at the blank walls of his apartment. This passage of distance had carried him from one home to another to find only an existence, not a life. Egypt had disappointed him, but family was there, friends with whom he had gone to school, people who knew him since he was a child. The gatherings where jokes were tossed back and forth into laughter. His family had held him in their grasp, and he knew they would catch him if he fell. Here, he was unattached, like a fragment of a sugarcane.

After three years at the hotel, he was promoted to assistant manager. "You're polite, you don't complain, and you do the work. I don't care what they say about Arabs," the manager told him when he offered him the promotion.

Two years later, he became the manager, but he found it difficult to embrace the congratulations others offered. The promotion made him feel stuck, as if he had been staked into the ground. The movement he had dreamt of slipped through his fingers. His life was now framed by the hotel, and his range of motion confined as it had been when he worked behind the grocery store counter. But he swallowed his fear and called his mother to tell her the good news of his promotion.

His cousin advised him to purchase a house, instead of losing his money to rent. The house he purchased was part of a new subdivision, disconnected from the town center, but it was not far from the hotel. When he walked into the house, the pale walls opened the space of each room, one after the next, and into the kitchen laid out with a counter that connected it to the sitting area. He didn't know what he would do with so much space, so he bought a mattress, placed it on the floor of one of the bedrooms and ignored the rest of the house. When his cousin and his wife came over, his cousin laughed and told him he would never find a wife with this house. His sister-in-law stood in the middle of the empty rooms and shook her head. The next week they came over with an old couch and table. They placed the couch in the living room and the table in the dining room, but the house seemed to swallow the furniture and retain its emptiness.

Time moved from the few months of summer to the long heavy winter months, when snow shrouded the world and he seemed to walk in slow motion. After four years of living in Canada, he received citizenship, and, wanting to give it some meaning, he began to take small trips to the United States, visiting what was within driving distance—Vermont, New Hampshire, Upstate New York. These excursions opened his days, adding rhythm, a few unexpected beats, and his spirits lifted. But he remained alone. He had not dated, unwilling to approach Canadian women, who tended to look through him, so he had to touch his face to assure himself he existed. And he was reluctant to speak for too long to any of the single women at the Coptic church, knowing any extended attention would result in interrogation and the assumption that he would be proposing marriage.

When his mother said, "the time has come, ya kareem. you're getting older," he didn't respond. Hearing his silence, she continued, "there's a girl. her name is basma. your uncle knows the family well. they live in the same apartment building. she has a degree, and she teaches at an international school. she speaks french, and her english is good."

She waited, let the quiet seep through the phone line, gave him the time he needed to respond. "tayeb, ya mama. i'll think about the situation."

The next Saturday, he called and asked for a picture of the young woman. The picture was sent, and Kareem bought his plane ticket, taking a vacation of three weeks that he had accumulated to return to Egypt for the first time since his departure.

His mother arranged for them to meet at Beanos in Zamalek the day after he arrived. He had requested that he meet her without the blanket of family. His mother consulted with the girl's parents, and everything was set up by the time he landed.

The plane ride from Montreal to Vienna—eight hours; a layover in the airport with voices, rolling suitcases, and intercom announcements all folding into one another to create a constant hum of sound. Then another four hours to get to Egypt, landing in the Cairo International Airport and finding two lines, one for foreigners and one for Egyptian citizens. He hesitated, both passports in his bag. The lines were of equal lengths, but the Egyptian line was moving faster, and there was less to explain.

The first morning, he slept until noon, finally waking to the sounds of honking horns, the call to prayer, the shouts of those pushing carts through the streets. He had forgotten how much sound there was here, the way the whole city entered you from the moment you rose. In Canada, he woke only to the hum of electric wires, but here, the city enticed you with its music of noise.

He sat with his mother at the table as she served him eggs and basterma, which he always enjoyed, but having grown used to cereal and toast, he found it difficult to eat and concentrated on the cup of tea she had made for him, although it didn't have the same effect as his usual Starbucks coffee. Afaf looked at him, seeing how he seemed to have grown taller and fuller, his body filling itself from the inside, the slimness of his youth gone. The echo of his former footsteps rising with each movement as he walked had settled its weight into the ground. His face had filled into roundness and his features reflected her own, his mouth with the same wide thin-lipped shape.

An hour later, Kareem was catching a taxi to Zamalek, crossing the 6th of October Bridge. The traffic moved slower than he remembered, and the streets clogged with cars, buses, minibuses, taxis. The population of Cairo had now increased to almost fifteen million. The radio in the taxi played the music of Fairuz, her Lebanese voice still resounding through the Middle East. He rolled down the window, and the energy of the city seeped in with a myriad of sounds and smells that assaulted the senses. He inhaled all of it as if he were smoking hashish.

"where are you from?" the driver asked, pulling Kareem out of his sensory revelry.

Kareem shook his head as if he had been dozing off. "here, from here," he answered.

The driver didn't respond, and a pause settled until Kareem added, "but i've been living in canada for a few years."

"ahh," the taxi driver said, nodding his head, "that's why."

Kareem turned back to the window. He didn't want to know what the driver had seen that marked him as different enough to motivate his initial question.

He was dropped off two blocks from the Marriott, its grand palatial structure forming an enclave for tourists and wealthy Egyptians who could afford its expensive rooms and its ten-pound hamburgers. He approached the entrance of Beanos and hesitated, taking in the movements of people revolving in his periphery as he considered the step he was taking. When he opened the door and walked in, the polished glamour of the café with the small tables and glass counters assaulted his vision. The place was mostly occupied by young people, ordering coffee, sandwiches, and pastries, sitting in intimate conversation. *this could be montreal,* he thought, with everyone wearing Western-style clothing and carrying their cell phones. Only their darker skin and hair distinguished them. A place without the specificity of location. It could fly up like the *Wizard of Oz* house and land anywhere.

* ⁂ *

I looked around but couldn't identify anyone who looked like the picture I had been sent. I couldn't remember what had made me agree to this meeting with a woman for the sole purpose of marriage. Perhaps it was just a desire for companionship, or perhaps it was just an excuse to return to Egypt. The artificiality of the situation hit me, and I thought of walking back out, but I didn't want to embarrass my mother. I stood in line, ordered a cappuccino, and when I looked for a table, a young woman sitting in the far corner waved toward me. As I walked in her direction, I could see her more clearly—an open face, bright eyes, and a mouth that had a slightly mischievous angle. The image was the same as in the photograph, but she had no makeup and her hair was not styled. It fell loose, draping over her shoulders. She stood up as I approached, reached out her hand to shake mine.

"hello, kareem, it's nice to meet you. sit down," she offered as if inviting me into her own home. I stumbled over my hello, taken aback by her forward confidence. "it seems this is the first time you've come to beanos." And I realized that she had been watching me since I entered.

"i didn't come to such places when i was living in egypt," I said, pulling out the chair.

"the country changes every day. we have mcdonald's, hardee's, pizza hut. amreeka has arrived," she said with a touch of sarcasm. She paused as I settled fully into my seat, the chair round and small, so I had to balance myself carefully.

"tell me about canada," she said just as I raised the cup to my lips. I put it down again without taking a sip.

I looked at this young woman, different from what I had expected—I thought she would be meek, obedient, or looking to emigrate, thinking she would be rich in the West. But this bright-eyed, forward woman—who had immediately taken the lead in the conversation and seemed to be interviewing me—was not what I expected. I decided to tell her the truth.

"it's not as good as i had hoped." And I continued, describing for the first time the cold, the snow, the long days of work, the empty house I had bought, the places where I sometimes went just to hear the sounds of life, my excursions to the northern states of America, the Canadians who seemed aloof and preoccupied with their own lives. For almost an hour, I spoke as if relieving myself of a burden I had been carrying, and she interjected with questions that kept me going, saying more than I had said to anyone over the past five years.

Finally, I looked up at her and said, "i'm sorry. i spoke too much, and i didn't ask you anything about yourself."

She smiled, took a sip of her cold tea, and responded, "it's not important. the day is long. are you hungry? what do you think about going somewhere else? it's our mothers who suggested we meet here. we can go to felfela for fuul and taamia. have you missed them?"

I laughed in response, startled by the sound of my own joy. We stepped out, leaving behind the glass mirrors of the café.

We took a taxi downtown to Felfela on Hoda Sharawee Street, going over the Qasr El Nil Bridge and into the hectic movement of downtown. Two blocks away, we asked the taxi driver to drop us off, deciding it would be quicker to walk. As we approached the restaurant, I could smell the taamia getting fried at the window that opened to the street, and my stomach growled in anticipation of tasting what I had taken for granted for so much of my life.

We sat across from each other, and between us were the plates of fuul filled with beans swirling in olive oil, garlic, and cumin; and the taamia, round and golden and filled with ground fava beans mixed with spices and sprinkled with sesame seeds; along with the tahini, pickles, and Syrian bread. I felt my breath lighten as I dipped the bread into the tahini, my own hands feeding me, rather than the sharp utensils that sat unused at the edge of the table.

After a few bites of beans, I felt brave enough to ask Basma why she agreed to meet me, to potentially marry a man she had never met and go so far from her life.

She looked up, still holding the pickled onion she had just taken a bite from. "is the taamia good?" she asked me.

My mouth was full, so I nodded.

"when you were eating it every day, did it taste as good as it does now?"

I hesitated at the question, trying to recall the way the fried flavor would enter my mouth. I shook my head.

"so maybe if i go to canada, egypt will taste better," she said, finishing the onion with one bite.

I looked at her, furrowing my eyebrows at her words.

"if every day is the same thing, then the flavor will disappear. we have to change our life, so we can truly taste its flavor." She emphasized her words by picking up a piece of taamia and waving it between us before taking a bite.

I stopped eating and stared at this woman whose words made me both want to laugh and reevaluate my life.

She continued, "maybe that's why we eat pickles," she said, "so we can remember how to taste." She laughed, picked up a pickled carrot and placed it at my lips so I had to take a bite. "enough philosophizing," she said. "what do you think? we meet every day for the next two weeks, and spend time together without talking about the future, then at the end of that time, we'll decide what we want to do."

Each morning, we met in Tahrir Square in front of the American University of Cairo, away from the prying eyes of family. We took turns deciding where we would spend the day. One day, I suggested the Giza pyramids, where we quickly grew tired of being offered camel rides and pyramid souvenirs. Another day, Basma suggested the Saqqara pyramids. There, we walked freely among the ancient structures, the first attempt before the success of the Giza pyramids. There were fewer tourists and only a handful of people trying to entice us to take camel rides. We waved off their offers until we came across a man with a donkey. "let's ride the donkey," I said.

And before Basma could object, I said, "yala," and went to negotiate a price with the man. Basma got on first, and the man took her around the largest pyramid. I walked along as the man told me he had nine daughters, all but the youngest married and settled. And he supported them all with the donkey rides he offered. When I got on the donkey, the animal raised his head and brayed, the leash slipping out of the man's hand, and the donkey ran off with me barely holding on. Basma stood laughing as the donkey ran in circles. When the owner managed to catch the leash and control the animal again, I got off as Basma kept laughing. "i never knew anyone could look so scared riding a donkey." The sound of her laughter rolled through the desert, releasing the tightness of my body.

We went to other places, visiting the Ramses Wissa Wassef Art Centre, the weaving school founded by the Egyptian architect; going to the Egyptian Museum, and even venturing into the mummy exhibit; spending a day in the countryside of Fayoum, until the last day of the two weeks, we opted for an evening felucca ride. The felucca floated on the Nile, guided by the boater's skillful hand as he stood in his white galabiya at the front of the boat, gently shifting the sail and using his oar to move us across the surface of the water. Other feluccas dotted the Nile, some with quiet tourists and some with families, music, food, and dancing. We sat quietly next to each other, the stillness of the sunset falling into the water. As the boat began to turn back toward the shore, I looked at Basma, and the days of the past weeks rose in my mind. A day in Egypt was so long. You could go to work, come back to eat and nap, and still have so much day left. If Basma came with me to Canada, our first days together would live forever—these shared images like flipping through a series of photographs—and I could retrieve this homeland in the midst of each cold day to survive in the barren landscape.

Dunya – 2011

The hum of the airport pierced a rhythm through Dunya, a whirl of sounds sustaining a steady level of noise interrupted by louder announcements over the intercom—"Flight 3581 to Turkey now boarding"; "Last call for Flight 281 to Greece"; "Passenger Rodney Glass, please report to Gate 4 in the International Terminal for a lost item." Dunya sat still, her back straight against the steel chair in the waiting area of Gate 4, Terminal E, Logan Airport. She had arrived three hours before the departure with her carry-on suitcase and purse.

Twenty years ago, beneath her father's bed, she had found three suitcases tangled in spiderwebs and layers of dust. It was clear that they had been there since she had arrived with her parents, Misha and Mariam, in 1954, at barely the age of two. She closed her eyes as she pulled out the suitcases and tried to hold her breath; still, the buried air found release once they emerged from the dark cavern beneath the bed. The disturbed spiderwebs untangled their weave and spread their threads into Dunya's face as dust entered her nostrils, and she was caught in a fit of sneezing and watery eyes. She stood up, placing some distance between her and these bags from a lost lifetime.

All three bags were identical, made of beige cloth, now faded to a shade beyond color. There were no wheels, no pull-up handles; you had to carry the full weight of each suitcase. She brushed them off with her hands, catching the dust that had accumulated over the past thirty-seven years. Framed by the three rectangles, she stood and looked from one to the other as if they could speak to her, but they kept the same secrets they had been holding since their arrival in 1954. She tucked her fingers beneath the handle of one of them, lifted it off the ground to feel its presence in her hand. It required a firm grip, a commitment to carry the bag to its destination. It was tempting to imagine using them again, taking them through airports, as if she were a traveler from another time. But she knew that would not work. The bags had been used only once on that long-ago boat trip. Along with everything else in the apartment, she would take them to Goodwill, and perhaps someone else might take them on another journey. Tomorrow, she would purchase a bag with rolling wheels that could move quickly from one destination to another.

* ⁂ *

Now, twenty years after that day and after so many trips, she was once again at the airport. When she went to check in, a purse over her shoulder and pulling one carry-on suitcase, the attendant pointed to the scale for luggage. Dunya shook her head. "Nothing to check in," she said. The attendant, an older man who had held his mouth in a tight pose as he checked her flight information, looked down, and she noted the corner of his lips rise in a quirk of a smile.

"Most people don't travel that light."

"I don't need much." Dunya breathed out the words.

He nodded, as if she had gotten all the answers correct on a math test. "Have a good trip," he added, "you'll find your destination."

The last words reached her ears after she had turned around, and, uncertain of what she had heard, she looked back, but the man was already helping another traveler.

She made her way to her gate and sat down. It was still two hours until her flight. Around her, most people bent over their phones, some flipped the pages of a book, and others stared out as if something in front of them was holding their attention. She got up and began to walk around. She had been in so many airports that they were now more familiar than any other location. Similar stores lined each concourse and a few cafés that offered alcohol. Everyone walked as if pulled by the destination that awaited them. She felt no compulsion to move with the same urgency as the other passengers around her. She stepped into one of the stores that sold a variety of small items: water, bags of chips, Boston t-shirts, neck pillows. She stopped at a display of travel-size items—a tiny lint brush, a small tube of moisturizer, a plastic packet holding a toothbrush and toothpaste. She had been living like this for the past twenty years: a life in miniature. Every time these small items ran out, she knew it was time to gather more and to travel to another place.

A coffee shop attracted her eye, and she stood in line and purchased a cup of tea and a blueberry muffin. Then she made her way to a counter where she sat facing the escalators and watching those who stood in motion on them: a man with a long beard that reached his chest, eating a salad from a takeaway box as he went down; a woman with short curly brown hair, carrying a flowered bag as if she were on her way to the beach; a young man with headphones over his ears, chewing gum to the beat of whatever music entered his hearing; a couple, each holding an infant in one hand and a suitcase in the other. A young girl approached, hesitant at the top of the escalator after her parents had already stepped on, leaving her to determine if her feet could remain steady on the moving stairs. Finally, with a forward motion, she stepped on, gripping the railing and looking down as if fearing the stairs would slip away from her feet.

Finishing her tea and muffin, Dunya got up to make her way back to the designated gate, joining the seemingly choreographed movement of people rolling their suitcases, sidestepping each other without contact. Each person or couple or family functioned like a singular unit, making their way through a predetermined maze. Yet all of them existed in the suspended space of this airport. Dunya took a deep breath and felt her shoulders relax as if a weight were being lifted off her body. For the duration of her trip, she would be nowhere, no location to bind her, no identity to define her, just as she had been living for so many years. This was her last opportunity to be another passenger in motion, and she wished she could continue making her way from one airport to another, catching flights, always in this state of suspended location.

She had made this decision to move to a place that held no thread to her past. Not the United States; not Egypt. She recalled two words in Arabic—"sakna" and "ayshaa." They were almost interchangeable, but not exactly. A slight nuance of meaning separated them. If someone asked "sakna fen?" they were asking where do you reside—as in, where is your dwelling? If someone asked "ayshaa fen?" they were asking where you live—as in, where is your life? Dunya knew she had only resided in the places of her past. The memory of her first two years in Egypt remained a smoky brushstroke like a cloud in an empty sky. Even before her birth, her father had planned on leaving, and so Egypt had been a place of residency from her first breath. And the apartment in Central Square that she had shared with her parents —her mother there for such a short time—the place she and her father had inhabited together for so long, a mailing address, a street name to put on forms, but not a place of living. She wondered if this new destination she had selected would be somewhere to live or somewhere to exist.

It was the expanse of ocean that made her choose it. She wanted to release herself from the walls that had attached to her peripheral vision for almost sixty years. From the apartment in Central Square to so many hotel rooms, she had exchanged one enclosure for another, and all those years of travelling had not given her the freedom she sought. Now, she hoped the ocean would free her vision.

* ⁂ *

She recalled her first flight out of the United States after accepting the job promotion. The sharp jolt of the plane as it released from the ground pushed her back against the seat. She felt a drop in her body and tried to catch her breath as she leaned forward to compensate for the tilt of the plane. Her mind lost grasp for a moment and felt the collapse of time, as if she were again being held tight against her mother's chest while the boat rolled over the waves.

"Are you ok?" the young man next to her asked, but he must have been asking a second time, as she heard the repetition of "Excuse me, are you ok?"

"Yes, yes," she said, the release of air from her mouth helping her to breathe.

"Is this your first time across the ocean?" he asked.

Dunya turned to look at him, a young man, perhaps in his twenties, perhaps a student, looking at her concerned. The truth was too complicated, and she settled for saying, "Yes, I haven't flown before."

He smiled, an almost sheepish curve of his lips. "It's not so bad once you relax into it. Sometimes, I just like to pretend I'm sitting in my living room."

"Thank you," she said. She had chosen an aisle seat, not wanting to feel crowded in by other people. But now she would have almost liked someone on her other side, something to keep her contained, so she would not feel as if she could tip over into the aisle and roll away.

* ⁂ *

After her mother died, Dunya searched for her. She would enter her parents' bedroom, lift the blankets off the bed and look beneath them; she opened the closet and separated the hanging clothes to peek between them; she wandered around the kitchen, opening cupboards—all as if she and her mother were playing a game of hide-and-seek. After a few weeks of this, her father sat her on his lap and said, "mama is not here." Dunya stared at his words as if dissecting them for meaning. He repeated them, adding "khalas," a word meaning "that's all, enough, the end, there is no more." Dunya understood, and after that, she stopped searching.

Her father enrolled her in a small private school where she remained through her elementary years. All the children started together in kindergarten and knew each other before they learned to perceive color and race and stamp labels of hierarchy on one another. Her school days repeated with a steadiness that kept her from faltering, a routine that helped her to keep the seesaw balanced.

She and her father wrapped their lives around each other. Each day, he went to work and she went to school, and each day they returned to sit across from each other at the small kitchen table to eat their meal. He asked about her studies, and she responded with an account of what she was being taught. He listened, nodded, affirming her words. Each day repeated itself, time standing still in the small apartment. Around them, the country spiraled —Kennedy's assassination, the escalation of the civil rights movement, the US entering the Vietnam War, Martin Luther King Jr.'s assassination. Later, Dunya would read about these events that took place during her childhood as if they were stories from another world. All she recalled of those years was the daily ritual of having dinner with her father, as if they sat on the axis of the earth while it revolved.

The one thing she recalled is how once a year, on January 7, her father would get up early to make a phone call to Egypt. The loudness of his voice would wake her from sleep. "aywa, aywa," he would repeat the affirmation. Then the back-and-forth of "we are good, alhamdulillah" and the question about everyone's well-being. She remembered her father at first asking about each person by name, but over time the matter of their well-being became a collective question. The conversation lasted only a few minutes, a punctuation mark in the steady days of each year's passing.

When Dunya outgrew her clothes, she and her father would go downtown to Filene's and approach one of the saleswomen in the children's department.

"My daughter," he said, nodding his head toward her, as if their relationship needed to be explained, "she needs clothes." He enunciated, pronouncing the *th* like a long *s*.

The saleswoman looked from father to child, passing over their two hands clasped together. With pity wiped across her face, she lifted her chin and said, "I would be happy to be of assistance."

She led Dunya through racks of brightly colored pants and dresses and blouses with sparkling fairies and angels. Dunya learned to shake her head and point at the neutral-toned items, selecting shirts that offered no fantastical images. By the time she turned eight, she told her father that she didn't need help, and they bypassed the salesclerk.

Middle school and high school were a blur of days, whispers behind her back about her dark complexion, her unruly hair, her unstylish clothes. She quickly learned how to drift in and out of classrooms, to sit at the desk in the front corner, to eat her lunch quickly at a table tucked into the edge of the cafeteria. The whispers diminished as if she had become invisible.

There were a few friends, or rather other students, who gravitated toward one another, sensing safety in each other's vicinity—a girl who had recently arrived from Haiti and whose face remained blank at the insults tossed in her direction; a tall, heavy girl whose body took up too much space, although she tried to tuck in her stomach and fold herself like an envelope; and another girl who held her arm at her side as if it were a weight she had to carry, her body slightly askew as she walked. They sat together in classrooms, in the cafeteria, at the required school gatherings and introduced each other to their parents to prove they had acquired friends.

In her second year of high school, Dunya cut her hair so the tangles that had fallen to her waist were trimmed away and she was left with short, dark curls. When her father saw her, the words "what have you done?" trembled out of his lips like pebbles. "i'm sorry," she said, her tone sincere, "but this is easier." He nodded. She kept the short hair for the rest of her life, the soft, dark-brown curls a simple frame for her face.

In her last year of high school, she identified another senior who strolled the hallways with his head down, absorbed in his own thoughts. He was known as a science nerd, often found in the labs after school with a teacher, and rumors said he was working on creating a Frankenstein monster. His shyness and his tall, lanky body kept him from interacting with girls. Two weeks before the end of the school year, Dunya approached him and asked if he would help her study for the chemistry final. A mumble escaped his lips as he nodded. She handed him a piece of paper with her address and the day and time when he should arrive. Dunya had taken AP Biology and learned how the body works, its intricate pathways, the way blood travelled through the veins, the way the mind controlled the physical being. There was no mystery to sex, she had determined. It was a biological action, predicated on certain needs of the body. And there was no magic to the act, only a series of interactions that went from cause to effect. That afternoon, Dunya and the lanky boy both lost their virginity. She had orchestrated the afternoon carefully. At the end, as she ushered the boy loaded down with his textbooks out the door, she felt relieved at having completed an assignment that she would not have to do again.

College took her to Boston University, a large, sprawling set of buildings. She continued to live at home, keeping the pattern of her father's days intact. Initially, she thought she might major in biology, but after one class, she decided that she understood all she needed. She attempted a philosophy class, but chasing after questions that had no answers left her exhausted. Having to fulfill a math requirement, she stumbled into a finance class. The numbers fit neatly into their boxes, and they could be moved like chess pieces to create different configurations. These numerals spoke to her, and she understood them with ease. Unlike the finite systems of the body, numbers offered endless possibilities; and unlike the unanswered questions of the universe, each mathematical problem had a solution. She decided to major in international business with a focus on finance, learning how money travelled across countries.

After she graduated, she began working for a consulting firm. She enjoyed spending her days reviewing the numbers submitted by companies and writing the reports that outlined the problems and solutions. After several years that came with promotions and raises, the president of the company called her into his office. Their interactions had never stepped beyond the usual "Good morning" or haphazard run-in with a mumbled "How are you?" Now she sat in front of his mahogany desk, uncertain of why she had been summoned.

"You're a bit of a loner," he began with no precursor, catching Dunya off guard.

She nodded, "Yes."

A smile flickered across his face. He looked the part of a company president with his gray hair, bright blue eyes that pierced the onlooker, and an almost-casual sportscoat that in reality was quite expensive.

"You prefer numbers to people?" He leaned in, allowing his elbows to balance on the edge of the desk.

Dunya began to understand his play and decided to respond. "Yes, they don't make emotional demands and they always offer a solution."

"All right, then," he responded. "No one can argue with that." And he went on to compliment her work, the praise he received from her clients, along with comments from her coworkers that she was always willing to offer help when they reached an obstacle in their own cases. Then, as if having finished a prepared speech, he paused to settle his gaze directly on her. "You're ready for the next step, to become a travelling consultant. You know what that entails—going to work with a specific company, sometimes for a few months, sometimes for a year or more. Are you willing?"

Dunya's mind lost its focus as images of planes and skylines and hotel rooms jumbled across her vision. She had stayed with her father in the same apartment, maintaining their evening routine. She rarely went out, and her encounters with men were always brief. Her mother's death had wrapped them both in a shroud. She could imagine travel, but she couldn't carry the image of her father sitting alone at the small kitchen table each evening.

One day, she had come home earlier than usual from work and heard music coming through the apartment door. She knew it was Umm Kulthum, singing "Enta Omri," repeating the refrain of "you are my life," a song her mother had loved and played often. She stood at the door, imagined her father sitting in the chair as the music flowed from the tape player, each extended word of longing entering him. She crouched down to sit, leaning against the door to the apartment, and remained there listening with her father until the song ended.

Refocusing her attention, she looked up and saw the president's eyes on her as if he had been following her thoughts. "I can't," she said, her voice just an octave above a whisper. "I . . . there are family responsibilities."

"It's too bad people are not as easy to manipulate as numbers," he said, leaning back. "I will hold my offer. Let me know when you're ready."

* ⁂ *

Three years later, she returns from work one day to find the apartment quiet, the kitchen exactly as she left it.

She approaches her father's bedroom, raises her hand to knock, lowers it, and instead turns the knob slowly and lets the door push in. The door releases from her hand and opens fully. From where she is standing, she can see her father's body in bed, but the room sits in blind silence. Walking toward the bed, she notices that he's lying on his back, the blue blanket pulled to his shoulders. She avoids looking at his face. Reaching, she knows before her hand touches him that he is gone. Cold, a vague tint of blue to his skin, his features soft as if he has released the burden of all his years.

* ⁂ *

After the funeral, the people that she and her father barely knew, mostly through the Coptic church, gathered to offer their condolences to her. There was no one to stand next to her, no husband, children, aunts, or uncles like other funerals where the line of people to be consoled extended. Each person kissed her on both cheeks, offered to provide whatever she needed, although she didn't know what to ask for. She had barely spoken to these Egyptian immigrants, most of whom came after her family. Her father rarely lingered after the Sunday service to engage in conversation.

When it was all over, she entered the apartment slowly, afraid of disturbing its ghosts. Standing in the kitchen, she heard herself say, "What will I do now?" At that moment, she could neither imagine staying in the apartment nor leaving it. She went back out, not bothering to change from her black funeral clothes. She walked through the streets of Central Square. It was no longer the rundown neighborhood it had once been. Gentrification had crept in, adding upscale ethnic restaurants, clothing stores, and coffee shops.

Dunya walked, catching her surroundings through the periphery of her vision. She thought that perhaps this was how she had always experienced this country, through peripheral vision, so she looked up, holding her eyes straight, allowing every nuance of light and color and shape to enter in—people she felt no connection with, a landscape of materialism that offered nothing, and elite academic institutions that meant little to her. She recalled how her father often took the walk from Central Square to Harvard Square, and she turned in that direction, following his footsteps.

Twenty minutes later, she stood in the middle of Harvard Square's frenzy of students, shoppers, and tourists. At Brattle Street, the traffic light changed three times before she crossed. She slowed her steps, taking a slightly less crowded side street. Finding an old diner that looked trapped by the other stores that had grown around it, she stepped in, sat at one of the booths, and ordered a black coffee. Letting the white ceramic mug warm her hands, she stared through the window of the diner out to the street. Through that window, she saw the smallness of her life. As a young child, she was taken across continents, but since then she had lived between school and apartment, college and apartment, job and apartment. She had not inhabited the space of this country. And yet she had little desire to immerse herself in it. Nothing about it felt like it belonged to her.

With her father gone, no one knew her. The people in the church came closest to family, but her father never brought anyone into their lives. They attended Sunday liturgy, weddings, and funerals, but their relationships with others never stepped outside the bounds of church ritual. She had no close friends, no lovers beyond the occasional flirtations that led to a single evening. Nothing held her here, not even the possession of a house. More than thirty-seven years had passed since she left the country where she was still tied to people by blood. Those who knew her would recall her as a two-year-old held in her mother's arms. Those who were born after she left might have heard of her only as a vague recollection in the minds of others. Nothing tied her to anyone or any place.

She looked around the diner—a booth with a single man reading a newspaper and eating a sandwich, another with a single woman reading a book. Unlike the streets, it was quiet, only the soft mumble of a few voices. And in her own mind, a voice told her it was time to live in the world, to live up to the meaning of her name.

She finished her coffee, left a generous tip as if thanking the diner for the moment of quiet it provided her. Walking back, she lifted her head, forced her gaze around her, taking in the brick facades of buildings, the urgent faces of those who had destinations. It was 1991, and Harvard Square was no longer the location of the hippie movement, the anti-war movement, or the place of free love it was in the '60s and '70s; the real estate boom had hit Boston, and Cambridge was now a prime location, with the most prestigious academic institution at its center. The world had changed while she was repeating the days with her father.

Back inside the apartment, she stood in the middle of the living room, inhaled the smell of dust that had layered over the years, the staleness of furniture that sat in the same place, the smothered air of grief that never left, and a slight aroma that drew her to the kitchen. She had forgotten that after the funeral one woman after the next had handed her a covered dish of food. It was the custom, although she knew that normally they took it to the house of the bereaved and sat with them. No one had entered their home, and at this point, it must have seemed a grave trespass to do so. Someone had taken the food and piled it into the trunk of her car. She had unloaded it in a daze when she returned and placed it on the counter.

She followed the smell, almost tiptoeing to the kitchen as if someone were going to come out and surprise her. She lifted the aluminum foil from one casserole to reveal the bechamel mixed with ground beef. In another dish, she found exquisitely fried eggplant, and another offered her rolled cabbage leaves, foods she had rarely eaten since her mother's passing. She felt the rumble of her stomach as each aroma mixed with her breath. She opened a drawer and reached for a fork, taking bites from each dish, filling a new hunger. The food assaulted her taste buds—cumin, allspice, and coriander seeping through each bite—reminding her of the women who cooked it. An Arabic phrase came back to her: *ye salem eadekee—thanks to the hands that cooked the food*. Her father would say it at every meal when her mother cooked. She recalled her mother standing in the kitchen, a place where she seemed content, and her offering as she set each plate on the table, and the way she sat next to her, cutting her food, giving her each spoon, although she could have fed herself at that age. Now, Dunya satisfied her hunger, eating directly from each dish.

She fell asleep in her clothes and slept without dreams until morning. In the daylight, the apartment looked worn, as if it had exerted too much energy over the years. She showered, dressed, made herself a cup of coffee, and stood in the middle of the living room, turned around like the second hand on a clock and out loud said, "yala!" She opened all the windows, some of which had not been opened for years, straining them upwards to release the hoarded dust. She turned on every light, combining the artificial and natural until the apartment shined with an eerie overbrightness.

She made her way to the hallway closet where her parents saved every box that held the items they bought during their first days in America—the one for the coffee maker, the vacuum cleaner, the toaster, the mixer. They couldn't imagine that such boxes were meant to be thrown away when in Egypt, even a plastic bag from America had value. She grabbed one of the boxes and took it into her parents' bedroom, knowing that this was where she must begin. She opened her mother's closet, the clothes almost trembling as she slid open the door. She took a deep breath and felt her own trembling hand as she retrieved each item, folded it gently and placed it in a box. She continued with the dresser drawers, disturbing the clothes sitting in paralyzed stillness for so many years. She went on to gather her father's clothing and personal items until the room offered nothing but its four empty walls and the open cavities of its storage.

Each day, she selected a room—the living room, with its assortment of knickknacks; the kitchen, with its pots and pans and dishes, keeping only the teapot; the bathroom, with its hoarding of old medicines and toothbrushes; and finally, her own room, judging each item with a critical eye to its usefulness, emptying the closet of most of her clothes, pulling the jewelry from the dresser, and discarding unnecessary shoes. On the sixth day, she gathered the boxes into her car, making five trips to the Goodwill to release the objects to their next destination. On Sunday, she rolled up her sleeves and pulled one item of furniture after the next to the hallway outside the apartment with a taped piece of paper saying "FREE." One by one, she squeezed out the couch, the kitchen table and chairs, the TV, the beds, the dressers. Word spread quickly, so that before she took out the next item, the previous one was already gone. The following day, she went into her boss's office and told him she was ready to accept his offer.

* ⁂ *

Sometimes she remained in a place for a few weeks, and sometimes up to a year for the larger international companies. At times, she was provided with a hotel room, and at times it was a fully furnished apartment. The surprise of a new place suited her, making up for all the years of coming home to the same place, each item in its secure location. They had never moved a piece of furniture or a knickknack. The only new things that entered the apartment was the food they bought and a few essential items. Her father had entombed their home, making it an eternal monument, and Dunya had not dared disturb his grief.

She carried home in her suitcase. Her carry-on bag held three pairs of black pants, two for business and one casual; five tops in assorted solid colors; one black blazer; one black sweater; a pair of sweatpants and a t-shirt for working out; one pair of pajamas; one pair of black shoes for work and one pair of sneakers; her basic toiletries; and three pairs of earrings and two necklaces in a pouch. Beneath the bottom lining of the suitcase, she kept a picture taken on the beach, her parents on either side of her holding her hands, her mother in a dress, her father wearing a sportscoat, and Dunya in a lacy outfit, as if they had misplaced themselves, but all of them smiling into the camera being held by a stranger who had accepted their request to take a photo. She put the picture in an envelope, then sealed it into a plastic bag and tucked it beneath the zippered lining of the suitcase, layering it in invisibility.

Occasionally, she would replace an item with another that she bought, but the contents of the suitcase remained essentially the same, maintaining her balance as she flew from one country to another. Her wardrobe exhibited a professional simplicity that travelled across cultures. And she found she needed nothing else.

For twenty years, Dunya travelled, from her first stop in Cyprus to Portugal to Panama to Brazil to South Africa to places she had to look up on a map. She accepted every possibility, settling into each job as if her presence there was preordained, and each time she left the company with clear numbers that added up correctly and a budget plan to keep them stable and profitable. She learned to enjoy what each place offered, trying mofongo in Puerto Rico, sadza in Zimbabwe, fish and chips with vinegar in London, allowing the sounds and smells of each place to surround her. The freedom of knowing it was temporary freed her from the fear of being captured.

In each place, men sprouted, and she enjoyed what they offered, the flirtation, the seduction. And also women, as she discovered that she could love both equally, embracing each body into her own with pleasure. Knowing she would be leaving gave her the freedom to enjoy the intimacy of each encounter without thought of a permanent relationship.

In some places, she blended in, another variation of the human landscape. She walked down the street, no one glancing twice in her direction, no one asking where she was from, and the anonymity of belonging lightened her steps. In other places, her difference was clearly marked, but once she said she was travelling for business, she was welcomed, a kind of tourist just passing through, not the possibility of a stranger remaining in their midst. Those who lived there pointed her to the beauty of their country, the sights she should visit. And so even in such places, her temporariness released her from the desire to attach herself. She walked—wearing her black slacks and her interchangeable shirts, her shoes flat against the ground—to mark a steady terrain through the world.

In so many places, her name gave her a passport to belonging—in Turkey, Pakistan, and Malaysia, "Yes," they would smile, "you are the world. Welcome." And she began to imagine herself a round globe like the one that had been in her elementary classroom, hinged to the stand, revolving with a slight push.

After almost twenty years, she resigned, knowing it was time to stop the motion. But was it possible to settle anywhere in the world that had felt like a moving plate beneath her? Now, at almost sixty, her feet stood still.

There was a woman who lived on the island of Gozo in Malta. Her house overlooked San Philip Bay, situated against the blue landscape of ocean. It had been built between the stone slabs and rocks that formed a barrier against the water. When Dunya met the woman at the company where she was assigned, they began a conversation that led them back to that house, where Dunya returned every night, the wind pushing at her back. She found peace in the arms of this woman who asked nothing, but the waves of the ocean summoned her memories. While the two of them sat, Dunya talked, forgetting the woman was there, telling herself the story of her past, resurrecting memories of a mother almost forgotten, recalling a wisp of hair, the smoothness of a soft palm against her back, a hand outstretched with a spoon to feed her. She fell into the lullaby of ocean and wind and her new lover's quiet listening.

That was three years ago. Now she sat waiting for a flight that would take her back to that island, a place unbordered by land, floating in endless water. Over the past three years, they had exchanged photographs with small captions: "Today's Sunrise," and Dunya saw the red and violet brushstrokes of the morning light rising above the ocean; "In London again," and Dunya clicked to send a picture of Buckingham Palace; the back-and-forth of the woman's photos marking the passage of seasons and Dunya's marking the passage of geography.

Dunya had returned to Boston to make the necessary arrangements for her retirement from the company. Her final stop in the city was the bank to close the safety-deposit box she had opened before leaving on her first trip. Inside, a turquoise ring that was always on her mother's hand and an envelope of photographs she had saved. She slipped the ring on her finger, felt it vibrate through her skin as if she had awakened her mother's spirit. She cupped her other hand over the ring until it quieted.

Outside the bank, the January air was icy, and she wrapped her scarf a little tighter around her neck. She pulled out her phone, snapped a photo of the ground—a gray slab of concrete—and typed "Looking for direction." Within a minute, her phone buzzed, and she looked down to see a photo of the woman's house, a white rectangle against the sky, with no message. Dunya stood in front of the bank as people entered and left, carrying out the transactions of their finances, the numbers she had worked with all her life sliding back and forth from one account to the next—a deposit, a withdrawal, a transfer. Oblivious to people muttering "Excuse me" as they walked briskly past her, she sorted through a number of clicks, squinting against the sun to see the screen of her phone until *Ticket confirmed* appeared, and Dunya messaged "On my way." Standing still, she waited, afraid to move, lest she disturb the precarious balance of the moment, until "Waiting for you" appeared on her phone.

The plane was already on the ground getting refueled and prepared for boarding to take its passengers to Malta. It was a twelve-hour flight, leaving at eleven in the evening with a stopover in Frankfurt. Since it was an overnight flight, she would arrive the morning of January 25. Dunya looked ahead to landing, embracing the woman and the land and the ocean with a desire that she had held in check for so long, fearful of what it would mean to commit to a place. She sat waiting for the call to board.

Fathy's Departure

When Fathy decided to leave, he asked me to drive him to the airport, knowing I would oblige. We had heard that he won the lottery and that he and his father, Farid, had argued. It happened quickly, and he must have worked hard to get all his papers together that fast. Someone told me he signed over the deed of his apartment back to his father, that he left it on the dining table without a word and it sat there for days.

His flight left the evening of January 24. When I went to the apartment to get him, his mother was urging him to have a piece of konafa before he left. It was his favorite dessert, and his mother had woken early to make it that morning. I could tell he was reluctant, but he obliged and accepted a piece, and I watched his throat clamp over the bite he took. He placed his suitcase by the door and approached the chair where his father sat. He awkwardly wrapped an arm around him and kissed his cheek. His father did not respond. At the door, his mother held him tightly, kissing each cheek again and again. "ya ibni, don't stay too long. come back again," she pleaded with moist eyes.

On the way to the airport, he asked me to stop at his sisters' homes, so he could say goodbye and hug each niece and nephew. Each sister asked him the same question, "motaked?"—one word encapsulating "Are you sure? Are you making the right decision? Please reconsider"—and in response Fathy nodded, swallowing his own uncertainties.

We drove through the streets, the sun slowly setting over the myriad buildings that rose out of the earth, a city watered by the Nile and surrounded by desert sand.

"something is in the air," Fathy said as he rested his elbow out the open window.

"only because you're leaving," I responded. "maybe you'll miss all this commotion," I said, waving my arm to encompass the eighteen million people and their incessant lives that boiled over within the confines of the city. "it's like ahmed adaweya's song," I added, "the world's crowded, our loved ones are gone, and there's no mercy."

Fathy shook his head. Something made his body twitch, as if the air stung. "i mean, do you think this uprising will happen?"

I shrugged. "it's all just talk. we like to talk but we're not a people of action. nothing will happen."

"maybe you're right," Fathy said, looking out into the quiet streets. "but be careful, ya fanous," he added. "just stay at home tomorrow."

I suspected that his nervousness was due to how quickly he had decided to leave, and perhaps he was having second thoughts.

"your decision is good," I said, "this country is not for the young. there are no opportunities. each day a door closes. and there is family in amreeka. boston has hafez and layla as well as hala and nessim, and their children are your cousins. here, nothing will change; mubarak's son will take over, and then his son after him. we are a monarchy of dictators."

Fathy nodded. "yes," he said. "maybe in amreeka i can open a door."

I looked at this young man, still in his thirties. I wasn't sure I believed my own words, but I felt a responsibility to send him off with faith in the future. The first time I had driven a family member to the airport, I was only in my twenties, taking Farid. America was grabbing our engineers and scientists because they didn't have enough of their own. A lot of Copts went because they thought it would be better there, that they wouldn't be discriminated against because America is a Christian country. But now look what America has become—attacking anyone who has dark skin. People ran to escape from one hole only to fall into another. Now I was in my sixties and still driving my family to the airport. This time, it was Fathy, who felt the betrayal of his country, and the weight of his dreams filled the car as the airport lights blinked in the distance.

Fathy – 2011

Fathy sat on the floor of the apartment that his father, Farid, had purchased for him. He placed one plank of wood, fitting it tightly against the previous one. He had finished putting in the flooring for half of the living room, and each day he added a few more planks, watching the dark oak color expand. He ran his hand across the wood before he placed it, relishing its smoothness, imagining the tree it had come from and the way it had been transformed from one state of being to another.

His father had told him he could hire someone to do this manual labor, that there was no need to dirty himself with such work. But Fathy enjoyed working with his hands. As the youngest child, with both of his sisters, Maha and Sonya, already in school, he had often accompanied his mother on her errands. She would go to El Mosky Market, where she could find everything she wanted. One day, when he was eight years old, they stopped at the stall of a man selling an assortment of small tables and stools. Fathy stood, mesmerized by the man's hands as they carved the wood into rectangles and circles. He watched the prickly texture of the wood turn shiny and smooth under the man's scraping. While his mother was busy making her various purchases, the man motioned him over and showed him what he was doing by his gestures. Fathy noted his hands, the knuckles enlarged, the fingers bent, and the skin calloused. He imagined that each piece the man made entered his hands, transforming their shape and texture.

When he told his mother that he wanted to do what the man did, she looked at him and said, "silly, why would you work with your hands and be poor?" Fathy tied his ambition into a knot and put it away.

As he grew older, he spent his days between home and school and family. But often, he was bored. He did his schoolwork quickly and a bit sloppily, not caring if his answers were correct. One afternoon, when he was thirteen, he wandered into the kitchen when their cook was beginning the preparation for dinner. The woman had been working for them for just a short while and had come from a Nubian village near Aswan. Her face was round and soft, and Fathy imagined that if he touched it, it would feel like bread dough. Her eyes were large and dark with long eyelashes. When he approached the kitchen, he had expected her to reprimand him and send him away as his mother did, but her soft mouth opened into a smile that encouraged him to enter. She was coring the eggplant, pulling out the pulp and seeds and putting them into a bowl.

"do you want to learn?" she asked.

He nodded and approached closer. She demonstrated how to hold the coring utensil and how to keep a firm grip on the eggplant, how to be gentle as he pulled out the pulp, so he didn't pierce the skin of the vegetable. His hands felt awkward as he attempted to imitate her actions. But she rewarded his efforts with a smile, and even when the tool slipped his grasp and poked through the skin, she did not reprimand him, only said it takes time to learn. After that day, he rushed through his homework so he could enter the kitchen each afternoon. One day, the house quiet and dinner mostly prepared, she looked at him and said, "what do you think, should we make bread?" He nodded, unsure of what that entailed but happy to learn something new.

His fist pushed the dough down as she had shown him, and he laughed when the stickiness attached to his fingers. He liked spreading the dough open and stretching it to see how far it could go. When the oven yielded the loaves they had made, Fathy inhaled the flour evaporating from the warmth of the bread as the cook smiled at him and said, "look at what you made."

His father had groomed him to become an engineer, to follow in his footsteps. He nodded when his father spoke, expressed obedience, but nothing about engineering appealed to him. He wanted to create something, to bring it into existence with his own hands. In his last year of high school, his father hired tutors for him, and he spent tedious hours studying for the final exams that would determine his future.

He sat in the large room filled with students sitting at desks, their heads bent over their exams. The prayers of parents waiting outside the building hovered above each student, along with the anxiety of undetermined futures and the judgement of numerical grades that would permanently mark each of their lives. Fathy knew the answers, knew he could achieve the necessary marks to enter the Engineering College, knew that his fate had been dictated from the day of his birth. He looked at those around him, pencils gripped in their hands, their bodies poised at this defining moment of their lives. He had not planned to answer the questions incorrectly; it was only that at this moment, for the first time, he felt some control. His father was not there, his tutors were not there; there was no one who could see his internal thoughts, no one who could know he was doing this purposely. He made his way through the questions, left his mark on the wrong answer just enough times to deviate from his fate.

When his father saw his marks, he pierced Fathy with his eyes, directing a glare of accusation. Fathy stood, eyes lowered in apology and disgrace. "after all the tutors, the money we spent on you, it's a loss," Farid said, turning his back and walking away. Fathy entered the business school, which offered a moderately respectable degree, and after he graduated, his father used his connections to find him a job. A meaningless job that required him to sit at a desk and present the appearance of working each day.

* ⁂ *

Technically he was still living at home in Mohandessein, since the Heliopolis apartment was meant for him once he married. But he made excuses about wanting to fix it up. He bought a bed, so he could sleep there, saying it was closer to his job. Spending time there allowed him to cook without having to explain anything. His parents never knew about his excursions into the kitchen, and the cook had never said anything to them. Now he wondered if she realized the illicitness of his trespass into this female arena and had protected him with her silence. She had stayed with them for a few years and then returned to her village, presumably to get married, and they hired someone else whose stern look did not encourage Fathy to approach her.

One day, he ventured to bring his family some bread he had made, claiming it was from a bakery near the apartment. They exclaimed at how good it was, praised its taste and texture. He had been practicing different recipes and once brought a large loaf of Italian bread with sesame seeds sprinkled on top; another time, he tried his hand at French bread, yielding the hard crust and soft center. But after a while, his family's insistence on knowing the name of the bakery caused him to say it had closed.

* ⁂ *

Fathy was in his thirties, and he realized that he could no longer hold up his youth as an excuse for his lack of direction. His parents were already scouting for an appropriate wife. One of his aunts once hinted that his father had wanted to marry a different woman, that he had been smitten by her, but she was not acceptable to the family. Fathy couldn't imagine his father as a young man in love. And he knew that the woman his father chose for him would be a checklist of appropriate qualifications. None of the women he had encountered interested him. He felt that they all followed a script of flirtation and coyness, and it was impossible to know if there was a real person beneath the role they had been taught to play. He couldn't identify what he wanted, only that he didn't want to duplicate his father's life.

Fathy still felt like a child, following his father's orders. He knew that soon his father would find him a wife, push for his promotion at the company, and he would be stuck in the box created for him. He wasn't opposed to marriage, but he wanted companionship, not just someone skilled at being a housekeeper, a cook, and a mother.

* ⁂ *

Once, while I was waiting for the metro when it was delayed, a young woman carrying several books sat next to me. I ventured to ask if she was a student. She answered yes with a confident voice and started to explain that she was getting a master's degree in economics at the American University in Cairo. And when I asked why economics, her face lit up as she explained how in the true study of economics, you looked not only at the large picture of big companies but also at the invisible layers of the economy—the women who sold limes on the street corner, the young girls and boys who ran after you to get you to buy a pack of gum or a packet of tissues, the man who enticed another man to buy a necklace of jasmine for the woman with whom he strolled along the Nile. It was this layer of the country's economy that most fascinated her, that showed the resilience of people. I listened and asked more questions, appreciating the passion in her voice. When the metro arrived, she slipped into the women's car, and I couldn't follow her.

* ⁂ *

Fathy saw how his father encapsulated himself in the shell he had created. He extolled the importance of keeping family close, intact. And on that basis, he pushed America away, his words spitting out against those who left. Fathy knew that his father never forgave Hafez for leaving and for taking his cousin Layla with him. But Fathy remembered that they came to visit when he was about eight years old and brought presents for everyone: scotch for his father, perfume for his mother, a giant box of chocolates for his sisters and him. In America, they had bought a house and a car. Fathy couldn't understand why his father denied their success. When he had watched Hafez and his father greet each other, he saw their muscles strain as if releasing them would unleash some force neither of them knew how to contain.

During that visit, Fathy and his cousin Yusef went outside to play, kicking the soccer ball and chasing each other. Out of breath, they sat on the steps. "you're lucky you're here," Yusef said. His Arabic had a slight twang to it, as if his mouth had to adjust itself each time it formed the words. "you're lucky you're in amreeka," Fathy answered. And they continued to play until Yusef's parents had finished visiting.

* ⁂ *

Each year, when they announced the immigration lottery in the newspaper, Fathy's father scoffed, rolled the newspaper and slammed the table with it as if he could scatter the words inside it. "amreeka likes to tease people," he said. "it entices like a flirtatious woman but offers nothing. there is nothing in amreeka."

Although he knew it was a mistake, one day, Fathy ventured to argue with him.

"but hafez and layla and hala and nessim and magda and lutfi—they are all there, and they're happy."

Farid glowered at his son, his face a fierce eruption. "all of this leaving traces back to hafez. he is the reason we lost our family."

Fathy started to turn away, realizing it was a futile conversation. But his father lowered his voice and called him back as if afraid he might lose him altogether.

"hear me," he said. "when hafez graduated in 1962, an architecture degree from cairo university still meant something. it had prestige, status—you were someone with that degree. people wanted to hire you. for seven years, he built a career, working for the top firms in the country until everyone knew his name. you couldn't drive down a street in cairo without seeing a building he had worked on. his stamp was everywhere. and the city was growing, buildings rising from the ground in every direction. hafez would've been a millionaire if he had stayed."

Fathy kept his voice calm, hoping his father might listen. "we were twenty-nine million in egypt in 1962, and look at us now: there are eighty million people in this country, and eighteen million of them in cairo. in 1952, nasser said the government would guarantee a job for each college graduate. now that's a joke—you're on a waiting list, and by the time your turn comes, you might already be in your grave."

His father continued almost as if his son were not there. "when hafez proposed to layla, he had already earned respect in his field, and his offer came with a nice apartment, and by then, he had bought the white fiat.

most men could only offer promises, but he had something in his hand. my cousin—she was young, only nineteen, and she spent her days reading romance novels by ihsan abdel quddous. she was captivated by hafez's green eyes and the success he carried in his briefcase. she imagined a fairy-tale life of parties, clothes, and travelling to europe. that's why she said yes."

Fathy attempted to alter the picture his father was painting, responding with "but you told me yourself how hard hafez worked, how after a full week at the company, he took the night train to menya to teach all day and then catch the train back to cairo, how he picked up extra jobs with private companies."

His father continued building his narrative like an architect's design. "and then hala followed her sister, searching for some vision she thought she could find in amreeka. nessim loved her or maybe he was enamored with her, her charm, her beauty, and he wanted to make her happy. she had that effect on you. she pushed and cajoled until he agreed. and we lost them."

Fathy was grateful when his mother summoned them to the dinner table, ending a conversation that could never resolve itself.

* ⁂ *

When Fathy turned thirty, he went to the American Embassy and entered the lottery. He thought of it as a spur-of-the-moment decision, but the idea had entered his mind a long time ago, perhaps from the moment he learned that his father left America. He wanted to see this country that his father abhorred so much. Still, he knew better than to buy into the illusions America exported. In 2001, he was twenty-three, and he listened to the rhetoric of America's leaders and watched the country retaliate against nations who were only guilty of being weak enough to be attacked. He knew its people couldn't tell the difference between an Arab and a Sikh or a Muslim and a Christian, but he also knew America was more than what appeared on the television sets.

The line at the embassy stretched out beyond the gates, and they only let in a few people at a time. When he filled out the application, he put down the address of the apartment in Heliopolis.

Fathy wondered if he only entered the lottery as an act of rebellion against his father, even though he had no intention of telling him. His father had thrown a blanket over America, making it an opaque illusion. Fathy dropped off the form and walked away from the fortress walls, leaving behind what he thought was a meaningless gesture.

He wasn't ready to go home, so he made his way through Zamalek, past the Cairo Opera House and the Cairo Sporting Club, observing the world in which he lived. The woman who was selling peanuts overcharged every foreigner attracted to her cart full of steaming nuts; the shoeshine man offered a gapped-tooth smile, saying "pay what you will" and kept his hand out for more; the bawab greeted each tenant with "ay khedma," offering his services in the hopes of an extra tip. Everyone had become a beggar—hungry for a breath of clean air, the possibility of feeding their families. A box of sweets for forty pounds a kilo, an English-language book for seventy pounds, a cup of tea for five pounds, a magazine for fifteen pounds—who could afford more than the most basic items, except those who frequented the hotels and the Citystars Mall, with its six hundred stores? Egypt had become a tiered society with each layer firmly tucked into its place, the lower ones holding up those on top.

* ⁂ *

It was toward the end of 2010 that Fathy noticed certain patterns in the posts on his Facebook: frustrations with the usual government bureaucracy, a reference to Mubarak grooming his son to be the next president, a parody of Mubarak depicting him as a pharaoh. There was nothing new in what was being said, but the visible articulation of it on Facebook stepped beyond the bounds of censorship that every Egyptian president had imposed. In December, Fathy noticed a sharp shift from frustration to a call for action with words like "organize, we are the youth of egypt" and "enough" popping up. They were calling for a day of rage on January 25, 2011. It was intended to coincide with the Egyptian Police Day, commemorating the battle between British troops and the Egyptian police in Ismailia that took the lives of many Egyptians.

The plan was to march to downtown Cairo and keep the protest peaceful. Instructions popped up on how to avoid tear gas and defend yourself against the anti-riot police. *nothing will ever come of it*, Fathy thought to himself. *this country is mired in its stagnation*.

When his friend Nabil approached him to participate in a gathering of young people to talk about taking action, Fathy declined, saying it was a waste of time. But Nabil was insistent, and he and Fathy had been friends since childhood, so he agreed. They gathered at the apartment of Hoda and Ziad, who had been married only a year. Almost everyone there was in their twenties or early thirties, a generation that had only known one president throughout their lives. Most were middle class, well educated. The words sprang out and soared across the room, until their existence became a concrete entity: "are you with us, fathy?" The voice did not register immediately and repeated itself, "fathy, are you with us?" Bodies twisted in his direction, eyes settling on him. "i . . .," Fathy hesitated, unable to reach any of the words that floated in the room. "we need you. you have connections. we want you to be one of our leaders." He felt himself caught in the net of his class status in a country where family defined your position and power. "of course," he said, "we are all together."

As they walked out, Nabil put his arm around him and drew him close, saying, "i knew we could count on you." They parted ways as Nabil headed to Shoubra, and Fathy to Mohandessein, a crossroads that marked the line between their class positions. Instead of heading back to his father's house, Fathy caught a taxi and went to the apartment in Heliopolis. As the taxi made its way through Tahrir Square, Fathy tried to imagine the protest discussed at the meeting. Would everyone really congregate and gather into a mass movement? Egypt was a solid rock, and it was hard to believe anyone could move it. The cab dropped him off, and as Fathy paid, the driver nodded at the generous payment and said, "thank you, ya pasha." He wanted to say something, to deny the man's evaluation of him, that he was somehow superior, that he deserved this label of respect. He wanted to dismantle the entire hierarchy of the country. But he said nothing as he walked away, toward the prestigious building where his father had purchased the apartment for him.

Inside, the emptiness of the space opened up and he felt his breath return. His father had said that once he married, it would be his wife who would choose the furniture for each room. That she would be "rabet el beit," the goddess of the house. Fathy wondered if that was why he avoided marriage, that it was perhaps an act of selfishness. He wanted to keep this place for himself. Although his father's money had purchased it, inside it contained nothing but what he put in with his own hands. He changed into the work clothes he kept there and sat on the floor at the edge of where he had placed the last plank of wood. With careful precision, he added one floorboard after the next, tucking one into the other.

* ⁂ *

After the meeting, Fathy found that he had been added to a private Facebook group, and the messages rolled in—plans, meetings, supplies. He had been pulled in, and he couldn't find a way to extricate himself. Nabil picked him up to go to the meetings, and he listened, saying as little as he could.

"we're going to bring the whole country to tahrir. and we will chant *erhal, ya mubarak* until we are rid of him. this is our nation, and we need to take it back, make it our own."

Each time he left a meeting and walked through the streets of Cairo, he saw how it had become a city of wealth and poverty rubbing against each other daily. Around the corner from luxury hotels and modern high-rises were the alleys of poverty where people lived without electricity and running water. Those who could afford it had moved beyond the city's confines, finding homes in gated communities sprouting outside of Cairo's borders. They lived their lives with satellite dishes, the internet, and trips to the various malls. Their children attended elite private schools, and they found entertainment at exclusive clubs. They created seclusion, encapsulating themselves away from the suffocating crowds and stifling air of the city.

At each meeting, Fathy heard the passion of another person's voice, and he saw the heads nodding around the room, but he felt nothing in response. Perhaps this had never been his country, his place. He felt no investment in its future; he was a mere observer in that room. He knew that he couldn't gather the naivete or bravery necessary to participate. But his status set the expectation that he would be a leader in this movement.

He was one of a handful of Copts at the meeting, and there was talk about how to bring Muslims and Copts together, to see this as a fight for all Egyptians, to create unity. Fathy's father was one of the few Copts he knew who didn't speak badly about Muslims, but in the gatherings with the rest of his family, he heard the bitterness and anger that came with living as second-class citizens in their own country, in the way the conversations trailed back to the invasion of the Arabs in 639 AD, the imposition of the Arabic language, the pressure to convert to Islam, and the fines required of those who didn't convert. The grudge of the past was still held close among Copts, remembered as if the injustices happened during their lifetimes. But as the meetings and online forums grew, more Copts joined, and the rise of "we are all egyptians" dominated the call to action. Over eighty thousand people pledged their support for the day of rage on Facebook.

He began to wonder if this could work. Could there be real change in Egypt? But Fathy doubted his own patriotism. Could he stand in Tahrir among other Egyptians? He felt removed, as if he were living the wrong life, in the wrong place, like wearing an ill-fitted suit with sleeves too long and pants too tight. He couldn't release the feeling that the thread of his existence wound back to the America his father had inhabited. But would America fit? Would it wrap itself around the configuration of his body?

After he entered the lottery, he began scrolling through the internet. He liked to look up woodworkers, browsing through their images. He was intrigued by the ones who worked with the natural shape of the wood, keeping its ridges, its gradations of color, creating a table, a chair, a desk out of its natural curves and texture. A synergy of nature and function. As he viewed the various websites, his hands would begin to itch as if searching for that sensation of touch, wanting to feel the grain of roughness turning to smoothness under his fingertips. Sometimes, he would become distracted by looking at the hands of the woodworker, the large, bent knuckles, hands that revealed what they had created. Many of the woodworkers seemed to be in Virginia and North Carolina, and that area began to intrigue him. There were workshops, classes, and apprenticeships. In America, you could learn anything. Could he erase the past, begin with a blank slate, like a tree trunk, and turn it into a new life?

* * *

ON JANUARY 1, 2011, A BOMB EXPLODES AT THE AL-QIDDISSIN CHURCH IN ALEXANDRIA. IT STRIKES THE CHURCH AROUND MIDNIGHT WHILE PARISHIONERS ARE CELEBRATING THE NEW YEAR IN WORSHIP. THE EXPLOSION IS SET OFF BY A SUICIDE BOMBER OUTSIDE THE CHURCH. TWENTY-ONE PEOPLE ARE KILLED AND AT LEAST SEVENTY INJURED.

THE CRASHING SOUND ERUPTS IN THE CHURCH TOWARD THE END OF THE LITURGY AS THE PRIEST INTONES THE FINAL PRAYER. THE GROUND SHAKES AND PUSHES EVERYONE BACK. THERE IS A CHAOS OF MOVEMENT, AND PEOPLE STRUGGLE TO LEAVE UNTIL THEY FIND THEMSELVES OUTSIDE WITHIN A CROWD OF WAILS AND SCREAMS. EVERYONE IS BEWILDERED, AS IF FLOATING ABOVE THE WORLD, THE SCREAMS STILL SOUNDING IN THEIR EARS.

That New Year's Eve, Fathy stayed alone in his Heliopolis apartment, drifting from wakefulness to sleep while the television hummed in the background. A little after midnight, the raised voices coming from the screen brought him to full waking. The erratic shouts and scrambling feet and blasting caught his attention, although the screen only showed smoke in the midst of broken pews.

Early in the morning, he caught a taxi and made his way to Mohandessein. The rest of the family had spent the night at his parents' home, celebrating the new year. They woke together to find the news that had already reverberated through the Coptic community, striking new fear. It unsteadied all of them, their sense of security shattered. Fathy's mother ran to ring her sister who lived in Alexandria, and the family stood around her, holding in their breath, ready to catch her should she fall. When the ringing finally stopped and their aunt's voice entered the phone from the other end, a collective release escaped.

Fathy walked away from the circle surrounding his mother's phone conversation. "this country will kill us all," he mumbled under his breath.

But his father caught his words and threw them back. "these things happen in every country. look at amreeka, with people who shoot children in schools."

Fathy turned to face his father, who was now sitting in his chair. His father's belief in his country boiled under Fathy's skin and gave rise to his voice. He knew that his father still believed Egypt was the mother of the world, "om el dunya," as everyone said. His father had grown up in the lap of a country infused with the cosmopolitan air of Jews, Greeks, Muslims, and Christians living alongside each other, exchanging the fruits of their labor.

Fathy looked at the man who had raised him, who had outlined his life even before his birth, and released his voice. “this is not the same country that you were raised in. the government doesn’t care about copts. they will protect us from nothing. all the people in this country are hungry. even those who have degrees are not making salaries that can satisfy their needs. no one is able to get married because they don’t have the money to buy an apartment.”

“you have an apartment. if you don’t get married, maybe we should give your apartment to someone who needs it.” His father’s words spat out across the living room.

Fathy’s mother and sisters stood at the kitchen doorway. His eldest sister opened her mouth, but her mother placed her hand on her shoulder to dissuade her.

“there is more than one way to live in the world,” Fathy said, lowering his tone.

“you’re a fool. when you get older, you’ll understand.”

“each generation is not like the last,” Fathy said, releasing steam with his words. “you took your life and arranged it as you wanted. now it’s my turn.”

“there’s no choice in this world.” Farid’s voice released itself. “there are rules and morals to be followed.”

“there are no morals. look at our leaders, each more corrupt than the other, and there is still a monarchy. mubarak has been in power for thirty years, and his son will come after him. they are holding the country in their fist and crushing all of us.”

“the smart ones always find a way to succeed.”

Fathy tried to hold the words in, but they escaped. “you succeeded through your connections. no one in this country succeeds through merit. you have to go to amreeka for that.”

“there is no gold on the trees in amreeka. you stay and build your own country.”

“can’t you see? it’s already crumbling. the country was shattered in ’67 and nothing has rebuilt it. we’re back to tribal wars, and copts are just the easiest enemy. you lived during the times of kings and queens. you were named after the last king when everyone wanted to be like british royalty. that freedom of ’52 came to nothing. and every revolution in this country will come to nothing.”

“we eliminated the british and won our freedom. the country is ours now. it has been sixty years and . . .”

Fathy stopped him before he ended his sentence. “sixty years and what do we have—poverty, overpopulation, people with degrees driving taxis, and only a few can reach the taste of meat.”

“i gave you everything—food to fill your belly, the best education, a job, an apartment. what more do you want?”

"the freedom to choose. i want to make something with my own hands, not be given something on a silver platter. you sit on your chair and think you rule the world. but you're not a king."

Farid heaved his body forward in the chair, his arm gesturing to encircle the apartment. "i built a home and a family, and now in your hand is an apartment, a car, a job."

Fathy looked at his father for a moment, a feeling of pity overcoming him. His father was in his early seventies, and, for the first time, Fathy noted the age in his body, the way his back naturally curved into the position of sitting every day. He wanted to say I'm sorry, but he swallowed the words. Instead, he spewed his anger, hoping for some relief from what he had been carrying.

"at least in amreeka, the poor can sometimes become rich, and honest work still has some value. at least one's future is not written at their birth. at least a human being can make something. i want to create with my hands, to know that by my own ability i have made something in the world, not this foolery of money exchanging hands, not this waste of a job with nothing to show what i have done. i want to offer sustenance to another being, a chair to sit on, a piece of bread that nourishes."

"you reject everything i've given you. emshee, go away, you don't deserve what you have."

After his father spouted the words, Fathy folded into himself, as if he could no longer keep his hand in his pocket hiding what he held.

"i'm leaving," Fathy said, his tone flat. "i won the lottery."

Fathy had told no one when he received the news. When he opened the letter, he saw a door opening, but it didn't seem possible he could actually walk through it. Yet, he had followed instructions, filled out and submitted the necessary documentation. A few weeks ago, he had gone for the interview. He knew that his education, his knowledge of English, his social status—all of which had resulted from what his father had given him—enabled him to be accepted. He had received the final approval only a few days ago. He hesitated, unsure of what to do, balancing on the seesaw between helping to plan for the revolution and preparing his papers for departure. He had slipped the letter in his pocket, thinking perhaps that was the end of it, that he would continue as if it had not happened. But now as he spoke the words aloud, he knew he had made his decision.

For a moment, the world held still. No cars honking their horns, no cart sellers shouting the value of their wares, no children in the street yelling their games. The father glared at the son, and the son kept his gaze steady. Inside the kitchen, three people held their breath.

"you've won nothing," his father said.

Yusef's Arrival

The call from Yusef came early on January 20 just as light filtered through the sky, clawing its way through the layers of pollution that had come to settle permanently over the city. I was an early riser even though I was now retired. My days no longer followed a routine, and I enjoyed the freedom that gave me. My grandson was not yet school age, and my son dropped him off each morning so my wife and I could care for him. I enjoyed having the child around. Even at the age of three, he showed an aptitude for mechanical things. We bought him a set of Legos, and he and I locked and unlocked the pieces together to create new shapes.

I ran errands for my wife, who preferred to avoid the hassle of the crowded streets and having to negotiate for each item. I enjoyed making my way from the butcher to the fruit seller to the fishmonger. People greeted me, laughing as they said "fanous, you light the world," playing on the idea of my name, which means "lantern." Despite the city's rising population and the depression that came with the escalating inflation, I managed to elicit a smile or a laugh from the vendors, who threw in an extra potato or a few additional oranges into my parcel.

That morning when I picked up the phone, expecting it might be my cousin Khalil, I heard a voice that I couldn't place, its Arabic somewhat stilted, yet the urgency of it let me know I needed to figure out this caller.

"i'm yusef," the voice repeated, and I tried to place the name within some context. Finally, the voice said, "the son of hafez and layla."

"yusef, ya ibni, are you well? are your parents well? is there anything wrong?"

Assurance came from the other side of the phone along with a request: "i'm in the airport. can you come get me, uncle?"

My mind couldn't match the voice with a location. "which airport?" I asked.

"here, here in egypt, the cairo airport."

"mish maoul!" I said, astounded at the impossibility of it, and added, "i'm coming, immediately. i'll meet you at the luggage area."

I arrived at the suitcase carousel and spotted the tall, slender man whose features carried the piercing eyes of his father and the easy smile of his mother. He seemed to sway slightly, as if even a soft breeze might cause him to move in a different direction. I didn't have to ask if it was him and immediately embraced him.

In the car, I rattled off my questions about Hafez and Layla and Hala and Nessim and Magda and Lutfi and why he was here even before we made our way out of the airport lot.

"they're well. everyone's fine. they send their greetings," Yusef answered.

He seemed hesitant, and I wondered if there was something he wasn't revealing. He rolled down the window and inhaled the city with its noise and pollution.

"the country has changed," I offered. "everything is chaos, not like amreeka."

Yusef turned in my direction. "have you heard anything?"

"what do you mean?" I asked.

Yusef tried again. "i mean the people are unhappy. there is talk of an uprising on January twenty-fifth."

I gurgled a laugh. "the people are never happy, and there are always plans."

Yusef seemed to swallow the rest of his questions.

"and what will you do here?" I asked.

He shifted in his seat and placed his hands beneath him. "i just wanted to visit. i missed all of you, and i had some vacation from work."

As we neared the end of Airport Road, it occurred to me that Yusef had not given me a destination. I looked at this young man who couldn't seem to settle his body comfortably, fidgeting in the seat, and was reluctant to release him.

"you have to stay with us," I said. "we have plenty of space. you know my son got married, and his room is empty."

Yusef turned to look at me with a sense of gratefulness as if I had just rescued him from falling into a hole. "thank you," he said. "if it's not a problem."

"we would love to have you," I answered, turning the car in the right direction.

Yusef / Joseph – 2011

When Yusef opened his computer on January 1, 2011, there were myriad messages coming through on his Facebook—talk of change, a new year, a revolution, a gathering to demonstrate. He wondered if this upheaval of desire for change would dissipate by tomorrow, if it was just fired up by the beginning of a new year. But the next day and the next, the messages multiplied, and a plan was taking shape. He knew that life in Egypt was not easy. He heard from his cousins about the difficulty of finding a job, making enough money to get married, the rising inflation that was squeezing them tight. "the frustration is boiling in the country," one person wrote. "we're coming together as a nation—copt, muslim, men, women, all of us are going to gather in tahrir. join us!" Those last two words stuck in Yusef's throat. He walked around with them, unable to swallow.

* ⁂ *

At the age of eight, Yusef held his mother's hand tightly, glad to have something to anchor him. He feared that if he let go, he would be swept into this sea of people and never found again. His older sister, Amal, was trailing alongside their father, Hafez, who was walking ahead. Yusef's imagination of Egypt had fluctuated between a room full of people who looked like his parents and a landscape of sand with three pyramids rising symmetrically in the distance like the pictures he had seen in his third-grade history book.

Instead, the noise and chaos of Cairo's airport surrounded him, a cacophony of incongruous instruments. They made their way to a line of people until they were moving in slow steps toward the desk with the officer.

Yusef found it hard to take a full breath, the smell of smoke and dirt and sweat filling his nostrils. He noticed there were two lines. In the line across from them stood people who all looked American, but something was different. They stepped from one foot to the other like a seesaw, they kept looking over their shoulders, and they whispered to each other in voices that hesitated. This was different from the people he was accustomed to seeing, like his teachers, who stood tall and spoke with strong voices, who never hesitated when they told him what he had to do.

He turned to look down the line where they stood and saw people who looked like his parents, well-dressed, their voices like air balloons, expanding with words. Outside of their house, when he heard his parents speaking English, their voices rose an octave, and each sentence ended in a slightly higher pitch as if it were more a question than a statement. Yusef looked back and forth between the two lines and felt the balance of the world shift.

He tried to listen, but the sounds came at him too quickly. He caught words he knew, but there was something larger he couldn't quite grasp. With his parents, he had spoken Arabic since he was a child, the sounds emerging from his throat like a continuous string of musical notes. He lived inside that language for his first years, his days spent with his mother until his father came home in the evening. When they saw other people, they spoke the same language, and only occasionally did he hear the utterance of an English word, but it was stitched into their own language, and he did not recognize the difference.

It wasn't until he entered kindergarten that English assaulted him. It came in the uproar of children running around a room without reprimand, no adult telling them to be quiet. It came in the monotone pitch of a teacher's voice, which made it difficult for him to distinguish whether he was being praised or punished. He responded with Arabic words, but there was no recognition on the listener's face, so he retreated into silence.

Finding himself in this swelter of new words, he learned to use his eyes, observe every movement, so when the teacher spoke, he focused on the other children, followed their lead and learned to imitate, standing in line with them and moving in the same direction or lying down and closing his eyes in the middle of the day. During recess, he cowered at the edge of the playground. If another child approached him, he shook his head, as he had learned that this would make the other child go away. He lived in silence for that year.

When he returned for first grade, the words around him began to untangle, and he found that he could decipher meaning. It was about halfway through the year that he heard himself speaking, finding new words in his throat.

Now, the sounds of Arabic beating against the walls of the airport came like a drumroll to his ears. This was more Arabic than he was used to hearing, and he had difficulty catching the strains of conversation around him. The line they were in moved steadily. When they reached the desk, his parents handed the officer four American passports. He looked at them and said something, of which Yusef only caught "masrieen," which he knew meant "Egyptian." His father responded with what Yusef could decipher as an excuse and apology until the officer stamped their passports and waved them off with "welcome to your country."

A frantic chaos surrounded the luggage area as people realized their suitcases had not arrived. His mother had spent the last three months with three suitcases open in their living room. For a while, she dropped the shopping bags she came back with almost daily in one of the suitcases as if they would pack themselves into an acceptable arrangement. In the end, the three suitcases had been fully stuffed with clothes being used to wrap presents.

Yusef didn't understand all the presents. When he inquired, his mother said, "this is the correct way." It was an answer his questions often received. Now they stood around the creaky carousel, waiting for the luggage to make its appearance. His father's posture was rigid, as if by his very stance, he could command the suitcases to arrive. His mother still held his hand, but not as firmly. Her glance followed the movement of the carousel, settling momentarily on each piece of luggage. Some bags had come unzipped, their contents poking out of the unexpected opening. Some were strangled with rope or tape, binding them to remain intact. His parents had purchased three new American suitcases that were meant to survive this journey. He saw his father reach for one of them, releasing it from the monotonous circle of movement. Then his mother let go of his hand to point to another one approaching them, and their father reached confidently to grasp it. Yusef wanted to find the last one. It felt heroic, and he wanted his parents to be pleased with him. But after a few minutes, the last one appeared, and his father moved to grab it before Yusef could point to it.

They left the luggage carousel behind with people's agitated voices rising in complaint at their suitcases not arriving. Yusef felt the relief escape from his mother's fingers as she held his hand again. When they stepped through another set of doors, his ears caught his parents' names, "hafez! layla!" He looked around to locate the voice. A man with the same large brown eyes as his mother and wearing a beret stood waving. He looked a little older than his mother, but his movements carried an unexpected energy. Yusef was engulfed into the weight of this man, who introduced himself as his uncle Fanous and kissed him on both cheeks, saying "mesh maoul, mesh maoul. akheeren." As if something impossible that he had been waiting for had finally arrived. Yusef stood aside as both his mother and father blended into the man's body.

In the car, he leaned against the window as they drove through the city. He looked at the rectangular apartment buildings that floated up and down, the balconies that hung over the sidewalks, and the water of the Nile that disappeared and reappeared as they drove. No thoughts passed through his mind; only images entered and entwined into the synapses of his brain. When they arrived at his uncle's house, his aunt embraced him and held him so long he thought his breath would suffocate. She was a solid woman who spoke with an air of authority, ushering them in, telling them they were tired and needed to sleep, that the rest of the family would arrive in the afternoon.

As soon as Yusef laid his head down on the small bed set up for him in the same room as his parents, his eyes closed into a dreamless slumber. When he awoke, for a moment he thought he was in his room at home, that he would open his eyes to see his jeans and sneakers on the floor, his desk cluttered with Superman comic books, and the window looking out to the pine tree in their backyard. Instead, the smell of onions and garlic entered his nostrils. His long lashes fluttered open, and his mind replayed the long flight, the stopover in London Heathrow, and their final descent.

He heard the clamor of voices outside the room and picked out the sound of his parents, although he noted the difference in their intonations. Their words came quicker, the rhythm stronger and more secure. When he entered the living room, he saw that the apartment had filled with more people. Someone noticed him, and he was passed from one to the other, embraced in arms and kissed multiple times until he felt like a puppet pulled by strings. Then he was pushed toward a group of children who looked at him quietly for a second until one of them said, "what games you play in amreeka?"

Yusef shrugged, unable to recall a game he had played with other children. "tag," he said almost as a question.

"ok," someone else said, "we'll play cops and robbers."

And they scrambled toward the door. Yusef stood confused by the movement until a boy about his age grabbed his hand and pulled him into the avalanche of children.

They took over the courtyard in front of the building, and Yusef was made the jail guard to ease him into the game. But soon he was chasing and running with the others, having figured out the rules. Arabic words tumbled out of his mouth as if they had been gathering there waiting to break free. At home, when he and his parents spoke Arabic, their words came out quietly with pauses, as if the sound of English all day had damaged them. He didn't know he could speak so fast or so loud. He heard his name shouted back and forth—not "Joseph," as his teachers and classmates called him, but "Yusef," as his parents had intended. In the hospital when they said the name, the nurse had looked at them quizzically. They explained that it was like "Joseph," and that was the name the nurse wrote on his birth certificate.

Once they were summoned back inside, he found himself sitting on the floor with a plate full of stuffed grape leaves, lamb, and potatoes. He picked up his fork but saw that everyone was eating the grape leaves with their hands, dipping them in the yogurt sauce, then plopping them into their mouths.

Within a week, Yusef had shifted worlds, and the America he had lived in for the first eight years of his life receded, never to fully return. Here, each day filled with family, and while he did not always understand his relationship to each person, he knew that he belonged. His cousins had opened a space and allowed him to enter. In America, he remained on the periphery, the other kids always wary of his darker looks, his inability to catch their jokes, his silence when they made fun of other kids.

They had come to Egypt for a month during his summer vacation, and each day he gathered with the other children. In the morning, his aunt cut a mango into squares for him, and he slurped it into his mouth, the syrup dripping down his chin. The days were hot with the sun beating heavily. His sweat smelled different, a heavier scent that was released when he took off his clothes. When his parents said they were leaving the next day, he stared at them as if he had forgotten there was anywhere else to go.

As Yusef headed to work, the rain drizzled steadily, the sky a pale gray fading into white. What few leaves were left on the trees fluttered, preparing to let go of the branches that still held them. He drove through the morning streets until he reached the high school in Concord where he taught.

Inside the classroom, Yusef looked at his students, heads bent over the surprise quiz he had just distributed. They were studying World War II, and he sensed that no one was doing the reading, so he gave them the quiz. The second half of the year was filled with wars—beginning with World Wars I and II, the Korean War, the Vietnam War, and the Gulf War—until they toppled over each other, gaining less meaning from one to the next. All these wars were distant both in time and geography for his students. They took place in some country they only imagined as a barren landscape. Events that changed the course of the world and people's lives held little meaning for the students who sat in front of him. Most of them were raised in this quiet suburb imbued with the meditative introspection of Emerson and Thoreau, who had also lived here. They grew up in spacious homes with parents who provided food, shelter, emotional support, and a belief that their existence in the world was guaranteed.

As his students struggled over the unexpected quiz, Yusef thought back to the '67 war—if it had not taken place, perhaps his parents would not have left, perhaps he would be the person he was meant to be. That war always stood at his back, pushing him. He had only heard about his uncle Kamel's death from his mother. His father never spoke of it, and his mother told him not to ask. It sat as an invisible layer beneath their lives. Wars changed the trajectory of people's paths, redirected them like his parents and others who felt the disillusionment of the war as permanent and wanted to leave it behind.

At the end of class, the students filed out, leaving their quizzes on his desk. He heard the shuffle of their feet, paralleling the rhythm of the rain falling outside. As the last two students stepped out into the hallway, he heard one say to the other, "History is so boring. Nothing ever really changes."

* ⁂ *

When they entered their house after returning from Egypt, Yusef heard his mother say, "it feels so different." And he understood that it did not really belong to them, that it would never be home. Yusef stopped trying to fit in with the other kids, kept to himself in the schoolyard, often bringing a Superman comic book to keep others from approaching him. For a month he had not spoken English, and now the words felt like sand on his tongue. He did not want to lose the Arabic words he had found, so he chose silence.

At home, when his father read the newspaper and said there was news about Egypt, Yusef would cut out the article and put it in a scrapbook. Over the years, he wrote letters to his cousins in Egypt and occasionally talked to them on the phone. Every time he heard their voices on the other end, a sense of comfort seeped into him. When email became available, he spent hours back and forth in conversation until each morning he had to remind himself where he was.

His parents promised they would make another visit, but each year, the scale of their responsibilities weighed them down. Something always seemed to be tugging at their finances—paying for new appliances, getting a car for Amal, saving for college tuition, buying a nicer home—so eventually Yusef stopped asking. Each time they made a call to Egypt, he saw his parents' faces open with joy until the conversation ended and a curtain fell over their features.

* ⁂ *

On January 7, Coptic Christmas, Yusef woke at six in the morning, which meant it was already one in the afternoon in Egypt. He got on Facebook to check the new posts. Along with wishes for a happy Feast Day, he saw that plans were taking clearer shape. He had joined a Facebook group for the revolution. A demonstration was planned on January 25, part of the movement to dismantle the government and oust Mubarak. Now, with these political developments, he began to read more about Egypt's economy, its transition from a socialist to a capitalist country, the influence of America's imperialism, and the IMF that gave money with one hand and made demands with the other. He followed the messages, the discussions, the gathering momentum, and for the first time he felt energized. Despite having spent only one month of his life in Egypt, the country called up a sense of loyalty in him that he could only describe as patriotism.

Yusef often wondered why his sister didn't feel the same way. She was born only a few months after his parents arrived in America, and they had named her Amal, for "hope." As soon as she entered preschool at the age of two, she came to be known as Amy and planted herself firmly in her new culture. Perhaps her brown hair and the green eyes she inherited from their father allowed her to move easily between school and home. She was pleased with whatever she was offered—food, toys, clothes. Everything gave her joy, and she took and gave easily. Even in preschool, she came to be known as the child always willing to share her toys. She had no fear of loss, unlike Yusef and his parents, who held on to everything even beyond its usefulness or beauty. Their basement filled with Yusef's discarded toys. When his mother asked if he wanted to get rid of a toy, he hesitated, reaching for it as if it might evaporate, and so it landed in the basement with so many other things—the broken blender they might fix one day, the crockpot they used only a few times, the frayed towels that might still be useful, the old window shades in case the new ones broke.

By the time they made their trip to Egypt, Amal was already sixteen, in the midst of adolescence. Unlike Yusef, who never made close friends, his sister brought friends into their home as if theirs was no different from any other household. She went to parties and was involved in after-school activities, pulling their parents into American life. In Egypt, she took in the family, the food, and the scenery easily, knowing it was only a moment before she would return to her normal life. After they returned, she bought their mother *The Joy of Cooking* for her birthday and gently guided her to American food, offering to help her. Yusef now came home from school to find an apple pie on the counter, a plate of chocolate chip cookies, banana bread coming out of the oven.

Amal went to Boston College, majored in biology, and went on to nursing school, adapting easily to the role of helping others. She eventually married an American doctor. They lived nearby, and already she had a son and a daughter their parents doted on. It seemed to Yusef that Amal had broken through something and come out on the other side. Her children had inherited just enough Egyptian traits to make them appealing but not harm them. Amal's daughter had the long lashes and full lips. Her son had piercing dark eyes. Both tanned easily, but no one asked where they were from. They blended in easily, and at home nothing disrupted their sense of belonging.

English was the only language in their lives. Hummus and pomegranates had made it to the supermarkets of America, and the fact that they ate them did not distinguish them in any way.

* ⁂ *

Yusuf attended UMass Amherst, and although he lived on campus, he made few friends, mostly those who also had homes in other countries. He dated a little but never went past a few dates, letting go before anything deeper could develop. He attended classes, found some good professors, did well, but he knew that no one would really remember him once he left. When he told his parents that he would major in history, the silence on the other end of the phone expressed their disappointment. "What about science or math?" his father asked, and Yusef could tell he tried to keep his voice from rising in judgement. "I'm just not very good at them," responded Yusef. They spoke in English, their words clipped, providing an emotional distance that kept the conversation from escalating. "What will you do with this major?" asked his mother. Yusef was only a sophomore, and he had not yet gathered some vision of himself as an independent adult, so he responded with the only thing he knew. "I can teach," he said.

It seemed a natural path. He found a small efficiency apartment in Dorchester and enrolled in the teaching program at UMass Boston. Then he acquired a job at the high school in Concord, and it seemed his life had settled. His parents were relieved that he had secured a job, although his father often asked how much he was saving, reminding him of the cost of raising a family, the importance of saving for retirement.

Yusef spent most of his spare time reading about Egyptian history. His knowledge of the Ottoman Empire, French and British colonialism, the 1952 revolution, and the wars that followed was extensive. But he had little opportunity to put any of that to use in his classroom, as the expectation was to teach his students a set of dates and events all related to US history that they could regurgitate on their tests.

Yusef thought of the city he lived in and tried to imagine spending the rest of his life in it. Boston had spread out beyond its center, each suburb becoming its own enclave, providing everything for its residents, so they could live secluded lives within the illusion of wealth and safety. When the housing market skyrocketed, people earned money overnight, creating a culture of materialism that fed on itself. Despite its diverse population, Boston remained entrenched in its racial segregation. His darker complexion and features marked him as an outsider everywhere he went.

Each day of Yusef's life passed as a flat note. He went to work, he had lunch with the other teachers, he went home to grade papers, and on the weekends, he went to see his parents. Nothing of significance distinguished one day from the other, and his life remained in a kind of stasis. His parents urged him toward marriage, but he never mentioned the few women he dated.

The last time his family had dinner together, Amal dragged him to her old bedroom and asked about his love life.

"There isn't any," he laughed.

"You know Mom and Dad want you to get married," she said, plopping down on her old bed and patting the mattress next to her so he would sit down.

"I haven't met anyone," Yusef answered, sitting with his back straight.

"You're always so secretive." Amal punched him playfully in the arm. "No one knows what you're thinking."

"Maybe I'm just not thinking," Yusef said, relaxing his posture.

"Well, do you want to marry an Egyptian or an American?" she asked.

"Doesn't it depend on the person?" Yusef said, looking seriously at her.

"I think it depends on the life you want. Our parents still live as if they were in Egypt, as much as they complain about it. Where do you want to be?" Amal ran her hand through her hair, pulling at the ends. Yusef had noticed that she had cut it up to her shoulders, and now she seemed to be trying to pull it back to its longer length.

"I don't know." And then to eliminate the question, he added, "Why don't you just let me know when you find the right woman for me?"

At dinner, he broached the subject of the revolution. But his father waved his hand as if it were a small fly to be swatted.

"nothing will change in that country. every year is worse than the one that passed."

"but there are a lot of people behind this revolution, and everyone is working together," Yusef said as his mother placed the fish she had made on each of their plates.

"don't be naive," his father responded, reaching for a spoonful of bulgur. "muslims and christians will never work together."

"but all of them want mubarak to leave," Yusef said.

There was a pause as his father chewed, and Amal and her husband focused on helping their children with their food.

Before his father could respond, his mother's voice chimed in, "and then what, someone else like him or worse than him will come?"

Yusef focused his eyes on his plate, picking the thorns out of the fish.

When he went home that night, he once again opened the Facebook page. There was heightened discussion about the goals of the revolution and the list of demands that would be presented to the government. The energy of the conversations seeped into him as he scrolled down until he came to a post that said "We invite all Egyptians in all countries to stand with us."

* ⁂ *

He had not returned to Egypt since his visit at the age of eight, and the possibility remained like a folded piece of paper in his pocket. At times, he felt as if he were still there, as if he had left himself behind, standing in the airport, waving to the other self that was leaving with his parents.

One night, inside of a dream, he found himself crouched on the floor of his apartment carving out part of the wall, cutting through the layers of plaster and wood to make a square opening. He crawled through it, and on the other side, he landed in his aunt's living room. His aunt invited him in as if it were all ordinary, as if it were that easy to step from one world to the other.

For the next week, he walked around as if he had dislocated himself. He had to ask students to repeat their answers, and colleagues had to call his name twice to get his attention. It became difficult to disconnect his worlds. The messages on social media shifted from general plans to particular details—where to meet, where first aid would be available, where water could be found. Everything was being organized by young people. It was estimated that seventy-five percent of the population was under the age of twenty-five. It was the revolution of the young.

Yusef wondered if there was a place for him in all of this. So many years had passed. He knew he couldn't claim knowledge of what it was like to live in Egypt. He had carried his parents' memories of Egypt, the brief visit he had made as a child, and the historical knowledge he had accumulated through his readings. But he knew life and books were not the same. Still, he felt something tugging at him as each day he became more immersed in what appeared on his screen.

He requested a week off, claiming a family emergency. *Just a week,* he thought. He wanted to see what would happen. If this revolution took place, what would it bring for the country? He wanted to be part of it, to experience this desire for change, for transformation, for the making of history. Within a day, he bought his ticket and packed a small bag. He didn't tell his parents or his sister that he was going.

* ⁂ *

During his layover in Switzerland, he went to a duty-free shop and purchased ten boxes of chocolate. He recalled his mother's frantic search for gifts when they had come years ago, and something told him that he should not arrive empty-handed.

He arrived in Egypt on January 20. For four days, he walked the streets, trying to overlay his childhood memories with what he now saw. The population had increased by millions, and he could feel the thickening of humanity as he moved through the streets. But he felt steady on his feet, as if he had walked the terrain of these streets and sidewalks all his life. As soon as he entered his uncle's home, he felt his family's embrace pull him in, as if a chair had been waiting for him all these years. The cousins he had played with when he was eight had grown like him, but their early shared experience bonded them, and he fit in again like they were still kids playing cops and robbers.

He had heard his parents reminisce about the easy pace of life when they were growing up, how the workday ended at two or three, so people could return home for the midday meal and a rest before going out in the evening. Now everyone worked longer hours and often had two jobs. Each breath the nation took rose from its breast, heavy with effort.

Going to the supermarket with one of his cousins, he saw evidence for the complaints about rising prices. He approached the deli counter and asked for a kilo of roomi cheese, remembering its sharp taste from his childhood, and found that it was fifty pounds—for him, that was ten dollars, but for his family, it had almost the same value as fifty dollars. He listened to his older relatives speak of politics, their vision extending beyond the thirty years that Mubarak had been in office. "we've gone from kings to presidents, but nothing has changed," they said.

When he talked about the upcoming revolution, no one seemed to believe it would happen, and he feared he had been gullible to have faith in what he had read on the internet. "it will not conclude in anything," they said. "everyone is frustrated, but what are we going to do? this is life." The resignation of their voices saddened him. He wanted to believe that something could happen. That this revolution would rise.

On January 24, he felt the country's pulse quickening. There was an urgency in people's movements, although nothing moved quickly. Cars made their way like snails in the congested streets, and a taxi ride from one location to another that should have taken twenty minutes extended through the heavy traffic, taking well over an hour. The roads overflowed with the old, creaking black-and-white taxis along with the new white taxis outfitted with air conditioning and working meters. It seemed every college graduate unable to get a job was driving a taxi through this maze of streets. Each time, he heard the same story—"i studied business at cairo university, but now this taxi is my business." Yusef wondered if this is what would have happened to him. Could he be one of these taxi drivers making his way through the winding streets of the city?

On January 25, Yusef woke early, before anyone else had risen, to make his way to Tahrir Square. As soon as he stepped outside, a piercing cold air entered his body. The quietness felt unnatural. Barely a car on the road, no taxis honking, no one walking. In this city pulsating with the movement of life at all hours, it felt unnatural for there to be so much space and silence. At the corner of 9th Street, he waited ten minutes until a taxi came by and he flagged it down. The cab driver responded to Yusef's "sabah el kheir" and then fixed his eyes on the road. Yusef could tell the older man was not inclined to talk, so he entered the quietness with the rest of the city. The driver let him off on Qasr el Aini Street by Garden City and said, “i won’t be able to get you any further than this.” Yusef nodded and handed him the fare.

Bashir and Salima – 2011

The light comes through the clouds of pollution and layers over the city on the morning of January 24. Buildings glimmer, and a draft of muted sun enters the shops. Bashir picks up Salima at the same house in Maadi where he had left her just under a month ago.

When he dropped her off, she had asked him to pick her up in four weeks, and he had given her his mobile number. When she called, he didn't recognize her voice immediately. Her Arabic flowed easily now, the words carrying the same harmony as those who had lived here their whole lives. She asked him to come a week earlier than planned, explaining that she had changed her flight.

"tabaan, tabaan. of course, i will be there," he said when she asked if he could take her to the airport.

When she emerges from the building, instead of the one suitcase, she is dragging two suitcases bulging with their contents. The new suitcase was clearly bought here, a cheap leather imitation with wheels already struggling under the weight and a zipper threatening to surrender its duties. Bashir looks at Salima and sees that her angular lines have filled in, achieving a soft roundness that reveals her beauty.

He approaches to help her, and she lets him take each suitcase and place it in the trunk.

"shokran, ya bashir," she thanks him as he opens the door for her, and she settles into the back seat.

"did you spend a good visit?" he asks as he pulls into the street.
"yes," she says and repeats it again. "yes, it was a good visit."

* ⁂ *

Only three weeks ago, Salima had knocked unexpectedly on Fanous's door. Even before the words "i'm salima" escaped her lips, she was engulfed into his arms. She recalled her uncle Fanous as a young, slender man, but now he had become solid and full. Yet, he moved with the confidence of having built his life with effort and pride. She knew he had become the official driver to the airport as one family member after the other left. Perhaps his body had grown heavier with each person he dropped off at the airport, as if he carried the heft of their hope and their ambition and the grief they left behind with their absence.

He insisted she stay at his house. That evening, Fanous's children and their families and Fanous's cousin Khalil and his children and their families all arrived. There was Fanous's son and daughter, Bassem and Deena, both married with their own children, and Khalil's two sons, Galal and Labib, also with their own families. Salima found herself embraced within a space of family as if a seat had been saved for her all these years.

For the next three weeks, her relatives took her into their homes, welcomed her back as one of their own. It was disorienting to be accepted so easily when her life in America had taught her to remain on the outskirts.

As Salima entered their lives, she came to know each of them. Fanous's wife, Salwa, moved with ease in the roundness of her body. But Salima could see that she carried her trials like a purse over her shoulder. Each day, her aunt cooked, and Salima ate the food of her childhood, from grape leaves to stuffed eggplant to molekhia. Khalil's wife, Mervat, who had grown up in Aswan, brought feteer that made Salima's mouth water as soon as she caught a whiff of its doughy aroma. They took her to the pyramids, to Khan el Khalili, and to Ain Sokhna, where she swam in the purity of the Red Sea.

* ⁂ *

"and how is your family?" asks Bashir as he makes his way through the dawn-lit streets of Maadi.

"alhamdulillah, they're good."

* ⁂ *

It was the closest she could come to an answer. Fanous and Khalil had built their families and joined them together. And she had thought that Farid and his children were all well when she visited them. The whole family had gathered at Uncle Farid's house, the table spread with an assortment of food that reached its edges. It was a gathering that stretched back to her grandmother Fayza and her brothers Sa'ad and Malek—bonds that lasted through time, stitching together the family in this living room. But toward the end of her visit, she heard that Fathy was leaving, that Farid would not speak to his son, that his mother was distraught.

It was seeing what was left of her uncle Hafez's family that sat uneasily with her. One Sunday morning, Fanous took her to the house in Old Cairo, where she was greeted by Amin along with his mother; his wife, Samira; and his daughter. They sat together between the empty walls. A Coptic calendar hung on the door of one room, the brightly colored figure of the saint the only splotch of color among the faded grays.

Amin's face was withdrawn, and he looked older than his age, the passage of time having marked him. He rested against the back of a wooden chair, wearing slippers and a jacket around his shoulders. His eyes followed his mother's every movement, and he guided her steps, handed her what she needed.

Samira sat stiffly on her chair and remained quiet except for saying, "we are so happy that you came. our daughter doesn't know anyone from the family." Her daughter, whom she had dressed in her best clothes, was polished and shiny, with her hair pulled back into a tight ponytail, her face eager as she greeted the aunt from America.

Amin's mother was pale and moved with slow steps. Her fingers were thin, an awkward contrast to the weight of her body, and her graying hair was pulled back into a bun. She seemed ill at ease, as if she were pulling at an outer shell to release herself.

They sat at the table in the small living room and offered Salima a meal of fried potatoes and chicken. Amin's mother asked if she knew about the appearance of the Virgin Mary, and she shook her heard. A few minutes later, she asked again if she knew about the Virgin Mary. Salima wondered if this was the beginning of dementia or the stale voice of someone who speaks to few people.

Salima felt uncomfortable. She kept her appearance simple, but she knew they saw her as a foreigner, from a place where the comforts of life could be taken for granted. They connected her to Hafez and his departure.

Without a precursor, Amin said, "my father did what was required. he stayed next to his parents and carried them through the last years of their life and into their deaths. and now, it is my turn." Salima could hear the heavy burden in his voice. He ended on a louder note, "my father's decision to not emigrate was the best decision."

Salima looked at Amin's daughter, wondered at her future. She saw this family as the last branch clinging to a dying tree, but they saw themselves as the tree and the family in America as the branch atrophying. Before she left, they took her to the balcony that overlooked Coptic Cairo and pointed out the churches to her, naming each one as if they were close friends.

* * *

"and what is your opinion of egypt?" asks Bashir.

* * *

The first day Salima stepped out of Fanous's apartment, her nostalgia was betrayed by the dirt, the garbage in the streets, the broken sidewalks, and the endless shade of gray that covered the city. This homeland made her wish for something else—a golden sun over a beach, a mosaic of light, a whiff of clear mountain air. But after a week, her vision shifted, and she noticed the rare beauty—a tucked-away garden, a woman hanging laundry on her rooftop, a jasmine bush hugging the side of a wall, a stray cat being fed by an old man.

A few nights after her arrival, Fanous and his children took her to Khan el Khalili, crowded with shops selling everything from belly-dancing outfits to statues of pharaonic gods. They taught her how to bargain through the stalls of the marketplace. She purchased an assortment of items—mother-of-pearl boxes, a backgammon set, Aladdin lamps, and small replicas of the pyramids. They closed the evening by eating at a falafel place tucked in one of the alleyways. Salima watched as the cook rounded and flattened each piece of taamia, then dipped his hand in the bowl of sesame seeds and patted them over the mixture before surrendering it to the hot oil.

Her Arabic came back quickly after that evening in Khan el Khalili, as if released from the paralysis of speaking English. Bargaining for each item almost erased the letters of the English alphabet and pushed her into dreaming in Arabic, everyone talking at once, negotiating memories and prices.

On Christmas Eve, she attended the liturgy at St. Mark's Church with her family. The two-hour service went on, the priest praying, the cantor chanting, the congregation responding. Her body couldn't help but respond as if to an ancient calling, and the song from which she could only decipher the words "from generation to generation" tugged at her as if the notes were playing inside her.

Each morning, she would wake before the others and make her way to the Saraya Pastry store, buying konafa with cream, a tray of glistening basboosa, small nuggets of baklava, petit fours with chocolate. She had quickly acquired a sweet tooth, and her cravings woke her each day. On her way out, she would greet the bawab guarding the front door of the building with "sabah el kheir," and when she returned, she would hand him one of the pastries she had bought. They said little to one another, only this exchange of the desire for sweetness.

Later, she would take her cup of coffee and step out on the balcony overlooking this city—tall apartment buildings, their rooftops dotted with makeshift homes, an unimaginable city rising from the sand, everything tightly interlocked.

* ⁂ *

Salima smiles at Bashir and says, "egypt is the mother of the world."

Bashir nods and repeats, "yes, masr om el dunya."

They settle into the drive as they make their way along the Nile Corniche.

"and how are you and how is your family," Salima asks.

* ⁂ *

Bashir blinks his eyes as if to replay the events that happened since he picked her up at the airport. Only a week later, he had come home to find his wife waiting at the door for him, holding a letter in her hand. Eman said nothing, just held it out toward him. He took it and sat down while she remained standing. He ran his finger beneath the seal and opened it, pulling out the paper and unfolding it. His eyes read the words, and when he finished, he looked up to see the question on his wife's face. He nodded, and she lowered her body onto the floor next to him.

For a while, they sat quietly, the sounds of the other apartments entering their home—a clanging of pots, a voice shouting, a child demanding. Until their daughter woke from a nap and found them. She glanced from one to the other and then said, "i'm hungry." Her parents looked at her as if she were a mirage until she repeated her words, and then Eman rose to enter the kitchen. Soon the boys came in from their playing, and the day continued with Bashir and Eman shrouded in quietness as their life moved around them.

In the evening, when the children had fallen asleep and they were in bed, Bashir stared in front of him and said, "what will we do?"

"as you see," she responded.

She placed the decision on him as expected of her, but he wished he could shake it off like an unwanted fly. He had dreamed of this for so long, of that letter arriving and opening a new door for them. Instead, he only felt burdened by the words he had read.

For the next few days, Bashir drove his taxi through the crowded streets, but his brain fixated into a static stillness. He tried to imagine going to

America but couldn't gather the details that would lead to such an action. He imagined letting his life continue as it was, but the accumulation of days sat like a heavy boulder in his stomach.

* ⁂ *

"my family's well, alhamdulillah," he answers.

Salima waits, wondering if he will say anything else.

A moment later, he adds, "i won the immigration lottery."

"what will you do?" asks Salima.

Bashir's mind goes further back in time, recalling his family's move from Kom Ombo to Cairo. "we left the village in 1973. i was twelve years old. each year, my father would sell a piece of the land, so he could pay the school fees for my brother and me, so we could celebrate the feast, so he could pay for his mother's funeral, so we could just live. and our land diminished to only a few feddans."

"that's a hard life," Salima responds.

A car edges toward them and Bashir maneuvers ahead into a miniscule space to avoid colliding with it. They are on Road 9 and the traffic has become heavier. He remains where he is, waiting for the other cars to move. Even if he finds a way to weave through and get ahead, he knows the movement will just stall again.

"and your aunt," he says, "you said she was sick. how is she?"

* ⁂ *

Every day, Fanous took her to see Aunt Afaf. The first day, she walks in and finds her in bed, her body drawn into the mattress. It's her neighbor who sits next to her, a woman who has lived across the hall from her for forty years.

Salima keeps the shock from reaching her face as the aunt whom she remembers as nurturing her now lies, barely upright in bed, the edges of her bones showing. But when Salima enters, Afaf's eyes brighten. "ya binti, ya binti, ya habibti," she says, calling her as she always has—her daughter, her beloved. Salima settles next to her and holds her hand.

She returns each day, watching her aunt's body fold into itself. The doctor tells the family it's pneumonia, and, given her age, it's uncertain if she'll recover. No one wants to call Kareem and tell him. When he calls, Afaf gathers her strength and talks to him, tells him she just has a cold.

Some days, when she's more awake and lucid, she fills Salima's mind with stories of the past. In her eighty years of living, she can recall the times of King Fuad and King Farouk to Nasser to Sadat to Mubarak. Salima listens to her aunt's stories, seeing her mother as a young woman, the jumble of her aunts and uncles, the women wearing the latest fashions on the streets that were not so congested during a time that she can only imagine as a black-and-white film.

When Salima says, "we've lost so much," Afaf turns to her and shakes her head. "no we have everything. we are wound around each other, and even the distance of separation cannot tear us apart."

Salima brings her what little food and drink she can eat, wipes her forehead, and washes her body. Each day, the hours that she is awake lessen. At the end of the second week, when Salima kisses her forehead, Afaf reaches for her niece's hand and says, "ya habibti, you must build your own family." By morning, she is gone.

The burial takes place the same day, as Salima learns that here the dead are ushered quickly into their rest. It's impossible for Kareem to fly back that quickly from Canada, and after Fanous calls him, he hands the phone to Salima. She holds it for a second, unsure of what to say to someone she barely knows, but when she hears the choked voice on the other end, she relays the time she spent with his mother and finds herself uttering words of comfort and saying how his mother spoke of him with love. How she held him as her greatest gift.

* ⁂ *

"she is gone," Salima answers.

"el bae'ya fe hayatek," Bashir offers the condolence, a reminder that the person who is gone continues to live in the life of those who remain.

"hayatak bae'ya," she responds, and they sit in silence for a few moments, the noise of the city a mirage of sound outside the taxi.

Once they approach the end of the Nile Corniche, the traffic heaves to a stop. Taxis and cars converge into a pattern of uneven lines that leave no space for passing each other. A short cacophony of horns ensues, blasting into the morning air then dying down, unable to maintain its momentum. Bashir looks over at the Nile stretching itself across the city. His heartbeat slows as the water flows beneath his vision. He recalls how his earliest years were spent in a village, his home sitting comfortably among others hugging the edge of the river.

"bashir," Salima says, and the pause after his name makes him turn around and look at her. Once his gaze has caught hers, she asks, "have you made a decision?"

* ⁂ *

A few nights after the letter arrived, Bashir turned to his wife again and asked, "what shall we do?" She remained silent for a few moments and then said, "do you remember when you came to ask for my hand in marriage?"

As a child, he had loved the feel of mud between his toes, running with other children in wayward directions, sure of the earth that carried them. They played soccer with a stuffed sock and ran along the road tapping an old bicycle tire. Each day offered joyous movement, and in moments of quiet, he watched the young girl who lived only a few houses away. She was the youngest of three girls, yet she seemed to hold the responsibility of being her mother's helper. He watched her in the early morning when she went to get water from the town well, returning with a full bucket weighing her down. And he saw her in the evening hanging laundry, handing each item to her mother because the clothesline was too high for her to reach. Midday, when everyone took time to rest, he watched her walk to the Nile, to a spot shaded by a few palm trees. She sat between them and seemed only to be watching the movement of water.

One day, he caught his bravery and walked toward her, shrouded by the quiet of the afternoon. He carried a stick, dragging it behind him in the earth, something to anchor him and create sound so he would not startle her. She looked up when he was a few meters away. His tongue caught in his teeth as he looked at her round face and the wisps of loose dark-brown hair.

"i'm sorry," he muttered, unsure of why the apology escaped his lips.

"it's not important," she responded, and she shifted her weight on the earth slightly as if making room for him.

He moved forward and sat next to her. After a few moments, she offered her name, saying, "i'm eman," and he answered, "i'm bashir." They sat together until the quiet of the afternoon shifted and the life of the village woke from its afternoon rest.

Bashir had kept track of time, and when he was twenty-seven, he asked his parents' permission to return to the village to request Eman's hand in marriage. He had not seen her in fifteen years.

The day after he returned to the village, he escaped into the early morning before most of the village woke. He sat on the green earth at the bank of the Nile, his pants rolled up and his feet bare, the soles flat on the muddy earth. The attention from the village at his return had surprised him. Naively, he thought that he could enter back into this world quietly as if he had not left. But his absence had been marked, and now his presence prompted a festival of rumors and conversations. He had forgotten how his village functioned as one, each member tied firmly to the center that held them woven together into a single entity. The loneliness of Cairo had made him believe he existed in isolation, that he could draw an outline around himself and call himself whole.

He looked out at the Nile, its water flowing almost imperceptibly, carrying all its secrets from the ancient to the present moment. He was just one man with his own hopes and dreams, and so many had been carried by this water that ran from one end of the continent to the other. He noticed a small rowboat resting on the bank a few meters away. His footsteps took him to it, and he shoved it out of the mud into which it had settled. Checking, he saw no damage. Pushing it toward the water, he stepped into it and began to row out.

The motion of rowing stretched his arms, and he felt his muscles expand as his strength moved the boat. His body swayed with the direction of the rowing, leaning forward and back. A smile filtered across his face, as he imagined having a rowboat instead of a taxi and moving people in Cairo by boat from one destination to the other. A sliver of light spread across the sky as the sun rose. Along the bank, the small connected homes rested, some shrouded by palm trees. He saw the laundry hanging across the lines stretched from branch to branch and the multicolored rugs that had been whipped clean draped over the low stone walls.

What if Eman did not accept his proposal? What if she said she couldn't leave her home? The sun leaped from behind the low buildings and flooded the sky with sudden light. Bashir lowered his eyes to the water to allow his vision to adjust. He pulled the oars in and let the boat float. The water was clear here, its blue color mingling into green, a transparent layer he could see through. He dipped his hands into the river and cupped his palms to fill them with water. Bending over, he brought his hands up and let the water splash onto his face.

"bashir! bashir!"

He heard the call of his name and looked toward the shore to see one of his younger cousins waving his arms. The boy cupped his hands around his mouth to extend his voice and shouted that the family wanted him.

Bashir rowed back to the shore and joined his cousin. By the time they had returned to the house that used to belong to his grandparents, it was filled with family eager to welcome him and hear his stories. The morning extended into afternoon as more people came and went. Those who had never been to Cairo inundated him with questions about movie stars and refrigerators and the glamour of what they imagined life to be in the city.

The women cooked throughout the morning and into the afternoon. For the midday meal, they brought out the feteer, the taamia, the fuul. Alongside, there was the tahini, tomatoes, cheese, and pickles that others had brought with them. Everyone circled on the floor and ate until the heaviness of the meal along with the warmth of the sun initiated their dispersal for the afternoon rest.

Bashir took a breath as the space finally cleared, and he could feel his own presence. Despite the day's activity and noise, he was restless. His mind struggled with why he had come here, and he felt his resolve sink. He was foolish to think she had feelings for him, that she was not already claimed by another man. He had resisted asking anyone about her, afraid to hear the answer.

He stepped out of the house quietly for a walk. The village was still in the midst of the hot afternoon. He made his way alongside the houses, unsure of his direction. His ear picked up the sound of a rebaba being played. It must be Moemen, he thought. As he walked, the music lengthened and grew louder. His footsteps moved in its direction, and he approached the Nile, where he could see Moemen sitting on a makeshift wall playing. He smiled and nodded at Bashir without a hesitation, his arm continuing the motion that created the music lifting above the water. Bashir walked toward him and paused for a moment to inhale a breath that contained the music of the rebaba. The instrument created more depth of sound than seemed possible with only its two strings.

Moemen's face was the color of rich dark-brown soil, etched into grooves by the heavy sun. He had come from Nubia, arriving already as an old man, when Bashir was only a young boy. People had watched as he walked through the alleys of the village, wondering at his destination. He made his way to the bank of the Nile to this place where he now sat, pulled out his rebaba, and proceeded to play. The sounds reached the village. A few boys who had been chasing each other stopped and ran to the Nile. Their energy calmed when they heard the music, and they settled for a short while. A father weighed down by the care of his family paused from his work in the small garden plot, resting for a few minutes to wipe his brow and look at the sky before returning to his task. A young wife carrying the burden of her first child in her belly paused in her cooking, taking a breath.

As the sun settled, a man who had an extra room in his house offered Moemen a place to sleep. People gave him what they could—a bowl of beans, a plate of rice and chicken, some fried potatoes, a piece of feteer drizzled with honey. Moemen slept and ate in the village, and each day he went to the bank of the river to play his rebaba. He lived on the kindness of others and in turn offered them this music that gave breath to their daily lives.

Moemen gestured his head toward Bashir to come closer.

"she's sitting in the center of the palm trees."

The words strung to the music so that Bashir couldn't be certain he had heard correctly. Moemen lowered his face and entered back inside the rebaba, his music stretching across sky and water to reach destinations beyond imagination.

* ⁂ *

I walked toward the circle of palm trees, my heart beating in my chest. From a little distance, I saw Eman, recognizing her from the tilt of her small chin and her long hair. I moved quietly. When I was standing close, she looked up and her face opened when she saw me. For a few moments, neither of us spoke. The words I had intended to say fell onto the ground, no longer needed. Eman placed her hand on the ground next to her, and I accepted it as a simple invitation that sealed our agreement even before we spoke.

"the yellow dates have filled the trees this year," she said.

"by the time they arrive in cairo, they have already begun to overripen," I responded.

"but their taste is still sweet," she added.

Before I could say anything else, Eman turned her face and looked directly at me, taking away the words forming in my mouth. "is your life good in cairo?" she asked.

I had planned to paint a bright picture, to describe the fancy hotels where I dropped off passengers, the large grocers that held an abundance of food, the new restaurants that sold hamburgers. And I wanted to tell her that I was planning to open my own business, become a rich man with a reputation. But my voice spoke without my permission. I told her about the long days in the taxi, my parents' weariness, the small apartment I had recently rented. I continued until my words ran out.

how could i ask her now? I thought after I had spoken so much truth. The silence fell again, and I felt defeated. A small breeze picked up, alleviating the heat with the palm branches that swayed above us, fanning the air.

I turned my face directly to Eman and reached for her hand. "i came back for you," I said.

Eman placed her hand inside mine and nodded.

* ⁂ *

"a difficult decision," Bashir finally answers Salima.

She nods, although she is not sure he can see her.

* ⁂ *

For the next few days after receiving the letter, Bashir continued to pick up and drop off his passengers. On Thursday, cars and taxis and microbuses converged on the streets, carrying those returning home from work eager for their Friday rest. The one day to breathe slower, move in accord with their body's rhythm rather than the dictates of the city that demanded a slow trudge through the monotony of inconsequential work. For some, wives were waiting at home with a midday meal and the promise of love; for others, there was the comfort of mothers bringing them a cup of tea.

The traffic stalled on the Qasr El Nil Bridge as the lights turned from red to green and back with no movement. They turned again like Ramadan lamps swinging and shining their light. One car honked, another added its echo, a taxi pressed its horn three times in even beats, another released a long note, and soon an orchestra sounded on the bridge, an outrage of disharmony, the cacophonous music rising over the Nile, its discontent carried from the beginning to the end of the continent.

Bashir sat in the midst of this chaos, and, despite his quiet nature, he added his own horn song to this protest of sound. He felt an urgency as his palm hit the taxi horn. One long note, and he lifted his hand, then pushed again, holding it longer, feeling exhilarated at joining this massive outcry.

A movement began and space opened, allowing the vehicles to make progress toward their various destinations. Bashir's taxi was empty, having just dropped off a customer in Zamalek. He had planned to pick up a few more fares, work into the evening to find those who preferred the excitement of Cairo's nightlife to the intimacy of their own homes. Instead, he turned right off the bridge and entered the street by the Nile Corniche and then turned left into the winding roads of Garden City to find a spot to park the taxi. He walked back toward the Nile Corniche, crossed the street when there was a lull in traffic, and stood overlooking the Nile. He leaned over the wall, the water flowing beneath, and let his heartbeat settle.

* ⁂ *

"you know," Bashir says, "i grew up in a small village next to the nile. my grandfather had two brothers who went to cairo, but he decided to stay. when things became more difficult, he encouraged my father to leave. my wife is from the same village. my grandparents' house is still there."

"my grandfather came from a village too," Salima says.

Bashir nods. "we are all from there. the origin."

* ⁂ *

A few nights after the letter arrived, Bashir asked his wife why she agreed to marry him. It was not something they had talked about before. She had told him that she continued to think of him after he left the village, and he had not asked for more than that. Now, he listened to her answer as she spoke through the night hours.

"after you left, i kept going to sit by the river in the afternoon while everyone rested. it was the only time when no one asked anything of me. i wished for the water to carry me to new places. i knew it reached cairo and alexandria, cities full of noise and cars and stores that sold magical things.

those who went there rarely returned. and when they did, it seemed like they were lopsided beings. their mouth moved in a strange way, as if their tongue did not know whether to twist the words into their city pronunciations or back to the rhythm of the village. after a few days, they left again with their crooked walk.

"when i reached the age of sixteen, the men started looking at me as if they were measuring me. i saw them coming to our house with their families, and i knew their intentions. after each visit, my father asked for my response. my two older sisters were married and settled into their own lives. as my mother grew in years, it became difficult for her to stand for a long period, her legs aching from all she carried. i helped her with the cooking, the washing, the cleaning, and i helped my father in our small plot of land.

"each time my father asked, i said no. i would find any reason—the man's mother looks difficult, his appearance is not attractive, he has no land. the reason was not important because i saw the relief in my father's face.

"one day, after i said no to a suitor with land and a good appearance, my eldest sister found me while i was hanging the laundry and grabbed my arm.

" 'look into my face, eman. what is the story? who are you waiting for? a hundred men come and ask for your hand, and with each one, you find a problem. who is the man who caught your heart?'

"it was as if she had unlocked my thoughts, and i told her that it was you.

" 'you're a fool,' my sister said, 'waiting for a boy, who was twelve years old when he left, to remember and return to you. he's in cairo, and that city swallows people and never spits them back out.'

"when i reached my twenties, they stopped coming. everyone assumed i would spend my life caring for my parents. when i heard you returned, i began to walk fast, as if i had somewhere to go. but i told myself that surely you must have married and were returning only to show off what you had accomplished. impossible that you even remembered me, especially now that my youth had passed. people said that you dressed like a foreigner in pants and a shirt, that you spoke like a cairene, that you were going to sell your grandparents' house and never come back.

"but i sat by the river and waited, knowing you would come."

* ⁂ *

As they approach the end of Salah Salem Street, the traffic stalls, cars honking their frustration at the eighteen million people who inhabit this city.

"what will you do when you return?" asks Bashir.

* ⁂ *

She had chosen adoption—it was a median between keeping the child and having an abortion, a point of balance. In Egypt, children exchanged hands frequently, everyone serving as a parent. They spent nights at the homes of relatives, ate from the hands of anyone who offered food. When they were young, Salima and her cousins were like siblings, running together from home to home. There was a cousin whose parents both died when she was still a girl; without negotiation or questioning, she was taken in by an aunt and an uncle, raised within the family. *Was this adoption really any different,* Salima thought, *just a passing from one family to the other?*

Salima had closed the door on the question of keeping her. Her parents would never accept it, and she and her daughter would have to wander in search of a home, cut off from what had created them. This is better, she had decided. Her daughter would be part of a family with no questions, not hovering above continents, not twisting her tongue around two languages, not always being uncertain of her right to a sense of home. In an American family, she could grow up belonging, laying claim to all she was given.

Salima imagined a middle-aged couple who might have been trying to have children for years until they finally surrendered and turned to adoption, a couple financially established with a house—perhaps they lived in one of those large homes in the Morningside neighborhood of Atlanta—and her daughter would grow up with the comforts of luxury. The couple would give her an American name, maybe Elizabeth or Catherine. She had resisted thinking of any names when she was pregnant, having already relinquished her claim to the child. But in the back of her mind, a name repeated: "Negma." It meant "star," and she thought how the same star could be seen simultaneously by people in different parts of the world. This child encompassed so much by the very act of her birth—the distance travelled by her grandparents so she would be born in a new country, the father whose ancestry mixed and diluted too many national boundaries to be able to lay claim to a single one. Every time the name came to her, she shook as if she could let it fall off her.

Once the child came out of her body, she assumed that everything would revert to what it was. Her stomach would deflate, her breasts would diminish in size, her appetite would return. She didn't anticipate the physical ache inside her, the phantom presence that remained there, the way she kept reaching toward her belly even though there was nothing to grasp, the way that absence could have such weight.

The night after she gave birth, there was a new nurse on duty. She was young, and it was her first week at the hospital. The nurses who had grown familiar throughout her labor didn't seem to be around. She took a chance, asked the new nurse if she could bring in the baby. The nurse smiled and nodded as if it were a natural request.

The nurse handed the child, who was bundled in a hospital blanket, to her. With the blanket around her and the small hat on her head, she could almost have been any child. Salima took the hat off to reveal a full head of black silky hair, and when she loosened the blanket to release the infant's arms, her hands fluttered in the air. The child's eyes were open, and she held Salima's face in her gaze. The darkness of her eyes made it difficult to detect the outline of her pupils. Salima's lips parted, and she spoke the name that had lain inside her, barely a whisper. The child whimpered and wiggled as if it had suddenly become aware of a discomfort. Not wanting to attract attention, Salima tried to rock her, and when that didn't work, instinctively, she brought her to her breast, and the child calmed as it found its nourishment.

She had requested a closed adoption, wanting neither the child nor the parents to know anything about her. She would undo what had been done and return to being a woman without children. There would be no trace of the event, no clues to enable the child to find her, to follow the trail back to her origins. Its only memory of her would be this trespass of intimacy.

For race, she had put down white. Technically, it was accurate and might speed up an adoption. Now, looking at her child's brown skin and full features, she knew that her daughter would always hold the question of her identity in her face.

The next day, someone from the agency came to pick up the child. She had been told that it would be placed in a foster home initially until an adoptive family was found, but they expected things to move quickly, with this being a healthy, desirable baby. The woman from the agency gave her a choice between having the child made immediately available for adoption or waiting forty-five days, during which, she was told, she could change her mind. Reaching to sign for immediate adoption, she wavered, the pen suspended above the line. The woman sitting by her bed reached toward her but did not touch her. "We generally recommend the waiting period," she said. Salima moved her pen to the other line and signed.

"there's something i forgot," she says in answer to Bashir's question, "and i have to go back and retrieve it."

"yes," Bashir says, "sometimes we have to retrace our steps."

Salima looks out at the city drifting into the fullness of day. Egypt is no longer the place of her childhood memories. Not the gathering of generations of voices. Her family here is dwindling. She can almost count them, and it frightens her to add up their number. The eldest have passed on and the younger emigrated, leaving those in the middle, now aging without parents or children. What if Hafez and Layla had never left? What if her parents had stayed?

The evening before her departure, Fanous's eyes settled on her as if he could detect her questions. "you know," he said, "when hafez and layla left, no one could imagine things could ever improve. you have to evaluate the time when they made their decision—what it was like after '67, the solid enclosure people felt, the complete hopelessness. perhaps immigration was the only way out of that enclosure. and your mother, hala—she always wanted to leave. her vision turned in the direction of the west—the movies, the magazines, the fantasy of a better world. even if her sister had not gone, she would have eventually found her way there. it's impossible to know if their decision was a good one."

Now, sitting in the taxi, Salima imagines how she will feel disoriented by the vast American landscape when she returns. Here, only a centimeter of space separates people from each other, not the open roads, wide fields of grass, cows grazing, the lone houses. So much space could paralyze you. Here the movement of the city propels you, pushing you into constant motion. A city living and breathing. Her body will refuse to release this place where she has spent only a few weeks, but where each day stretches itself past the normal lapse of time.

She will arrive with three days to claim her daughter.

* ⁂ *

At the airport, Bashir squeezes the taxi into a spot and gets out to help Salima with her luggage.

"shokran, ya bashir," she says, handing him the fare with a generous tip.

He puts up his hand in an attempt to refuse, saying, "it's on me," but she has learned how to insist, how to offer three times.

Before she turns to enter the airport, she asks again, "bashir, you didn't tell me. what will you do?"

Bashir smiles as the cars congregate around the airport. "we're returning to the village of kom ombo, and we will complete our lives there."

Salima nods. "tabaan, of course, a good decision."

"shokran," he responds, "and if, one day, you come to kom ombo, please be our guest."

"maybe," Salima says, "maybe i will come. and if one of these days you come to amreeka, you will stay with me."

* ⁂ *

As Bashir drives to pick up his family and take them all back to the village, he recalls the last day of the previous year as it turned from 2010 to 2011. He had decided not to work that night, unable to call up the energy needed to make it through the congested streets of the New Year's Eve celebrations. He and Eman and their three children joined thousands of other people pressed on the Qasr El Nil Bridge, the smog from the standstill cars shortening their breath as they walked over the Nile. Their daughter felt sick, and Bashir's throat couldn't keep the smog at bay. It did not feel like a celebration, only a mass of people invading the streets to exert their existence for another year.

At midnight, the cars on the bridge sounded an orchestra of horns announcing the new year, their urgency strong enough to make the police officers trying to control the traffic relinquish their efforts. It was only the people who could keep the flow of this city from stalling and push everyone into the upcoming year.

Dunya, Fathy, and Yusef – January 24–25, 2011

The TV screen in the waiting area clicked through a series of images, but no one was paying attention. Until the word "Cairo" caught Dunya's ear and she looked up to see the image of Tahrir Square on the screen. It was midday in Egypt, and the camera panned the square filled with so many people that they could barely be distinguished from one another. It was a conglomeration of shapes moving. The announcer's voice: "An unprecedented number of people . . . Gathering in Tahrir Square . . . Antigovernment protests . . . Demanding the resignation of President Mubarak . . ." Dunya watched, entering into the screen's images.

Her father had always talked of Egyptians as an apathetic people who were only concerned with their next morsel of food, but what she saw now contradicted the image of a dormant nation. For a moment, the newscaster quieted and the sounds coming from the square emerged: "erhal! erhal!" they chanted. Then she heard "laa le mubarak!" and understood the call to oust the president. The camera retreated to the outskirts of the crowd to show a reporter holding a microphone, explaining where he was and the name and title of the person he was interviewing, which Dunya didn't quite catch, as an announcement was being made in the airport.

Her attention settled back on the screen that now filled her vision. A young man with black hair, a slim physique, and sharp brown eyes took the microphone the reporter had been holding for him and spoke directly to the camera as if he could see his audience. Speaking in clear English, he said, "We are a stubborn people and we will not stop until we achieve our goal." Another intercom announcement broke through the chanting crowd where the television camera had returned. Dunya felt movement around her as several people gathered their belongings and stood into a makeshift line. The newscaster was back on, and unable to explain fully what was taking place, he retreated into history, recounting the 1952 revolution and the presidencies of Nasser and Sadat and the Camp David peace treaty and Sadat's assassination and the start of Mubarak's presidency.

* ⁂ *

On January 24, Fathy closed his suitcase and handbag. He had packed clothes, a few photographs, and a couple of books. He knew he was allowed two suitcases, but there was nothing more he wanted to take. He walked out of his room and placed his luggage by the front door. He would embrace his mother with tears in her eyes, leave the keys to his apartment on the table for his father, who would never forgive him for not rejecting America as he had, and stop to say farewell to his sisters. Fanous would arrive exactly at seven in the evening as they had agreed. His flight left at ten, and, with traffic, the drive to the airport would take at least the hour they had allotted.

* ⁂ *

As Yusef approaches Tahrir Square, the voices reach his ears. He can detect the chanting of "erhal! erhal!" rising from the crowd, demanding that Mubarak leave. Once he enters the square, his body attaches itself to the throng of people gathered. He tries to stay on the edge in case he has to detach himself, but the movement of this many people creates a force that pushes him in, and he can no longer detect the way out.

The people have become larger than the buildings that frame this square—even the Mogamma, that huge, rising gray structure that towers above the city each day, mocking Egyptians with the bureaucracy it holds within its modernist architecture. For every license, every stamped piece of paper, Egyptian citizens have to climb into that building and be swallowed by it. Tourists pay little attention to it, their gaze directed at the Nile Hilton that offers a luxurious stay for those who can afford it. Nearby stands the Egyptian Museum, antiquities filling each floor, their cases dusty and the labels misspelled or missing altogether. Across the square stands the old AUC building, a palace that housed the prestigious Westernized university until just two years ago, when it relocated itself to a sprawling campus in New Cairo. This square holds in its grasp the history of Egypt. Now it erupts with the presence of thousands of people rising up to create a new history.

Yusef senses someone pushing against him, and when he turns, a man hands him a bottle of water. He takes it, says "shokran," drinks a sip, and passes it on.

* ⁂ *

Names her father had spoken—Morcos, Farid, Khalil, Fanous, Afaf—crowded her mind. Dunya wondered if those names were in the midst of Tahrir, if she might have a cousin holding up a sign and chanting. Or perhaps she had an aunt sitting alone in her apartment, scared. Where were they, this large family her father had spoken of? Although he was an only child, he always talked of family as an extension of himself. He referred to everyone as "cousin"—he would say, "the son of my aunt or uncle," using the Arabic terms to indicate whether the cousin was paternal or maternal. More specificity than that, her father had explained, was irrelevant, adding "everyone is family woven into a rope of knots from which, no matter how far away you travel, you cannot untangle yourself."

She wondered if she resembled anyone in the family, if someone else had her dark-brown curls. Her eyes returned to the screen to watch another young man being interviewed. He spoke in English, saying, "We are staying in Tahrir. We will regain our dignity and determine our own future."

* ⁂ *

The family's apartment had closed in on itself since Fathy announced his departure. His father's stare into the wall, his mother's mouth pursed into loss, and his sisters' accusatory stances. The day of his departure, he approached his father, who neither looked in his direction nor stood up to say goodbye. Fathy opened his mouth, expecting words to come out, to say something that could allow him to leave with closure. But his mouth remained empty, and he stood transfixed in silence. His mother clutched him to her chest, her sob emerging into a cry for her son, "ya ibni." She did not let go until Fanous knocked on the door.

* ⁂ *

Yusef feels himself tossed into the crowd, and the collective energy makes his heart beat faster. He is among his own people, in his own country. This is where he belongs—not in the frigid streets of Boston. His voice rises out of his body to join the chanting of the crowd, a voice that had subdued itself to the rhythm of soft English syllables. Now, his fist pushes into the air, and he shouts "erhal! erhal!" in perfect sync with every other voice in the crowd. He chants his loudest, his voice reaching its full power.

Yusef's eyes catch the faces of other men, and he sees himself multiplied a million times. These men and their frustration are his own. He belongs inside this struggle, shouting his love for Egypt, a patriotism greater than the mere display of a flag. The crowd surges with a spontaneous energy, and he becomes seamless with everyone shouting in the square.

They march and protest until a ripple of tension passes through the crowd, and Yusef feels himself jostled back and forth. "police," he hears someone saying. "police, damn them." Water falls on him, and he hears someone saying "water cannons"—and then the smell of tear gas, then coughing. Around him, people step backward, and Yusef finds himself propelled forward without having moved.

* * *

"Last call for Flight 334 to Malta." The intercom voice pulled her out of her reverie, but Dunya's ears couldn't translate the sounds into comprehensible words.

All these years, she had never chosen where she went. Her parents made the decision to come to America, her father made the decision to stay in the apartment, and even when she chose to take the position that led her to travel over so much of the world, each destination was determined and arranged by others. She only had to pick up her ticket and follow the itinerary given to her. And now Malta, with a woman waiting for her at the house on the ocean with an offer of love.

"Last call for Dunya Michelle Sa'ad Salim. Last call for Dunya Michelle Sa'ad Salim."

* * *

Fathy knew that he had to leave before January 25, before he would have to act on the promises he had made. That morning as crowds gathered in Tahrir Square, creating a single body out of so many, their strength filling the space to push the country forward, Fathy stepped off the plane and walked through the accordion tunnel into the Raleigh-Durham International Airport. He entered into the crowds, the noise, and the rapid movement, feeling relieved to find himself alone and anonymous.

* * *

Yusef hears someone say "we are not afraid," and he joins the voices as together they heave their weight as one body against the police. Two walls collapsing into each other. Yusef feels the power of his own physical presence until the blow to his shoulder topples his balance. Those behind him push forward, and with the next blow to the side of his head, he collapses, his body sinking into the crowd. The sounds of voices calling him a martyr hold him until everything subsides to nothing.

Dunya stood up, swung her purse over her shoulder, pulled up the handle of her suitcase, and walked away from the gate, certain of where she wanted to go.

Fanous – 2011

I grew up with two sisters, multiple first cousins, and more cousins further removed. We spent our childhoods together. Every week we gathered at my uncle Sa'ad's house, and we ran wild, chasing each other until the adults tossed us out to where we had more room for our games. My cousins were as close as siblings. We forgot which parents owned us; we only knew that we belonged to each other.

When Misha left, and then Hafez and Layla, it was like pulling a thread that unraveled us. After we lost the war, no one could imagine things would improve. The military was the first priority, and people could barely find enough to live. Nasser closed the country, held it in his firm grip. When Hafez made his decision, we were surrounded by a solid enclosure. Maybe it was the war and his brother's death, maybe someone was trying to harm him because he was successful and a Copt. Maybe he panicked.

If he had stayed, he would have done well after '73. With Sadat's Open-Door Economic Policy and the move away from Russia, opportunities became more abundant. You could work in the private sector, where your qualifications could get you promoted. Those private-sector jobs pay well, although they demand long hours and more labor. People used to work from morning until two or three, then go home for their midday meal, a nap; then in the evening they could go out, socialize, and get together with family. Now, a man works each day until evening and returns home to collapse, with Friday his only day off. The private sector expects more of its workers. We've become like America, demanding full commitment in exchange for money that allows us to consume more material goods.

Some believe it would have been better if we had stayed under the control of the British with kings ruling us. There was a sense of luxury and abundance that filled the country, but perhaps this is only the nostalgia for the past. When independence came, it only seemed to restrict us, crowd us into the tight spaces created by leaders who claimed to have a better vision. We felt our lives shrink, and when the door opened to another place, some took flight, pulling apart the tapestry of our nation.

Under the fluorescent lights of the airport, we gathered to say goodbye. Each mother held her child tight to her chest, as if she could imprint her body into theirs. The father would grasp his child once and release them too quickly, as if they were already gone. Some went to New York or California or Boston. It was all America to us, and we assumed they would have each other close.

Still, we worried as we had for Misha. We remembered when he called to tell us Mariam was gone. He was there alone. No family to stand with him, to comfort him. That was the first phone call that reached us with bad news, but others came, and we learned to detect the foreign ring of the phone, anticipating the news arriving from that other place.

And then Shafiq, a distant cousin who was my age—the one I chased when we played cops and robbers, the one I told the first time I kissed a girl, the one who consoled me when my mother died—he left too. America wouldn't take him. They never told him why, just said his application didn't meet their requirements; he wasn't suitable. He sulked, his face fallen, and for months, he moved as if trying to kill the ants under his feet. Then one day, he told us all he was immigrating to Australia. No one had gone that far. I had to pull out a map to find it floating in the ocean alone, as far away from us as land could exist. We pleaded with him to change his mind, to try for America later, to at least consider Canada or Europe. But his mind was decided. I received one letter from him, a few months after his departure, to tell me he had a place to live and a job. That is all he gave me. I've heard nothing from him for almost thirty years. I don't know if he's alive or dead. What sense does it make to take yourself so far away, to a far-flung land where you have no one?

After Farid's eldest brother, Morcos, died, only three of us first cousins remained. Farid stays with his own family, presiding over them. We rarely see them. So it's just two of us now, my cousin Khalil and me. Like me, Khalil decided to let his roots spread in the same earth where he was born. If everyone had stayed, there would have been children and grandchildren filling our house with the joyous cries of youth. Our families should have been growing together, intertwining into a fabric knotted into a tight bond. Khalil and I gather each Christmas and Easter with our children—my son and daughter, his two sons. We keep our two families close, but those large family gatherings when we were all here and our voices rose in celebration are gone; they are only the nostalgia of the past.

When our children were young, we would watch them play and recall our own childhood. Back then, there were more children than adults, and we felt like we held the world in our fists. Our children only know this small gathering. It's a repetitive pattern for them, not the excitement we anticipated when we were young. They don't know the laughter and the exhilaration of being a tribe. Even when all of us are together, the house settles into quietness, and the children's play is softer. There are uncles and aunts they have never seen, myriad cousins whose names they don't know. They are as remote as the characters they read about in storybooks.

Our family evaporated, each person who left sucked by the airplane's engines into a void. We watch American movies, and we search in the background to find our relatives—a man that has my elder cousin's crooked gait, the way he would lift one leg a little higher as he took his steps; or my sister, whose elegant high heels clicked a perfect rhythm, turning her walk into a dance. But America never returns what it takes. Now we make family out of two, and when we gather for each occasion, the empty chairs sit with us. We are left here with a mirage of what our lives might have been if we could have kept each other.

Each holiday, the phone releases that long, choppy ring, and we know someone from America is calling. We pass the phone to each hand to sound out our greetings and questions of well-being. "ezayekom?" we ask over and over again, as if the question might elicit a different response. But we only say that we are well. I said nothing when they found a lump in my wife's breast. I stayed silent when I discovered I had diabetes. And I wonder what news there is on the other side of the world that stays hidden. Still, this line keeps us connected so the thread doesn't break, even as it stretches across the ocean.

When I have time, I drive out to the corniche and walk along the water, sometimes making my way from Maadi to the island of Roda. I watch the feluccas, the fishing boats, and the occasional rowboat. I stop, lean over, and something of the length of that river enters me, as if taking me to a place I know only in my dreams. *Kom Ombo*. I wonder what life I might have had if my grandfather Salim had not left the village. Would I have grown among family in a home that expanded with each marriage and each birth, living under the shadow of the temple known as the Gold House? Here, it is the city that expands, sprawling its streets further and further out, grasping for more land to contain the additional people that arrive every year. Some are swallowed whole by the city until they feel themselves in a crocodile's mouth, while others follow the falcon and fly into the distance.

Printed in the USA
CPSIA information can be obtained
at www.ICGtesting.com
LVHW091954130524
780196LV00003B/383